STRANGERS IN THE NIGHT...

Now, what about this sleeping arm that weighed so gently on his breathing? Ah, yes. Her name was Marjorie. She too was a newcomer to Chicago, looking for a job; last night the desk clerk at the Y had assigned them to the same room. Behind the front desk was a big sign reading PURE THOUGHTS ARE THE MARK OF A DIRTY MIND. And they weren't trying to be funny either; they were really that old-fashioned here. They had a strict rule requiring at least two people in every bed. . . .

LOVE CONQUERS ALL

Books by Fred Saberhagen

THE VEILS OF AZLAROC

THE HOLMES-DRACULA FILE

LOVE CONQUERS ALL

THE MASK OF THE SUN

AND the BERSERKER saga:

BERSERKER
BROTHER ASSASSIN
BERSERKER MAN

from
ACE SCIENCE FICTION

SF

LOVE
CONQUERS
ALL
FRED SABERHAGEN

SF
ace books

A Division of Charter Communications Inc.
A GROSSET & DUNLAP COMPANY
360 Park Avenue South
New York, New York 10010

LOVE CONQUERS ALL

This novel originally appeared in the November 1974, December 1974, and January 1975 issues of Galaxy Magazine, copyright © 1974 by UPD Publishing Corporation, Inc.

An ACE Book

Cover art by Bob Adragna

First Ace Printing: January 1979

Printed in U.S.A

I

ARTHUR RODNEY walked through his little California house, calling his wife's name, but only music answered him. The hidden sensors of the hifi system marked Art's passage from room to room and as he passed the system changed the music for him, blending each piece more or less smoothly into the next. When he entered the children's room, where the two beds and a scattering of toys reposed in a somehow ominous stillness, there came from the speakers a cacophony of metallic sounds that bore an intended resemblance to a baby's cry. Little Timmy and Paula had wanted that teenage stuff for their room, and he and Rita had agreed, though the kids were really far too young, but never mind that now, no one was there. The discordant metallic baby cries cut off when Art went out.

In the master bedroom he was fed the music of pulse-beating drums, fit for a wild and wiggling dance that must find its appropriate end upon the bed. No one here, either. The glass in his wide windows (looking out over his neighbors' desert landscaping, complete with plastic iguana) had darkened itself almost to

opacity against the force of the California sun,
but the sun was getting into the bedroom anyway, reflecting blue and green through the
depths of the inside-outside swimming pool.
By this water-mottled light that quivered in all
of the bedroom's many mirrors Art saw that a
small piece of white paper had been propped
against the massage unit on his bedside table.
He tossed his box of handcarved Staunton
chessmen rattling onto the large circular bed,
set his digital tournament clock down gently,
and picked up the note, which was in Rita's
handwriting.

Darling, please believe that I love you as
much as ever, but I must go away for a time.
The kids are with me and will be okay. I
really am pregnant again and Dr. Kuang
says he has had to report my pregnancy to
Family Planning. It's the law, as he says,
and I guess that I can't expect him not to
report it. I will call you or at least write you
soon so try not to worry.

                                Love, Rita

As he read, Art's knees went weak with fear
confirmed, and he sank down on the edge of
the round bed. He glanced up at the overhead
mirror, but learned nothing from the sight of
his own slightly pudgy, dark-bearded face,
pale and enigmatic in its shock. He looked
down again and re-read the note three times
and dropped it on the bed beside him.
Putting his weight on the bed had quick-

ened the heartbeat of the hifi drums, though if he sat still the system would soon switch to soothing, lulling music and in a little while he would be granted silence. He could get up and turn the thing off but he felt too numb. Where to look for escape, for guidance? Where else but on the short bookshelf built into the wall beside his bed? The words of Eros are those of the true heart. Shortly he reached over and pulled out a well-fingered gray volume with *Philosophy of Pleasure* lettered on the cover in a beautiful and lively pink. But then he sat there holding the book unopened.

It was obvious that Rita had run off to her sister-in-law in Chicago. She would not have taken the children to leave them with anyone else. Rita meant to go into hiding somewhere and bear an unwanted child, even if she had to put it up for secret adoption later. Just the kind of thing that sister-in-law Ann would encourage her to do; quite likely it was Ann who had suggested the scheme to her in the first place . . . thought faded out into pain and shock. His wife was gone.

How far pregnant was she? It couldn't be more than ten weeks or so, he thought. He tried to remember when she had last gone off the pills for a menstrual week, but he had trouble keeping the dates in his mind, because his mind wanted to forget it.

So it would have to be about six months before she bore the child, assuming she could remain in hiding and get away with it. If instead, as seemed more likely, the FP caught up with her and gave her her abortion anyway, she would probably go to jail. So it was in the cases one read about. In any case she was going to be gone for months. As well as being the mother of his children she was Art's favorite sex partner, too. He opened the book and began to make plans for the changes in his sex life that would be brought about by Rita's prolonged absence. After half a minute he realized what he was doing, threw the book aside, and went back to re-reading the note, hoping without real hope to find some less terrible interpretation of its words. But there was none.

Pulling the phoneplate toward him on the bedside table, Art started to punch out the number of Ann and George Parr in Chicago. They had recently moved into a new house there—business at George's karate school was evidently good—and the new number was still fresh in Art's mind. He had looked it up for Rita last weekend. But when he was halfway through punching, he hesitated and then hit the blankoff key. Rita had been gone only a few hours at the most, and probably had not yet reached Chicago. Talking to George was not likely to do any good since Ann would be the one most actively helping Rita—and arguing with Ann about anything was, in Art's experience, certain to be futile. Anyway it was not the kind of thing Art wanted to talk about over the phone. Best not to call at all but to go straight after Rita and for her own good compel her to behave sensibly. And the sooner he caught up with her the better.

He reached for the phoneplate again, and this time tapped out the number of the Chess Director's Office, in the mid-California branch of the Bureau of Arts and Games. There was a wait, with evanescent rainbow static on the plate. Then a man's florid face appeared.

"Oh, hi, Art," the face said. "What's up?"

"Listen, Nick, I just called to say you'd better not pair me in for the first round of the Quarterly. I'm taking a little trip and I don't know if I'll be back in time."

"Oh, okay. Let me know about the August Monthly, hey?"

"Certainly I will. Go'th Eros."

"Goodbye."

For a moment Art continued to stare at the blank phone. In spite of his larger worries he found himself irritated by the Chess Director's offhand manner. Bureau of Arts people were supposed to believe in the importance of what they were doing; they should show at least a little formal regret when a rated master withdrew from an event. Nick had seemed as indifferent as a factory foreman checking attendance.

The thought of factories reminded Art that in courtesy he should call his own place of employment before he left, but the chime of an incoming call forestalled him.

On the plate appeared the face of a young woman, full-featured and of flawless skin. "May I speak to Ms. Rita Rodney, please? I'm Ms. Lazenby of the Bureau of Family Planning."

An unpleasant contraction in the stomach. "This is her husband. Ah, Rita's not in the house right now. Ah, she's out shopping somewhere, I expect."

Ms. Lazenby smiled, a friendly smile that could become sympathetic if the need arose. "Actually, the reason for my call concerns you too, Mr. Rodney, and your two children." She paused just enough for Art to have gotten a question in if he had felt the need. "Will you ask Rita to call me back as soon as possible if she returns home during business hours? We're open until five. Or otherwise to call me in the morning at her earliest convenience?"

"I will, yes, I'll tell her that."

"Thank you," Ms. Lazenby blanked off.

Art sat clutching the phone. Dr. Kuang had smelled trouble coming, had called in Family Planning right away, reporting Rita as a problem case. Call back tomorrow, Ms. Lazenby, and you'll probably get no answer, and you'll be very suspicious that something's up. But call back two or three days from now and you'll have a willing Rita here to talk to you, I promise you that. Or maybe you'll never have to call again, maybe by then the Certificate of Abortion will already have been fed into your FP computer banks.

What next? Oh yes, his job. Art punched out the number of the Macrotron Electronics plant in San Bernardino, and then the personal extension number of Pete Kinelo, his boss in the test-equipment maintenance and engineering department.

The plate showed the Macrotron trademark, and then the taped image of a girl who was nude or nearly so, it being impossible to tell at the moment because she was partly concealed behind a receptionist's desk. A small vase of roses stood before each breast, so that her nipples were just concealed. "One moment, please," the girl said, smiling pleasantly. "Your party has not yet answered his or her personal phone. We are continuing to page your party; thank you for waiting."

The music of *Swan Lake* began. The girl affixed an electrostatically clinging sequin to each of her nipples, coyly displayed a G-string and wriggled into it, and then writhed up from behind her desk in an erotic dance. In a moment she was dancing along the shore of a lilypond, and then in and out of the curtain of a small waterfall.

Art waited impatiently, looking at his watch. There were several other calls that he should make. One was the bank, to see how much cash was readily available, in other words how much Rita had taken; fortunately he had come home today with the check for first prize in the Weekly in his pocket and so should at least be able to buy a ticket to Chicago. Another call would be to the Office of Transcontinental Transit, to see how soon he could get a seat on a tube train.

At last the dancing girl was replaced by the face of Pete Kinelo. "Art?"

"Hello, Pete. I can take next week off, too."

"Oh, good." Pete beamed through his thick

glasses. "Then I can bring another substitute engineer in for a week. That'll put us in real good shape on employee utilization. Say, there's nothing wrong, is there?"

"No, no. Ah, I've been winning quite a few prizes and I've got my nerve up. I'm going to try some of the big tournaments coming up around Chicago."

"Great. Fine. Be sure and let me know if you're coming back week after next."

The transcontinental train, a string of sealed metal cylinders almost windowless and almost silent in their movement, hurtled eastward through its buried tube at a steady supersonic speed. On three-dimensional stages at the front of each car, feature-length tridi programs were being shown, a hangover from the days before competition with the airlines had been virtually ended by the latter's susceptibility to hijacking, accidents, and weather. In Art's car the life-sized, solid-looking, almost-real-looking images were enacting a play set in Victorian England, the locale of a lot of fiction these days.

The story had something to do with the romantic pursuit of a prim London nursemaid by a young leftenant (in the play they pronounced it that way) freshly returned from India. Obsessed as Art was with his own real problems, still the trashiness of the play aroused in him an automatic disgust. There was no apparent limit to what they could get away with showing these days. Every second or third shot, or so it seemed, was a long lingering closeup of the heroine, showing her swathed almost from chin to ankles in clothing that was not only loose-fitting but practically opaque. Only just enough of her shape and skin showed through to keep the Bureau of Arts censors from clamping down. Doubtless the producer would argue that in real Victorian England *nothing* had showed through, but, thank Eros, that was evidently not yet accepted as a valid argument by the censors and the courts. Ann, when he met her in Chicago, would probably be wearing something like this heroine's clothes. Rita wouldn't, though. She had better not.

What would be the very best first words for him to say when he caught up with her? What kind of look should he put on his face? He thought a moment and then decided there was no use trying to plan in such detail. Details would have to depend on the circumstances of the moment, on what her own attitude seemed to be. Of course he would have to be absolutely inflexible about terminating the pregnancy. No room for argument there. Rita could be stubborn, as he well knew, but this time he would be more stubborn. Maybe if he had taken a firm stand earlier, things would never have come to this pass . . . maybe. The trouble was that he could discern no single turning point; they had just drifted into it somehow.

Of course, pregnancies did happen. There was really no shame in getting pregnant, for the third or the thirteenth time, the only

shame was in not doing something about it.
Yes, pregnancies happened, all right. They
certainly happened to Rita, ever since he had
known her.

He had been teaching high school electronics when he met her; she was a student,
though not in any of his classes, and eight
years younger than he. They had been casual
acquaintances until the Senior Prom for Rita's
class, at which Art had happened to be one of
the chaperones. At the Prom—it had been
held aboard a tube-train basically like this
one, only a local, chartered to keep running in
a closed loop around mid-California for a couple of days—the graduates in keeping with
tradition broke out of their own age-group sexually for the first time, and Rita had spent a
good deal of the Prom in the bedroom car with
Art. He had felt a little guilty later about being
distracted so much from his chaperone's
duties, for there was some stargazing trouble
in the baggage car—well, that sort of thing had
happened before, and would again.

A few weeks after the Prom, coming back
from a vacation trip, he had accidentally—as
he then thought—run into Rita while visiting
the school for a one-day seminar. Later he was
to realize with a warm glow that she had made
a determined effort to locate and meet him on
that day. In the course of casual conversation
she mentioned to Art that she was pregnant.

"That's too bad," he commiserated mildly.
In general he disliked hearing people talk

about their ailments. "Do you suppose it happened at the Prom?"

"I think it must have happened there." Rita
smiled at him, and brushed back her naturally
blond, almost platinum hair, for which Art
had declared his admiration a number of
times, and which today seemed to have been
newly curled. "Maybe it's a little present from
you."

"I suppose it quite possibly is. The Prom
was great fun, though, wasn't it? I hope your
escort wasn't too put out with you for spending
so much time with me."

Rita dismissed the problems of her Prom escort with a wave. "Great fun!" she agreed, but
in the next moment smiled a little sadly. "Now
it looks like I'm leaving my good old school
days all behind."

Art was surprised. "Surely you're going on
to junior college at least?"

"I had planned to, but a pregnancy sort of
changes everything. At least for me it does."

"Why, won't you be over all that before the
fall term starts? Are there complications?"

"I'm going to have the baby, Art." About
halfway through the Prom her calling him Mr.
Rodney had stopped forever.

"You're *what?* I'm sorry, it's none of my
business, of course, but . . ."

"Going to bear the baby." This calm determination was a side of her he had not seen
before.

"But why?"

His shock dampened her enthusiasm, if that

was the right word for her attitude, but not her determination. "That's what my parents keep asking. It's hard for me to explain to anyone. It's as if there were already a tiny baby inside me, depending on me. Though I can't even feel it moving yet, of course."

"Hormonal changes are proceeding early, I suppose," Art muttered, to be saying something. As he had already said, it was none of his business—unless, he realized with a shattering silent flash, unless he wanted it to be.

He had tried, as he thought, a lot of things in his life, but never marriage. Now it was getting to be time for marriage. And he liked this girl, liked her better each time he saw her.

He said: "I suppose your parents have pointed out to you that having a child already is bound to make things harder for you when the time comes when you want to get married. Not to mention the difficulty of raising it by yourself."

"I know, you're absolutely right." Her frown admitted that it was a problem. "I guess most men want to raise two kids that they think they might have fathered themselves."

And she, too, was right of course. It was a rare man who was certain of being the biological father of his wife's two children. It took the trouble and expense of genetic testing to make sure, and few were that concerned. You might as well accept the first two healthy ones that came and raise them as your own. If one of your neighbors' kids was especially strong or smart or handsome, why you might nurse a hope that you were the sire. Conversely, if your wife gave birth to a child that seemed a little inferior, even though acceptably free of defects and certified human, you might tell yourself that someone else had fathered it.

The really pertinent question was, would Rita Parr make him a good wife? From observing his married friends Art knew that you always wound up spending a lot of time with a marriage partner. It was also an important step to take because getting into and out of marriages all the time added up to a lot of trouble and expense—and you wanted the children, when they came, to have a stable home.

He said: "Rita, I wish I knew you better."

They started dating regularly. He got to know her parents, and her likable brother George. He considered the idea of marrying her from every angle, or tried to. On the few occasions when he saw his own parents he hinted at the prospect of coming marriage, and detected a mild glow of approval in response, which, of course, was as much as he could expect; it had been a long time since what he did was of deep concern to them, or vice versa.

He and Rita were together more or less constantly for several months. He became convinced that she wanted very much to marry him. They quarreled, and then made up. In the spring her Timmy was born and Art sent flowers to her at the hospital and a few days later came to pay her a visit at home.

Rita, sitting in a rocking chair in her bedroom and feeding the baby from a nursing bottle, said to Art: "You know, I still think he's yours. I have that feeling about him, and I'm glad."

Studying the small wizened face, still bruised from the violence of birth, Art could find in it no resemblance to himself. But he realized that he was hoping to find a resemblance and, giving this some solitary thought a little later, he decided it was enough to tip the balance. A month later he and Rita, now legally, financially, and socially united in the bonds of matrimony, moved into a new apartment with little Tim.

After marriage, as before, he and Rita preferred to spend most of their free time in each other's company. After marriage Art experienced only one or two orgasms per month with anyone except his wife. And while he wasn't sure, he had the impression that Rita's sex life was even more intensely concentrated on him. He should have made a point of finding out. Such concentration of lust was one of the danger signals that the popular psychologists were always harping on, a sign that one's sexual attitudes might be somehow warped.

They had been married, quite happily for the most part, for two years when Rita surprised him with the announcement that she was pregnant again. It was really a surprise because they had both been taking anti-fertility pills, which certainly should have given protection. But, as Dr. Kuang explained, the pills were not one hundred per cent certain. Anyway the pregnancy was no real problem; they had caught it quite early and he could do a menstrual extraction right now in his office if they wished.

Oh, no. Although Rita, too, seemed surprised and not at all as calm as she had been about her first pregnancy, she was if anything even more determined that this one should produce a baby. To her the fetus was a person inside her belly, as if someone had taken a real baby and stuffed it in there. Her new baby was alive already, and she must protect its life. As far as Art could tell she had not absorbed this dogma from any of the few religious or "humanistic" sects which still maintained it as official doctrine. She had arrived at it by herself.

Naturally Art saw more of her during this pregnancy than he had during the previous one, and by now could more easily read her moods and guess her thoughts. What he saw this time began to frighten him. The first time he had thought she was simply being stubborn on the subject, acting in an immature, adolescent way. This time she seemed in the grip of some enormous force, a force bent on using her for making babies. Indeed, she refused even to discuss the possibility of getting an abortion. She even refused to take the tests that would predict whether her fetus was likely to grow into a deformed child; deformed or not, she said, it was her baby still. If Art persisted in trying to talk to her about it she quivered and suffered, seemingly outraged to the point of pain.

Well, Art had always more or less expected his wife to have two children. And people said it was more convenient if your two kids were about the same age. They could play together, and you got the diapering and the rest of the messy business over with once and for all. Since Rita was so determined to have this one, why not?

A couple of days after Paula was born Art called Dr. Kuang to talk over the best means of insuring against another pregnancy. Frowning from the phoneplate, Dr. Kuang told him that Rita's psychological profile showed that surgical sterilization was definitely not indicated in her case. He would prescribe new pills for her. "And of course having a vasectomy yourself will help. And, with male partners who are known to be strongly virile, she should choose sex activities other than copulation."

One trouble was that sex activities other than copulation were not much fun for her. One good thing was that she so rarely brought any man but Art to orgasm. He hastily got his vasectomy; in six months or so the residual sperm in his duct-work would presumably all have had their chance and he would be permanently and completely sterile.

He had done all he could, or so he thought. Meanwhile he had switched from teaching electronics to working at it, for Macrotron; also he had begun to spend more time away from home, improving his chess rating and winning more prizes. And then one day he came home and found a note.

II

THE SUGGESTIVE dialogue of the pseudo-Victorian play nagged at Art's attention, pulling him away from the fruitless game of trying to guess how he might better have managed his life with Rita in the past. He looked for the set of earplugs that should have been attached to his seat, intending to drown out the play with music or a soothing waterfall of gentle noise, but found to his disgust that one plug of the set was missing. Its connector of steel-jacketed wire had been neatly severed by some vandal, who seemed to have gone to the trouble of using a cutting torch.

He was not going to be able to avoid hearing the struggle of Phyllis and Rodney (the nursemaid and leftenant, respectively) against their mutual lust, a struggle in which he was sure they would eventually be victorious, but at least nothing forced him to watch the repulsive sight. Art now kept his face turned most of the time to the small window beside his luxurious chair. In the buried tunnel there was of course nothing to be seen except advertisements, the kind that were now starting to be called flickersigns. These were glowing adjurations that might be a hundred kilometers long, lettered in elongated characters designed to be intelligible only to one hurtling past them at a distance of a few centimeters and a speed of hundreds of kilometers per hour.

Art was reading one such ad, without absorbing an iota of its meaning, when without warning the train was thrown into violent deceleration. It was braking at emergency rate from jet-aircraft speeds, seemingly coming to a halt. In an instant the great plastic flowers of airbags bloomed before each seat, their multiple release coming with the sound of a single explosion.

A second after they had bloomed, the bags were soft and deflating once again, sagging into plastic detumescence. "Phyllis," said the tridi leftenant's voice, loud and clear in the first breathless moment of alarm among the passengers, who were only now reacting to being slammed in the face by plastic bags, "I am not an animal, to hurl myself upon you."

Phyllis's reply was drowned out by a general commotion among the passengers. In Art's car about half the seats were occupied, and the people were now exchanging exclamations, questions, and comments. As Art rubbed his nose where the bag had stung him a woman seated across the aisle looked over and asked him, almost pleadingly: "It must be just something wrong with the machinery, don't you think?"

Bracing his arms on the seat before him,

against the continuing heavy deceleration, he tried to give her a reassuring nod. "Yes, it must be." But he recalled the missing earplug; the Transon tubes were not immune to vandals, not any more at least, and therefore probably not immune to apes, or to terrorists of one persuasion or another. Glancing at his wristwatch, he determined that at the moment the train must be somewhere under the Great Plains, only a few hundred kilometers from his destination. Now the deceleration eased markedly. A look at the blur of tunnel wall and flickersign outside the little window indicated that the train was now moving not much faster than an automobile.

As the train continued to slow toward a full stop, the tridi play was interrupted. A man's voice, strong and reassuring and probably recorded, issued from the speakers on the momentarily empty stage. "Ladies and gentlemen, there is no cause for alarm." The voice paused as some decision-making process, human or electronic, selected the next phrase. "A technical difficulty has arisen. To minimize your inconvenience until your trip can be safely resumed, you will shortly be conducted to the surface by company guides. When the train stops, please remain seated until the guides arrive at your car. There is no cause for alarm."

Immediately a girl's tremulous voice added: "Rodney? I—I've always wanted a—a large family." A moment later Phyllis's image, as heavily garmented as ever, was back on stage, confronting the image of Rodney, who was standing in such a way that his uniform's flat lack of any bulging codpiece could not very well be ignored.

The airbags by now were nothing but wrinkled draperies on the seats. The passengers, who had quieted to get whatever news they could from the recorded announcement, were now babbling again and some of them were standing up. The woman across the aisle was once more addressing herself to Art but he could not hear her in the general noise. Now she got up and approached Art, to stand hovering over him. He unthinkingly took this as a sexual invitation and began to caress her hips, bare except for a G-string, but she gave only a perfunctory wiggle of response and he realized that her intent was to peer out of the little window beside his seat.

"Is that *water* in the tunnel?" she asked in a loud, clear voice, looking out. Other passengers heard her words and echoed them, and alarm began to mount.

Art took a turn at the window, trying to squint down at a difficult angle along a curve of dim concrete. The tunnel was circular in cross-section, as was the train, which filled it nearly from side to side and top to bottom. It was hard to see anything but Art thought there was at least some wetness on the concrete wall.

"Yes, it was a Thug who strangled him," groaned a grayhaired senior officer in full dress uniform upon the stage, "but I am the one really responsible for my son's death."

And that was the last of the play. The phantoms vanished from the stage again, as behind it, with a hiss and a clack, an emergency door opened in the front of the car. In a moment a man in a blue translucent uniform had come through the door and climbed upon the stage. Looking at first no more real than Rodney or Phyllis, he wore a hard helmet of blue plastic, with a clear faceplate, and carried some kind of pistol holstered at his belt. His stern expression eased into a professional smile as soon as a quick glance through the car assured him that all was peaceful. He stepped down briskly in front of the stage, making room for two more men, similarly dressed and armed, to mount it from behind.

The man who had entered first, and who wore stripes on his sleeves like those of a military sergeant, leaned casually on one of the front seats and addressed the passengers in a loud but friendly voice. "There's nothing to worry about, folks. The company regrets the inconvenience. We'll just have to walk a few steps through the tunnel, that's all. Will you all follow me out, please, through the front of the train?"

Eager as they were to get out of confinement and on their way again, the sergeant had no trouble keeping them moving past him and onto the stage and over it, while his two aides went on to the rear of the car, presumably to start evacuating people from the next car in that direction.

"Nossir, there's no flood," the sergeant re-

assured a man who had mounted the stage
ahead of Art. "It's no more than a puddle. Just
some kind of equipment breakdown. Keep
moving. This way out, please."

A few people were burdened with enough
luggage to make getting over the stage a struggle for them, and Art felt like offering a hand,
but he would have had to back up or push
ahead in line to do so, and he judged it better
to keep the evacuation moving smoothly. So
far all was going well enough, considering.

He and his fellow passengers had to pass
through two cars ahead of the one they had
ridden in, surmounting another tridi stage in
each, before an open door in the very front of
the train let them descend a short, steep, folding emergency stair into the darkness of the
tunnel. Maybe the sergeant had spoken too
soon about there being no flood, or maybe he
had simply been lying to prevent a panic.
From somewhere ahead, beyond the point
where the file of passengers preceding Art vanished in the gloom, there came a sound of
heavy splashing, as of wading, shuffling feet.
And now he could distinguish another watery
noise, as of a minor waterfall. The tunnel
seemed to slope downward gradually ahead of
the train, so it was natural that the water,
wherever it was coming from, would be deeper
there.

A pebble's toss ahead of Art one of the
guides—they were really Transcon's uniformed private police, of course—was shining
a pocket flash about, and someone else was

doing the same thing much farther on. The
only other illumination was that which shone
feebly from inside the train, and from a dim
red glowing line embedded in the tunnel wall
and stretching crooked and broken into an in-
determinate distance. Art realized that this
was an elongated flickersign symbol; if he had
been compelled to guess, he would have said it
was a question mark.

Following the vague form of the passenger
ahead, he felt the water rise to slosh about his
ankles. Now in the glow of the flickersign he
spotted the water leak, or at least one leak.
From a small crack in the concrete near the
tunnel's curving top, a kitchen-faucet-sized
stream came burbling down the concavity of
wall. But at least swimming was not going to
be necessary, for now just ahead another sergeant with another pocket flash was lighting
the file of evacuees into a doorway set into the
curved concrete of the tunnel wall. When Art
neared the door he saw just beyond it the steep
steps of a service stair ascending in a tight
helix.

He climbed in the wet footprints of those
ahead. At a landing that Art hoped was near
the top, but later proved to have been approximately halfway up, another policeman was
stationed to urge them on. It was a good thing
there was nobody in a wheelchair. "Step right
up, folks. When you're all assembled on the
surface we'll see you safely across the river,
then get you on another train. Sorry for the
inconvenience. This way . . ."

A black woman past middle age, gasping
from the climb, wearing gigantic false breasts
and an obvious merkin of false pubic hair beneath her transparent gown, stepped out of
line to argue. "River? What river is this? Why
were we halted here, for sex's sake?"

"It's the Mississippi, lady," said the officer,
politely gesturing her upward, then when she
still delayed, taking her arm with easy firm-
ness and propelling her along. "You're almost
in Chicago. Don't be alarmed, we'll get you
through in good shape."

Maybe three hundred kilometers to go, Art
estimated. As he climbed on, he could still
hear the guide's voice from behind: "Have to
keep moving, folks. No telling how high the
water'll come up these stairs if the tunnel
should collapse down there. Step along, please.
If you should see a little light rioting on the
surface, don't let it throw you. Just assemble
where you're told, and we'll see you through."

Of course there was adequate lighting on the
stair, but still it was good to finally distinguish daylight coming from above. At its
top the stair delivered its stream of refugees
into a graceful low concrete structure that was
open on three sides to the late summer afternoon. The structure looked as if it might serve
as a picnic shelter on more peaceful days. It
stood surrounded by a half-wooded, park-like
area. The near bank of the wide, placid river
was little more than a stone's throw away, at
the bottom of a broad gentle grassy slope. The
sun was lowering over the woods behind Art's

back as he faced across the river toward a solid
array of wooded bluffs that rose above the distant shore.

In and around the shelter lay many pieces
of freshly splintered wood that might very recently have formed picnic tables and benches,
and nearby a trash container lay on its side,
meager contents scattered. But there were no
rioters in sight. Some forty or fifty passengers
with their luggage, apparently all who had pre-
ceded Art up from the tunnel onto the grass,
were standing in loose formation close by the
shelter, like some motley levee of inducted
troops about to begin their training. A single
uniformed policeman stood casually before
them, giving them something to look at, at
least. Three more police, one wearing in-
conspicuously on his collar what Art supposed
was an officer's insignia, were standing inside
the shelter. One of these carried a radio buzzing with distant messages. With the three police was a shivering middle-aged man wearing
a translucent coverall and thick, tough-looking clear boots with mud dried on them. For a
moment Art thought that this man too was
armed, but then he saw that the holstered object at his waist was an electronic calculator.

Following the gaze of these men, Art saw
that the park was becoming not so peaceful after all. Down near the water people were emerging at a run from the concealment of some
trees. The people were mostly men, running
like clowns in twos and threes and half-dozens,
whooping and waving. There were twenty or

twenty-five of them altogether, and they might have been playing a game, or just scampering in high good spirits. One was waving a festoon of what appeared to be cables or plastic tubing.

The man with the calculator at his belt was talking rapidly to the police; with a little sideward glance he included Art in his audience, and went right on. "So we had our boat close in toward the west bank here, taking sediment samples, and just as I turned to say something to Carl, why pow, this rock went by my head and missed me by about a centimeter. And then I heard this mob up on the bank start yelling. Sex, once you hear a yell like that you know what it is, it means a bunch of people have all gone ape. Carl had his helmet off, see, but he still had his diving suit on, and it must have looked almost opaque and they must have thought we were from the monastery. I gunned the boat to get out from the shore, and then we must have hit something, a log or a piece of junk. When I came up for air that mob was heaving more rocks, there were splashes all around me. I ducked under and swam and waded, and came downstream about half a kilometer and climbed out here when I saw the uniforms. Never saw what happened to Carl. I hope he managed to grab his helmet and tank before he went under."

The capering people near the riverbank had disappeared into the trees again.

"Looks like they've got her burning, finally," one of the police said, squinting to the north, where the bank of the river on which they were standing mounted higher in tree-clothed bluffs. Rooted somewhere among the trees atop the bluffs, an ominously burgeoning growth of black smoke towered like the djinn of riot above the countryside.

"Must have been an old building," another policeman remarked.

"Did someone say it was a monastery?" Art put in, shocked at the indication of bigotry without being surprised by it.

"Yes," the river engineer (or whatever the man with his calculator was) answered. "Oh, not Church of Eros. One of the old Christian ones."

"That's hardly an excuse." Art watched the plume of smoke grow fatter. All this time a continuing trickle of passengers was continuing to emerge from the stairhead and straggle into place in their loose formation on the green.

"Well, I live around here," one of the police commented. "Not right for people to take the law into their own hands, but what can you expect? The rumor has been going around that the monkeymonks up there have been carrying on some kind of experiments with abortion specimens. Not just the kind where the scientists gain knowledge from them, but creating some kind of monsters. Chastity, I don't believe all I hear, but how do you expect people to take it when they're so mysterious?"

No one said anything for a little while. A poor attitude for even a private policeman to

take, thought Art, practically condoning rioting and vandalism. But it would be futile to
argue.

Shortly the engineer remarked: "Here come
a couple more refugees." Hiking across the in-
viting park, from the direction opposite the
smoke, came a couple who had evidently been
picnicking, for he carried a red plastic picnic
cooler and she a small outdoors pack and a
folded translucent blanket.

The man was tall, lean, thirtyish, and
freshly sunburnt. The girl was a full-bodied
brunette of eighteen or twenty. As they drew
near, Art saw that what he had at first taken
for sunglasses on her face were really artificial
eyes of what must be an advanced design.
They might have been opaquely dark sunglasses except that the thickness of their bulky
frames was molded in flush to the skin, all
around her eyes. She was neatly and modestly
dressed in a sports bikni of the latest style, her
translucent bra extended in twin peaks by
finger-long cones of pinkish nipple-colored
plastic.

As the couple approached the shelter, the
man spoke to the police in a husky, somewhat
hurried voice. "Officers, we're very glad to see
you. I hope you can provide us with some kind
of escort back across the river, or get us on the
train to Chicago if possible. Our boat was destroyed, you see." The girl said nothing,
looked around nervously, and stayed close to
her companion. She looked at Art, but he had
trouble reading her expression; the artificial

eyes functioned like a mask. Faint cat's-eye gleams shone in their dark lenses, and the plastic frames were studded with artificial jewels. Or could those stones possibly be genuine?

"Sure, you can come along," the officer with the collar insignia said. "Got your boat too, hey?" He changed his position and stretched as the last rescued passenger, sitting in a wheelchair (so there had been one, after all) was heaved into view at the stairhead by a team of puffing police. "I guess we're all here now. Let's start getting these people over the water."

The two saved picnickers walked beside Art to join the other evacuees. As the whole group with its escort of police began to move, the girl let out a sudden, choked little cry, and Art saw her actually begin to tremble. Following the direction of her gaze, he beheld a new eruption of rioters boiling out of the woods and cutting across the passengers' path, evidently with the intention of intercepting them before they could reach the river. Art now also saw in midstream a large launch that had evidently just been called from across the river and was now heading in to the near bank where a small dock waited at the end of the passengers' present line of march.

The march continued. The officer barked an order or two, and his blue-uniformed men, now about a dozen strong, closed in beside the much more numerous troop of people they were convoying, their screen forming most tightly at the point where the threat was greatest.

There were perhaps thirty people in the mob approaching. Half a dozen or so were women, and these were screaming loudly, urging on the men. Most of the men wore the gaudily colored and oversized codpieces favored these days among the youth of the Basic Income class. One who was so garbed, a large, florid young man with close-set eyes, went right up to the police line and peered over uniformed shoulders at the shrinking sheep behind as if about to choose one for slaughter.

"Any triplet priests in there?" the florid one demanded. "Any sublimatin' vivesectionists? We got one already, but there's some more experiments we'd like to try." He seemed on the point of trying to push his way through the protective line, and one of the bigger police shoved him roughly back. When he demonstrated anger at this treatment he found himself looking at a drawn handgun.

"We're just passing through, bigmouth," the policeman told him. "Now you just pull your jaw out of our way and let us pass."

There were no firearms visible among the rioters, and indeed Art could not see that they carried weapons of any kind. The sight of the gun knocked them back almost like a physical force. Moving like the cells of some multiple organism, keeping together as if under the control of a single mind, they fell into retreat.

One we got already. The words echoed in

Art's mind. But maybe they were only brag and bluff.

The passengers with their convoy of police moved on unmolested toward the dock, which was now only about a hundred meters off. The immediate threat was apparently over but the girl with artificial eyes, walking beside Art, continued to breathe as if on the verge of hysteria. Her escort held her by the arm and kept speaking to her in a low voice, but his efforts to calm her had little effect.

The police, evidently to keep a prudent distance from a patch of dense woods into which the rioters had retreated, had bent the convoy's line of march almost parallel to the river. Now in those infested woods another outbreak of shouting rose up, blended with the noises of running feet trampling the undergrowth. The girl moaned and moved away from the noise, leaning against Art like a frightened child. He put an arm around her full body and squeezed it in a polite caress. "My name's Art, by the way. What's yours?"

He would scarcely have been surprised to receive no answer, but one came. "Rosamond. Rosamond Jamison. Oh!"

Now from the woods came a man's voice shouting, but words indistinguishable but pain, fear, and despair all blended in. The man who was walking on the other side of Rosamond Jamison froze in his tracks, so quickly that those walking behind him had trouble avoiding a collision. "That was Steve," he said to himself in a low voice that Art nonetheless overheard distinctly. In another moment Rosamond's escort had caught up with the police lieutenant and was grabbing at his shoulder. "Did you hear that? A man's in trouble over there. Aren't you going to do something?"

The voice shouted again, this time in terrible wordless agony.

The lieutenant, who had started to say one thing, began again with something else. "I've got my own job to do, getting these people safely on their way. That could be some kind of trick, just to get us into the woods."

"No it isn't. Didn't you hear that scream just now? You think that could have been a trick?"

The lieutenant, inflexible, shook his head. "I've got my orders, my job. That's it."

"You can't just go on."

The lieutenant turned away.

The tall, sunburnt man, anxiety unabated, hurried back to Rosamond. "Here." To her he gave the weighty-looking picnic cooler. She took it automatically and carried it with some difficulty as she continued moving forward with the refugee column. The man said to Art: "Try and look out for her, will you? See that she gets on a train to Chicago?"

"Of course, I'll try to help. But what are you —?"

Muttering some last, unintelligible phrase over his shoulder, the man was gone. Moving with unexpected strength and speed, he had pushed his way through the police escort on

the inland side and was running toward the
woods before anyone but Art became aware of
his intention.

"Halt!" the lieutenant bellowed, when he
did catch on. "Come back here! Don't be a
sublimatin' fool!"

The fleeing man did not pause or turn. In
another moment he was out of sight in the
woods. Rosamond, struggling forward with her
picnic cooler, looked after her companion only
briefly and then faced forward again, concentrating her efforts on keeping up with the
convoy's rapid pace. She was having a hard
time doing so now. In the rear of the column
shifts of volunteers were practically carrying
the wheelchair and its terrified occupant.

Art put a hand on the cooler's carrying grip.
"Let me help."

"Oh, thank you." But she seemed reluctant
to let him take the weight. When he did so,
however, they made better time.

The boat, which was moored at the dock by
the time they got there, proved to be some sort
of sight-seeing craft, evidently commandeered
for this occasion. With all the refugees aboard,
it was quite crowded, and some had to sit or
squat on the deck between rows of seats. Most
of the police remained behind on shore, and as
the boat pulled away from the dock Art saw
them beginning to march in loose formation
back up the slope toward the emergency exit
from the tube. Other trains would be arriving
behind his, Art realized.

Along the eastern, Illinois shore the woods

looked wilder and less park-like than those of Iowa just left behind. When the boat scraped bottom on the eastern side, the police pilot made an announcement, straining to be cheerful. "Folks, will you all wait right here in this area, please? We have to take the boat back across the river and pick up some people from another eastbound train. Then we'll get you all on your way to Chicago very shortly. Get off the boat promptly please, step right into the water there. It's not deep." There was no dock here on the eastern shore and one policeman was in the water himself, handing passengers off into the knee-deep Mississippi. Plenty of volunteers rallied around the wheelchair again, with grins and jokes. People were sometimes marvelous.

A few steps had to be taken on the oozy river bottom to reach the muddy shore. Once on solid ground most of the passengers gravitated inland, as if hoping, in spite of what the guides had said, that there might be another tube terminal right at hand. Thirty or forty meters inland a narrow unpaved road roughly paralleled the river, but traffic seemed nonexistent. Beyond the road and behind a wire fence, the tree-covered bluffs rose up unpromisingly. The passengers who had probed the farthest soon came back with unhopeful reports. There was apparently no place to go and nothing to do but wait as they had been told. No one knew where the point of access to the eastbound tunnel might be.

Art and Rosamond, having the cooler to carry and both of them lacking any desire for an aimless hike, remained somewhat behind most of the other passengers as the latter drifted up to hang around the road. The two of them sat down upon a grassy bank where the sun, now lowering close over Iowa, still shone brightly. Rosamond was quiet, and seemed less fearful now, though she was still looking intently back over the river.

"He'll probably come over in the next boatload," Art offered, trying to be comforting. "He's probably all right and they'll be able to pick him up and bring him along."

She turned to him and reached across the cooler to tickle the palm of his hand, and smiled at him beneath her enigmatic eyes. "I think I would enjoy some sex right about now."

"Of course."

They spent an enjoyable ten minutes at it, with Art's paper shirt spread over the rough grass beneath their bodies. Afterward as they lay together together relaxing Rosamond began to shiver; the sun was so low that it had lost its heat, and a cool breeze had come up. In a little while she sat up and pulled her discarded bikni on again but of course it was too small to provide any real warmth. Art picked up the paper shirt, now notably wrinkled and soiled, and held it out. "Afraid this is the best I can offer you. There doesn't seem to be a clothing vendor anywhere around."

"You'll be cold, won't you?"

"I'm a little fat." He stood up and adjusted his codpiece and transparent trousers. "I guess that helps to keep one warm."

Rosamond pulled on the shirt, and then sat down in the grass again with her legs crossed, feet and all tucked completely in under the garment so that it fell around her like a small tent. The shadow of a bush fell over her now and in the dulled light the shirt was practically opaque, and she was concealed and shapeless from the neck down. Now it was Art's turn to shiver slightly, and his shiver was not caused entirely by the cold. Unwholesome thoughts had come unbidden to his mind. He controlled himself, however and, like a gentleman, looked away.

Just as he thought he had the temptation to repression really squelched it popped up again with a new ploy. The poor girl was still shivering, wasn't she? He should do what he could to help, right? "Want my trousers?" he asked. It was incidental, he told himself, it was not important in this emergency, that removing the trousers would mean taking off the codpiece too and this would mean stripping his detumescent body of his proper sexual emphasis.

She appeared not to find anything wrong or suggestive of sublimation in his offer, but declined it all the same. "No, this is fine, thank you. You've been a wonderful help. I hope I can repay you some day."

He slew a mosquito on his bare shoulder. The river before them was beginning to reproduce a sunset. Around them on the riverbank a number of the other stranded passengers had also paired off and were embracing or resting between embraces. The presence of these others made real impropriety unthinkable and helped Art put temptations from his mind.

There were more boats in the river now, police or other official crafts of some kind, and their searchlights were beginning to play over the far bank. Groups of people were still moving around over there. They had improvised banners to carry, and rhythmic chants to sing. From where Art sat on the eastern bank the words of neither song nor sign could be distinguished, but the powerful tones of the chanting carried across the water.

III

AS THE train began to slow for the Chicago terminal, Rosamond leaned across the seat arm and snuggled once more against Art's shoulder, while one of her hands, like some small animal seeking shelter, strayed inside his tattered shirt. "Art, are you sure you can't take the time to meet Daddy tonight? I know he's going to want to thank you for helping me."

"I wish I could, but I'm really anxious to catch up with my family." Of course he hadn't told her why he was trying to catch up with them. He glanced at his watch; it was nearly midnight. "Some other time."

"You be sure and call us while you're in Chicago. I mean it." She dug out a pencil and a piece of paper from the pouch attached to the seatback in front of her, and scribbled a number, using the top of the picnic cooler as a desk. When he touched the plastic top, in reaching to pick up the paper, it felt at least as cold as ice. Like her eyeframes, the cooler was perhaps more expensive than it had seemed at first sight; whatever picnic remnants were inside were probably frozen solid.

As he emerged from the tube car into a vast

cheerful cave of ceramic tile and warm light, Art looked around to wave goodbye to Rose, and caught only a glimpse of her in the crowd, being met and welcomed by a couple of men. Strange girl. But he forgot about her quickly in heading for a huge electronic display describing the city's public transportation system.

It was late enough for the traffic to be light, and the taxi he had chosen as the probable fastest means of transport made good speed through the well-illuminated streets. Still Art shifted restlessly in his seat, and pulled at his beard impatiently. He had the feeling that minutes counted, that even now Rita might be taking some irretraceable step toward an illegal parturition. The feeling was no doubt irrational; any actual birth would have to be months away, of course. But there was some kind of federal law against even conspiring to commit an illegal parturition. Midwifery, as the news media usually called it. Art didn't know exactly how far one could go without running afoul of the law. He didn't know exactly what the law said. It was one of those things he hadn't wanted to learn about, probably because all along he had been subconsciously afraid that someday it would menace him and Rita.

How could she do such a thing, get them into this kind of trouble? In her note she had said that she still loved him. She had used the word twice. But now he was being rhetorical with himself; he knew his wife, and she was perfectly capable of doing this thing, loving him or not.

While waiting for a traffic signal to change
the cab driver turned in his seat and glanced
back at Art through the bullet-proof partition.
Through the intercom speaker the driver's
voice asked: "Someone meeting you?"

"Yes." Art stretched the truth. "At the
block entrance. It's a block of townhouses."

The cabbie faced forward again without answering. Art had just killed his hopes of collect-
ing an easy bodyguard fee, in what the cabbie
must know was a good neighborhood.

They were moving again. Now the building
walls that had lined both sides of the street fell
back. The cab was entering a section of the
city that had a look of newness, of having recently been rebuilt. Under new streetlamps
that closely simulated daylight, tall elms
warmed their fine June leaves. On each side of
the wide, gently curving boulevard were new-
looking stone walls, smooth enough to be un-
scaleable but still with enough irregularities in
their texture and color and shape to give them
almost the look of natural formations. The
walls were windowless, two or three stories
high, and Art knew that they enclosed
townhouse blocks, about the size of the old city
blocks they had replaced. The pedestrian entrances, never more than one on a side, were
narrow-mouthed and well-lighted; inside each
entrance, Art supposed, there would be a security guard in a protected booth. Vehicle
ramps curved down from the street to enter a
subterranean level of each block.

The cab stopped in front of one such entrance, and Art put money into the slot in the

partition, got back his change, and disembarked. He walked right into the bright rocky tunnel of the entry, through block walls that looked as thick as those of some ancient castle —or cave, perhaps, where the first men had sheltered from the terrors of the night they could not understand.

He came quickly to a place where the bright-lit narrow passage was blocked by a gate of steel grillwork, heavily functional despite its ornamentation of nymphs and cupids. In a booth built into the wall beside the gate sat a gray-uniformed man who looked out at Art through a small window of bulletproof glass. Through the window Art could see that this guard had before him rows of buttons, and closed-circuit TV monitors, and a pistol within easy reach. The guard was eyeing Art with alert suspicion, no doubt sharpened by the lateness of the hour.

"I want to visit George Parr," Art said. "Tell him Art Rodney is out here." He checked the time on his watch and began to wait.

Less than three minutes passed before George came into view beyond the iron gate, which slid open at his arrival. He was smiling and holding out his big-knuckled hand. Aside from the callus pads over the base knuckles of forefinger and middle finger, there was nothing peculiar in the feel of George's hand, lethal weapon though it was supposed to be. And George was rather short. Sturdy, but not bulging or rippling with muscle inside his trans-

parent shirt. His pale hair, almost the color of
Rita's, was crew-cut to the same length as his
neat goatee.

"How's it going, Art?" George didn't look
upset about anything, but then Art could not
recall that he ever had.

"Well, I'm upset, naturally. I want to talk to
Rita right away."

"She's been here, but now she's gone again."

"What?"

"That's right. Come in." With gentle pressure on an arm George steered him through
the gate. Speaking to the microphone below
the guard's window, George added: "My
brother-in-law. He's going to be staying with
us for a day or so."

Art let himself be steered inside, though he
wasn't at all sure about the duration of his
stay. "Where is she now?" he asked impatiently. "Couldn't *you* have talked to her?"

George simply continued to smile in his
likable way. "Come on in and have a look at
our new home. We can talk the whole situation
over. It's not something that can be settled in
a couple of words. Ann's fixing up a bed for
you."

"All right." Art sighed, abandoning whatever hope he had left of somehow catching up
with Rita tonight. Let Ann fix the bed. He was
willing to bet she would never offer to share it
with him, which was fine with Art. He would
make polite gestures of lust at her, whether or
not she had the good manners to reciprocate,
but in truth she aroused him not at all.

Another few meters of tunnel and they had reached the interior of the block. It looked just about as Art had expected, but still he was impressed. Most of the interior was a single open space, wide and pleasant, green now with summer grass and trees and shrubs. This central park was mostly in darkness now, but was surrounded by the lighted windows and patios of the block's thirty or so townhouses, which were all backed against the block's encircling outer wall and were probably integral with it.

Shaded lights on knee-high poles gently illuminated curved paths of flagstone paving that branched off into the balmy night in several directions. Crickets sang of summer and tranquility. In spite of his worries Art found himself pausing, soothed by the peaceful scene. He said: "It looks like you have things nice in here."

George pounced gratefully on this retreat to banality. "I tell you, it makes me feel a lot easier about the kids. There's even talk about getting our own elementary school started right here in the block." He gestured the direction for Art to take and they walked on. Somewhere nearby, people playing string instruments were rehearsing a melody, starting and stopping and trying again. Somewhere else a wild party was in progress, but its uproar came heavily muted from some deep interior place, and to the musicians inside their own house it must be entirely inaudible.

"Yes, very nice," said Art, following where George led.

"We have our own emergency power generator, too," said George. "In case vandals knock out the city power or there's a breakdown. That's happened a couple of times in the last year."

"Good idea." Art's sandals scraped on the slight unevenness of the flagstones as they walked a pleasant curve between the houses' vine- and bush-screened patios and the openness of the central park. Each house was surprisingly private behind its trellises or open-work wall or vines. Art wondered if Rita might be sheltering at this moment in one of these discreet dwellings, hidden by friendly conspiratorial neighbors until Ann could throw the persecuting husband off the track with some halfway plausible story. "Yes, this is a beautiful place."

"Costs an arm and a leg and a testicle too," said George, his voice now turning grim. "I don't think there's a man in the block who doesn't have a job—I mean a *good* job—or his own business. In fact I'm repressin' sure there isn't." Talking man-to-man, George would sometimes use strong language. In front of ladies, Art had noticed, he never did.

"How are things at the dojo?" Art asked. Then he turned his head at the unexpected sound of a splash, followed by a trill of feminine laughter. Way out in the middle of the common park the lights of a swimming pool glowed in the soft, safe darkness, and he saw the wet tan gleam of a bikinied body. What were possibly the lights of another pool

were almost completely blocked off by in-
tervening shrubbery.

"Oh, good enough, I guess," said George.
"Here's our happy home." He walked behind
a vine-covered trellis to a patio. Ann, as if she
might have heard them coming, was peering
out with a hospitable smile from her doorway
of white stone and Spanish-looking ironwork.
Stalking across the Parrs' hedged-in patio on
thin metal legs, a kneehigh electric bugkiller
lured flying creatures to itself with a nervously
flickering eye of yellow light and a whisper of
attractive noises. It broke its whispering with
zapping hiccoughs as some of its larger victims
were ingested.

As Art had expected, Ann's dress was radical. Her skirt fell almost to her knees, and her
blouse almost completely covered her breasts
and left only a narrow strip of midriff bare.
Both garments were loose-fitting and practically opaque. Also as he had expected, Ann's
chin was lifted high in challenge despite her
smile; she would be glad to have him stay in
her house for a day or so and argue; maybe she
would be able to convert him. Her face was
reasonably pretty, and her hair a curly brown.
She was small and strong, like George, and her
strength was even more subtle than his.

"Rita thought you might come after her,
Art," she greeted him. "You didn't bring a
bag? That's all right, there's a clothing vendor
right here in the block. Of course you're
staying with us, we have a spare room. My
brother was here for a couple of days, but he

moved out when Rita showed up." Ann shrugged away her sibling's behavior.

"Fred's here in Chicago too?"

"Yes. The day he finished high school he just had to apply for Basic Income, like a fool. Couldn't see going to college, or even trying to go. He wants George to give him a job, or so he says. Come and see your children, they're asleep."

Inside the townhouse the furnishings were rather sparse and disorderly, indicating that the Parrs were not yet done with the job. Evidently they had barely time to unpack in their new house before a series of their crazy relatives began to arrive from California. Following Ann to some ascending stairs, Art noted an electric fireplace in the living room, where the floor looked like real hardwood. He could well believe that only the prosperous lived in this block.

After gesturing for silence in a second-floor hallway, Ann slid open a door. Art went in to find Timmy and Paula curled up in their usual positions in the strange bed, child-bodies clothed in opaque pajamas like unopened flower buds all sheathed in leaves. Across the room in another bed were two small mounds that would be George Jr. and his younger brother Enoch. On the wall Art noticed a version of what he recognized as a traditional Christian statuette, depicting the putative founder of the sect fastened to a wooden cross. The figure was quite large for the little room, and crudely but strongly carved in some pale wood. He wondered if Fred might have done it.

"Don't wake them," Ann whispered, as Art bent over his own two children. "They're worn out from traveling."

Art, who had not intended to touch them and risk an awakening, now gave each a kiss. They were not as deeply asleep as he had thought, for Paula reached up to tangle baby fingers in his beard. Then, as if reassured, she slept again. Tim, almost three years older, murmured: "Daddy."

"Go to sleep," Daddy whispered. And Tim did so, for once.

Art walked downstairs again with Ann. "So," he commented, "Rita's gone into hiding somewhere. How long does she expect the children to stay here?"

"Art, you know we don't mind having them in the least. Husband George, where are you?"

"That wasn't what I asked."

"Black Russian?" asked George from below, appearing in the doorway of what was evidently the recreation room, holding a couple of plastic bottles in his hands.

"Thanks, I will," Art answered. Inside the rec room was a bar, and a second fireplace, with a tap marked INSTRUCTIONS still hanging from one andiron. Art sank down with a sigh upon a leather-like couch, and received from George a glass with ice cubes floating in a dark and powerful fluid.

Ann had vanished, apparently to the kitchen, for there drifted in sounds suggesting the preparation of food. From out there somewhere she called: "How do you like our medieval fortress? I'm very happy with it. The kids have a safe place now."

"It's very nice," Art called back, downing his first swallow of Black Russian. "I think I saw two swimming pools, didn't I?"

In a chair opposite the sofa George sat, or squatted, pulling up his sandalled feet and folding his legs in an effortless contortion. "The pool in the bushes is more Ann's than anybody else's. She's always wanted a nude pool available, and when the blockhouse corporation was being formed she kept standing up in meetings and demanding."

"Well, why shouldn't I?" Ann, smiling, was in the doorway, already pushing a serving cart laden with sandwiches and cups of soup. Had she been expecting Art? "You know me, Art."

He thought he did. While moving clutter from a small table to make room for some food, Art got a good look at the covers of some of Ann's radical magazines. The cover photos featured startlingly shrouded bodies, and bold print promised that the articles inside were of shocking frankness, detailing what every adult ought to know about the history of celibacy and the ancient, once-honorable techniques of self-control. Art took these to be the kind of magazines that promised more in the way of obscenity than they usually delivered. He would have expected a more sophisticated obscenity than this on Ann's coffee table. He thought that she was watching for his reaction to the magazines, and he tried to show none at all. Maybe they were just left there as argument pieces.

Art didn't much like the idea of his children staying here, but where else was he going to put them while he searched for Rita? And they were too young, he supposed, to be much affected by Ann's morals—or lack thereof. He liked to think of himself as fairly liberal, but this woman just had a dirty mind. It was as simple as that. He could imagine being marooned in a long orbit with her, and her wearing long opaque coveralls continuously, and refusing sex through all the months and years.

He had thought he was conjuring up that image as a private expression of his scorn, but somewhere in its ugly heart a kernel of attraction lay, which made Art angry when he realized it. Repulsive woman! He could feel sorry for George, who was a gentleman, except that George must have known what kind of woman he was marrying and George still seemed very well satisfied. George in his own quiet way was evidently pretty far out himself.

"You know, old girl," said George, the squatting guru, "your ways are actually more old-fashioned than your opponents' are. You go back to the twentieth century. Or was it the nineteenth when everybody pretended to be chaste?"

Ann took a seat on the sofa next to Art and gave him a look intended to show comic exasperation with her husband. "I'm hungry, let's eat," she said. "Oh, George, you know it's

not what's new or what's old-fashioned. I
know things go in cycles. It's not whether people wear suits when they swim or don't wear
them, it's *why* they wear them or go without."

"Ann." Art set down his glass, which had
somehow become empty. "Ann, where is Rita?
Where did you send her?"

"Art, listen to me. I'm not going to tell you
where she is, because I don't know."

"Don't *know?* Come on. When is she coming
back to get the children? As soon as I leave?"

Ann, with maddening assurance, ignored
the question. "Art, I suppose you realize that
she's expecting the people at Family Planning
to make trouble for her."

"Of course I know she's in Family Planning
trouble. Why do you imagine I'm here?" If he
hadn't had the drink he would be shouting at
Ann by now. "She left me a note, I know she's
pregnant. I even had a call from the FP before
I left California." He repeated as well as he
could the few words of Ms. Lazenby's
message.

Ann listened in sympathy and indignation,
as if the FP agents had broken down Art's
door. "Well, if and when our third one comes
along—I take my pills and pray it never does,
but if and when—I'm going to do just what
Rita's doing. No court or no doctor is going to
murder one of mine, I don't care what the laws
say."

"You have that right," affirmed George in a
low voice.

She flashed her eyes over at her husband,

glad of support though not needing it, and plunged on. "And no one's going to make me call it unwanted, either, not once I know that it's alive!"

Drink or not, Art's nerves were worn and his voice got louder. "Most people would say that you yourself have rather a murderous attitude toward the wanted people of the world. The ones who are alive right now, including the babies. You're talking about adding to the crowding. Remember Calcutta. Remember Rio. Where will this year's cannibalism be?"

George had begun on a cup of soup with apparent good appetite. Now he reached in between the disputants for some crackers. "Peace, brethren, peace, sistern," he said, smiling genuinely. "Art, how was your trip?"

"Oh, exciting." Art sat back and took an interest in his own soup. Arguing general principles with Ann was certain to wear him out and get him nowhere. Let the atmosphere cool off for a minute and then he would return to the subject of his wife. He began to tell the Parrs of his adventures.

The attack on the Christian monastery was naturally a shock to Ann, and he let her see the real sympathy he felt for any victims of persecution. "I suppose we passengers should have stopped and demanded that the police do something for that man who was screaming in the woods—but they were only Transcon's private police, and I suppose they had their orders, as they said."

Ann looked at him wanly, mystified. "But

why was the monastery being attacked?"

"One of the people there said something about the monks' performing experiments on some aborted fetuses. Some absurd, muddled story about creating monsters. Of course a lot of scientists work with fetuses." Ann for some reason seemed shocked, perhaps even frightened; she was sitting quite still and listening intently. Art went on: "It *does* strike me as rather inconsistent for these monks, who are presumably as opposed to abortion as you are, to use fetuses that are still biologically active in their experiments, whatever research they're really doing. Of course that's no excuse for violence, for mob action."

Ann and George exchanged a look. Then she brought her attention back to Art. "Who was this girl you said you helped?"

"Oh, her name was Rose something or other, lived in Chicago. She was really frightened, for which I don't blame her."

Ann was upset. "There doesn't seem to be any safety for anyone any more. I'm glad we've got this place. Art, you and Rita should think about getting into a townhouse like this. I don't think California is any safer to live in than Illinois."

"I'm sure we have a lot of problems out there, too. I'll talk over our housing situation with Rita after I've found her again. Now tell me where she is."

His voice was not threatening but it was grim and determined enough to shake Ann back into her anger mode again. Her eyes

brightened and her chin lifted. But before she
could speak George put out a peremptory
hand and got to his feet with a neat quick un-
tangling of his legs. "Ann," was all he said, but
to Art's surprise, she closed her mouth.

George set down the empty soup cup that he
had been turning round and round in his fingers for some time. "Art, I'm satisfied that
Rita's in good hands."

"Then you know where she is. If you know,
you're going to tell me."

"Let me finish. Let's say that I know my
sister. I believe she knows what she's doing.
Isn't that enough?"

"Not for me." Art was inflexible. "You
knew she was trying to do something wrong,
and dangerous, and maybe you could have
stopped her but you didn't try."

There was a pause that seemed long. Ann,
evidently still considering herself commanded
to silence, was biting her tongue. Her husband
still held the floor, dominating the room
without effort, unconsciously rubbing his
enlarged knuckles. "I know it's dangerous,"
George said unhappily. "She could go to jail
for what she's doing. But she wants to do it.
She made a free decision."

"What about me?" Art demanded. "Don't I
have any say about how many children I
have?"

Ann's headshake snapped a decisive No.
"Not if it means killing."

"*Killing?* How can you call an abortion—?"
But it was no use. Even if it had been desirable

to argue with Ann, he could have found no words. Ann's reality was so far from the commonly accepted view that there seemed to be no place to start. At least Art could not find the place, not after midnight, not after a day of wife-chasing and strain and rioting and Black Russians. Somewhere along the line George had refilled his glass and by now it was half empty again. "I wish we could forget about our differences," Art went on, lowering his voice. "Rita's welfare is the only thing I'm worried about right now. All else is secondary."

"We know that," said Ann with impulsive honest sympathy.

"Eventually I'll find her," Art insisted. "You know I'm going to bring her home. You think I'll just let her drop out of my life for six or seven months? And what about the children, are they going to stay here for that length of time? Timmy should be starting kindergarten ... it's an insane scheme and I won't allow it. In any case Family Planning will put a stop to it if I don't. Don't you suppose they can quickly track her down? Isn't there a law against conspiracy to commit parturition that they could prosecute her under already?"

"Not without more evidence than her dropping out of sight for a few days," Ann said quickly. "Not without a lot more evidence than that."

"For a few days? I don't understand. What does she hope to accomplish by doing that?"

Ann fell silent again. George waved a hand

and seemed about to speak, but then only sat down again and stared into his new fireplace.

"Will somebody tell me, please?"

"You see," Ann began slowly, "once nine months have passed since conception, no doctor is allowed to put the baby to death for any reason, without the direct petition of the mother or other surviving next of kin. The Supreme Court was very clear on that several decades ago, and the decision still stands. And what does a conspiracy indictment matter to a mother who can save her baby's life?"

Baby? Oh, of course, she was talking about the fetus. Art was no longer sure that anything being said made sense. It was well after midnight, and they must all be tired. He was, certainly. Eros, but Rita too must be tired this midnight, wherever she might be.

Ann said: "Art, your room is ready. Whenever you want to go up."

"In the morning, then," Art told her. "But never doubt that I'm going to find her and take her home."

IV

FRED LOHMANN woke up with someone's smooth arm thrown across his bare chest and someone's delicate breath snoring gently in his left ear. Where was he? Oh yes, the YPPC hotel, in Chicago. Yesterday he had checked out of the Parrs' plush new house, more or less urged on by his sister Ann, and anyway not anxious to get himself involved in whatever had brought Rita Rodney in weeping from California. Rita had looked pregnant, far enough along to show a little. Say, didn't the Rodneys have two kids already?

Anyway, all that was none of Fred's affair. He had big problems of his own, and important events were scheduled for today. First of all, this morning Fred as a newly independent and adult citizen was going to collect his first Basic Income check from Uncle Sam, the check covering the month that had passed since his graduation from high school in California. And that first BI check might well be his last; he sublimatin' well hoped it would be anyway, for this afternoon he was going to have a real workout with George and if things went well at the dojo he might be a jobholder

by tomorrow. And that would prove a lot of
people wrong.

Now, what about this sleeping arm that
weighed so gently on his breathing? In a moment he remembered, her name was Marjorie.
She too was a newcomer to Chicago, looking
for a job, and last night the desk clerk at the Y
had assigned her and Fred to sleep together.
The atmosphere at the Young Persons' Play
Club was certainly different from what it was
at the Parrs'. Ann and George might get a
chuckle out of it when he told them. Behind
the front desk in the lobby was a big sign on
the wall reading PURE THOUGHTS ARE THE MARK
OF A DIRTY MIND. And they weren't trying to be
funny, either, they were really that old-fashioned here. They had a strict house rule requiring at least two people in every bed. Marjorie, though she herself was by all indications
a conservative, well-brought-up, lascivious
girl, had agreed with Fred last night that the
sign was funny, and they had shared a little
laugh about it. She was a good sex partner, too,
so things had worked out all right. He might
have been paired with someone a lot less con-
genial.

Fred disentangled himself from Marjorie's
naked body and got out of bed without awakening her. The bed folded down on both sides
of the wall that separated his tiny room from
hers. Ingenious, Fred thought. When the bed
was raised it completed the wall and the rooms
were separated, allowing either party to have
privacy for business or social reasons. A hole

was created through the wall, connecting the rooms, whenever the bed was lowered for use. Last night Fred had discovered that the bed mechanism made it impossible to raise or lower either side independently; if you wanted to lie down, you had better be ready for sex, or at least a polite attempt at sex, with your appointed partner. George was going to have a good laugh when Fred told him. Except George seemed to have a lot on his mind just lately.

After a quick visit to the alcove that held his toilet and shower, Fred came back to the center of his small room, studied his tall, muscular body in the wall mirror, and did a few light exercises, just loosening and testing a little, making sure the knee and elbow joints moved freely and with plenty of snap. He tensed his corrugated belly muscles and snapped his rocklike fist at his solar plexus, leaving a small red mark. He told himself he looked older than eighteen; the beard was coming along okay. But he hadn't really worked out in more than a week, and though he tried not to admit it to himself he was scared by the thought of this afternoon's pending test with George.

Would George take his word for it that he really had a brown belt ranking, or might George call California to check, and catch him in a lie? The idea was to do really well in the workout, show George some real good moves, and he wouldn't bother to check up. He would hand Fred a brown belt to wear and put him to work instructing novices. Meanwhile he would work out all he could, and in a few months start to think about moving up to black . . .

Marjorie stirred in her sleep and seemed on the point of waking up, and Fred hastened to get his codpiece and shorts from the chair and put them on. She seemed like a nice girl, and so Fred was treating her with respect; he wouldn't want to display to her his unmannerly shriveled lack of arousal on this nervous morning.

. . . all the same, though, you never knew. Some guys who had been around said that the nice girls like this one could really be the coldest chillers once they let themselves go. Looking down now at Marjorie's still-sleeping form, Fred could easily imagine it covered, blurred into sexlessness. Her figure was almost boyish in repose, without the padded bra that she had thrown off last night, and it was years since he had felt any lust for boys. He could picture her eyes opening, their clear and penetrating gaze (so he imagined; last night he had not noticed) pushing lust aside, piercing through his hard male body, seeking to touch *him* . . .

Fred gave himself a mental kick and looked away. Not that he felt guilty. Twins, every normal guy had thoughts about chastity and sublimation, and enjoyed them, too. It was just that today Fred didn't want to get himself into a difficult emotional state.

Still it was impossible not to notice how childlike Marjorie looked in her sleep. In his imagination he found himself putting a long, snowy, opaque gown around her . . . he kicked himself again, and went on getting dressed.

She woke up, turning and stretching, before he was ready to leave. He looked around at her and swallowed hard, for suddenly the clear-eyed gaze he had imagined was quite real.

"Good morning—Margie. You don't mind if I call you by your first name?" He had forgotten what her last name was.

"No, I don't mind. Uh . . ."

"Fred, Fred Lohmann."

"Yes, certainly, Fred." She rolled over onto her back and gave a routine wiggle of her hips. "Burning with lust this morning, that's me." But her tone made the invitation no more than a polite form.

"Me too." His tone was even more casual than hers. "Too bad, but I gotta get an early start on some business today."

Her eyes seemed to chill, sending something like a sensation of real cold along his back. She murmured softly: "What is a poor girl going to do, when the man she's with says he just won't screw?" The verse from which the line came was latrine doggerel, ancient and more than mildly dirty.

If Fred had ever heard encouragement, this was it. Even Basic Income and karate could wait. "Well, then, how about it, girly?" he asked boldly. "How about you and me just frosting things a few degrees?"

He had been too bold too soon. "Just don't rush it," Marjorie said crossly, with a curve of her spine becoming all sex again. Who could tell anything about women? She rolled out of the bed on her side, into her own room, where she reached for a transparent robe.

"I'm sorry," Fred muttered, bending slightly to look at her through the bed-gap in the wall. "Don't get sore." Sublimation, was she going to complain to the management now? Would he be thrown out?

Somewhat mollified, she paused in the act of raising the bed between them. "Just don't rush things, okay?" Her eyes had lost their coldness, but at least she was smiling.

"I'll be around tonight!" Fred called through to her. He helped her lift the bed-barrier into place, and gave his side of it a jovial pat as it sealed him off.

An hour later he had found his way to the nearest branch of the Social Security office and was standing in line. Having no permanent address since leaving California, he had arranged to have his first Basic Income check held for him in the Social Security data bank until he called at an office somewhere to pick it up. For whatever reason, a number of other people seemed to be making similar arrangements. The line was eight or ten people long, and not moving very fast.

The jobholders in the office sat snugly fortified behind their desks and counters and computer consoles, or else walked by, giving the impression that they were up to something important. Chastity, it was just that they had some kind of political pull, or they'd be the ones standing in line. They seemed to have little regard for the people they were processing so slowly. Fred lit up a small cigar.

Now the window at the head of the line was being closed for some reason, and a man came to divide the line and lead its fragments to different windows.

"No smoking in here!" he snapped at Fred. He was a paunchy, waddling man who reminded Fred of a particularly unpleasant high school teacher he had suffered under only a few months ago. "No smoking, I said! Put it out at once or you'll have to leave the office."

"I got a right to my check," Fred muttered, but so weakly that it was doubtful if the officious man even heard him. At the same time Fred was crushing out his cigar on the sole of his sandal, for he knew very well that he was never going to win an argument with the paunchy jobholder. Not here. Now, if they ever met somewhere else . . .

Fidgeting and waiting, thinking vague and sullen thoughts, Fred inched forward with the line. At last he reached the window, gave his name and federal identity number, and held the tips of his fingers on a scanner-plate. After a few seconds there came a machine-gun clacking from a printed device beside the clerk who was processing Fred, and some official looking papers emerged.

"Well, this is your first check, Fred. Do you have a permanent address to give us yet?"

"No. I'm staying at a YPPC now."

"Address?"

"It's here in Chicago. The one on North State Street."

The clerk made a note with a stylus on a computer input plate, then pulled more pieces of paper from beneath the counter. "Take these booklets, Fred, they'll tell you more about your rights and responsibilities under the Basic Income law. If you win more than two hundred dollars' prize money in any state or national lottery or government-sponsored competition in any calendar month, *or* obtain gainful employment, *or* acquire ownership of more than fifty shares of corporate stock, you are required to notify us so that your Basic Income can be adjusted. There are penalties for failing to notify."

There was a little more he had to listen to. When at last they released him by handing over his check—he supposed it was enough to scrounge along on for a couple of weeks until the next one came, if scrounging along was your idea of life—he hurried from the office, dropping the booklets into a trash receptacle as he went through the door. He'd notify them, all right, as soon as he moved up to jobholder. The sooner he could tell them that, the better.

Since he had such a good chance for a job, there was no use hoarding his money like a miser. Two weeks' scrimp-along money could buy a couple of nights of real fun. After that ... well, nobody starved.

A kind of gravitational pull was leading him onto a particular slidewalk, one that would carry him in the direction of a run-down

neighborhood he had noticed not far from the
Y. There he should be able to hit a coffeehouse
bar or two. He could get some lunch there as
well as anywhere. There was plenty of time
before he had to meet George at the dojo. And
Fred wanted to see about getting hold of some
gladrags, in case it turned out tonight that
Marjorie was not just teasing but was really in
a willing mood. If you went to the right place
and asked the right person, a few dollars could
always buy a pair of plastic cloaks, thin, but
stiff and perfectly opaque, folded together into
a pocket-sized carton.

Art awoke with a start in the Parrs' guest
room bed, looked at his watch, and saw that it
was a little after nine o'clock. He sat up blink-
ing. On the barren tile floor in one corner of
the sparsely furnished room lay a pair of
men's translucent disposable trousers, apparently used and ready for the discard. The
length of one extended leg indicated that the
garment would be too big for either him or
George. Oh yes; Fred Lohmann had been
staying here, before Rita. Conceivably Fred
would know something of her present whereabouts, if Art could find a chance to question
him. Art remembered him as a wild-looking
adolescent, tall and awkward.

Before retiring Art had bought himself
some disposal clothing from the block's vending machine, and now after a quick shower
and beard-trim he dressed in fresh shorts and
shirt. Still only a quarter after nine. While

buttoning his shirt he peeked into the
children's room and found the four of them
still sleeping. Must have been allowed to stay
up late last night, playing together. A door
chimed and very shortly thereafter voices
drifted up from downstairs, one Ann's, the
other belonging to a man whom Art did not
recognize. Standing in the upstairs hall he
could understand only a stray word or two.

Going down as soon as he had finished
dressing, Art turned first into the kitchen. He
was liable to feel sick unless he ate something
as soon as he got up. In the refrigerator he
found a cinnamon-flavored protein bar, and
on the elaborate new stove he dialed himself
coffee. Five minutes, while the low dialogue
continued in another room, and he had the in-
dispensable minimum of breakfast in his
stomach. Chewing on a toothmint, more or less
ready to face the world, Art walked into the
living room.

The low voices stopped. A lean, stooped
man wearing a conservative transparent business jacket above his shorts was standing just
inside the door that had been closed last night
and which Art now realized must provide access to a lower-level garage. The man looked
up at Art with keen interest, or perhaps he was
only glad of any interruption.

Ann, her pretty chin somewhat higher than
usual, turned with arms folded from her
stance of confrontation with the visitor. "Art,
this gentleman claims he's a Mr. Hall. From
Family Planning. George has gone out." Her

tone managed to imply that George, if at home, would have beaten this probably fraudulent intruder to a pulp, and Art was welcome to do the same if he liked.

"My name *is* Hall, and I am from the Family Planning office." The intruder had a determined voice, though not angry or flustered (Aha, Ann, have you met your match at last?), and his eyes were sharp. "I take it you're Mr. Rodney?"

"I am."

"I was hoping to run into you here. Our California office has asked us to make a routine investigation into your wife's case."

"Her case? My wife hasn't broken any laws."

"That's fine! Then if you'll tell me where I can get in touch with her, we can clear all this up promptly and with as little inconvenience as possible."

The protein bar in Art's stomach had suddenly gone lumpy. He supposed that criminals must have terrible chronic digestive problems. Or maybe they got used to it. He could think of nothing to say to Mr. Hall, and just stood there like a guilty fool.

Hall's determined voice kept coming at him. "I understand you didn't accompany your wife to Chicago, you followed her here?"

"I—yes, what of it?" Surely, thought Art, he had the right to refuse to answer these questions. To talk to a lawyer first, at least. But once he refused to answer, Hall's suspicions, that possibly were no more than suspicions now, would surely be confirmed.

"Mr. Rodney, is there some reason you don't want to tell me where your wife is at the moment?"

"I don't know where she is." It was Ann's fault, and George's, and Rita's too, that he had to conduct this argument in ignorance. Their fault, not his, if he got them all in deeper trouble. Meanwhile he marveled greatly at how fast the deadly pits could open beneath one's feet in the dull corridor of life.

"You don't know?" The interrogator's tone implied that Art must be a fool or a knave, or both, to hope to get away with such an answer.

Art folded his arms in unconscious imitation of Ann. "That's right."

Mr. Hall glanced toward Ann, who with her own arms still folded was obviously quite ready for him. He appeared to stifle a faint sigh, and then turned back to Art. "Mr. Rodney, our California office has received medical testimony indicating that your wife is pregnant for the third time."

"Yes, I know about that."

"We have no record that she's made any appointment with a physician to have this pregnancy terminated. And the first trimester must be nearly over."

"I, ah, know nothing about that."

"Well, I'd like you to at least give me your opinion on the subject, Mr. Rodney. Do you think your wife is planning *not* to have it terminated normally, to carry it on to parturition?"

There was no way he could admit it. "No, I don't think that," he had to say. Then he had to pause, for a nervous, choking swallow. Ann was just standing by, letting him flounder, confident that they had told him no secrets and so there were none he could betray. Triplets, but he hated her at the moment.

When he had his throat under control again he said: "I'm sure Rita means to have it terminated properly, she's, uh, probably just gone away by herself for a few days to think things over. You see . . . our psychologist has recommended against her being sterilized. After Paula, our youngest, was born, Rita had an IUD inserted but her body kept expelling it. She always takes her pills. I'm sure there was just a chemical failure somewhere. I'm sure she didn't plan the pregnancy. Unless it was subconscious." There seemed to be stories in the newsprints every day about apes avoiding prison sentences by pleading their subconscious compulsions. If they could do it, why couldn't she? Lay the groundwork for it now. But he was talking too much, he had better shut up.

As soon as he quieted, however, Hall was after him again. "Mr. Rodney, is it like Rita to go off by herself for days at a time? When was the last time she made a similar disappearance?"

"I . . ." He was cornered. Once he started making up a string of lies, Hall would have it knotted around his neck in no time at all. "No, I can't say it's like her," he said in desperation. "I tell you, I don't know where she is. If

I knew where she was I'd be with her right now."

Mr. Hall shuffled his feet, which were no doubt tired from standing, and glanced again at Ann, and sighed once more, more openly this time. "Mr. Rodney, will you walk me back to my car?"

"There's no need for you to do that, Art," Ann put in.

"All right, Mr. Hall," Art said, since the alternative was to go along with Ann's instructions.

Ann was not going to argue with him, not in the face of the enemy. "I'll have breakfast for you when you get back," she promised, holding the door. She gave Art a ritual kiss as he went out, but offered no kiss or caress to Hall, who in turn contented himself with a barely polite pelvic thrust in her direction.

As they were walking down the stairs to the garage, with no one else about, Hall said quietly: "Mr. Rodney, I hope you don't think of us at Family Planning as out to *get* your wife. Believe me, we'd like to help her; I think she's a woman who can use some help."

Art was silent. They emerged at the foot of the stair into the garage. A variety of vehicles were berthed in a series of numbered, gate-protected stalls. Other areas were marked for delivery vehicles and visitors' parking. At the moment there was still nobody else in sight.

Hall stopped, facing Art. "If I can't get a chance to talk to your wife, it's going to be awfully hard for her to stay out of trouble. And you yourself can be in trouble if you're deliberately withholding information. There is the federal conspiracy law. We may not like the world in which all these laws are necessary, but it's the only world we have."

"I've been telling you the truth."

"Another thing." Hall very slowly resumed his walk toward the visitor's parking area. "Giving birth is a somewhat risky proposition at best—I'm sure you realize that, as the father of two legitimate children. In some of these birth-mills a full-term parturition, or even a fetiparous one, can be downright dangerous, believe me."

This time it was Art who stopped, a few slow paces later. "Even a what?"

Hall was silent. He seemed to be trying to read Art's face.

Art repeated: "Even a what? What kind of parturition, live birth, is there except full term? Do you mean premature?"

Hall continued his intent gaze at the mystified Art for a long moment, and then relaxed. "I think you and I are really on the same side in this case, aren't we, Mr. Rodney?"

"I want my wife at home with me, not getting into trouble. And I don't want the world overcrowded with my progeny, I'm willing to respect the rights of others."

"Fine." Hall was suddenly more relaxed and friendly. "Then I'd better tell you something you may not know about. Just recently there has come into use a method for removing a first-trimester fetus or embryo from the womb in such a way that it can be kept alive. The midwifer usually freezes it—"

"Alive?"

"If you can call it that. Alive in potential. It can later be reimplanted in the woman's body again, or in the body of another woman, or put into an artificial womb, and it will grow and develop eventually into a child. In experiments on animals normal young have been produced by this method for several decades now."

"Oh."

"You begin to see. Now if we at Family Planning seize a frozen fetus or embryo, our legal situation is tricky, because federal law states that if nine months have passed since conception, the fetus has become a child. The law goes back several decades to when termination of surplus pregnancies was first required in this country. Some women who were about six months or so along claimed that they were already in labor when their pregnancies were terminated by FP doctors, and there was a lot of fuss. The law is really outmoded now, but we're still stuck with it."

"I don't quite see . . ."

"The thing is, we can't legally destroy a frozen fetus unless we can *prove* it's less than nine months old. Calendar age, not stage of development, is the way the law reads. We're trying to get it changed, of course. There have been several articles lately in the newsprints on all this, and stories on television. I would have thought perhaps you would have heard or read something about it."

"I've been busy," Art said. "Not keeping up much with the news." Probably it was another example of his subconscious avoidance of hearing or remembering, like the exact wording of the federal conspiracy law.

"You see, with just a frozen fetus in our hands, we have a purity of a time proving its exact age. Can't even take a tissue sample for proving the parenthood, since that would constitute damage. If we can't prove it's a superfluous third, and nobody claims it, why then believe it or not it has to be regarded as an unidentified orphan child. Treated as a human being in potential, which means taking it to an orphanage. Some of these religious and so-called humanist institutions will take them right in. They're building artificial wombs at a furious pace, without permits of course, and they have plenty of money and manpower for clandestine research on freezing and revival techniques, or so it seems."

"Uh-huh."

"You may have heard something about the riot just recently in Iowa, where a Christian monastery was destroyed. I understand the ringleaders of the riot are now in jail, as they should be. Can't have people taking the law into their own hands. But there'll have to be proper legal action against those cultists too. Some of their priests were out there building cryogenic devices and freezing fetuses."

Art, without realizing it, had started walking again, on newly shaky legs. Cultists. He

thought of the carven image on the wall above
the children's beds. He knew Ann. He thought
of the scream coming out of the woods, and he
thought of Rita. "But then . . . suppose, as you
say, that the fetus is thawed and put into an
artificial womb and a child results. What
then? Could the mother claim it?"

"Probably not without spending a prison
term, and undergoing sterilization." Hall was
looking at his watch. "I suppose there might
be all kinds of devious means, adoption and so
on. But a third live birth is still a criminal offense by the woman, no matter what sub-
terfuges she employs. I really can't understand the woman who does such a thing. Setting aside the legal problems, anywhere that
she and her husband live afterwards, the
neighbors are going to be able to count: one,
two, three children. You couldn't very well
pretend one of them is adopted. There aren't
enough adoptable children to even match the
childless couples who want one, let alone go to
people who have two of their own. So it'll be
obvious to all that the parents had three kids,
and pretty soon that third one is going to know
that he or she is superfluous and unwanted by
the world. That's a very cruel thing to do to a
child, in my estimation."

"Mine, too."

"No, I just don't understand these women
who go to midwifers." Hall had reached his
car and now he unlocked a door and pulled it
open. "There's just one more thing I wanted to
mention to you, Mr. Rodney. Several times a

year we in Family Planning get a massive de-
tailed population forecast for the whole world,
and for our own areas in particular; we get it
right from the UN computer center. Right now
the latest forecast is several days overdue; the
rumor is that it's been delayed for re-checking,
because it's a real shocker."

"I suppose so."

Hall got into his car, slammed the door,
and then peered out the window. "I hope I can
rely on you, Mr. Rodney."

"Certainly I *mean* to do all I can—"

"That's fine." With a tiny wave and a half-
smile, his mind probably already at work on
his next case, Mr. Hall upped his window,
faced forward, and drove off.

—but I don't even know where she is. Art
stared in silent protest after the car already
zooming up the exit ramp.

V

AFTER HALL'S departure, Art wandered to an escalator and rode it up from the garage, emerging just inside one of the block's pedestrian entrances. He was jogged partially out of his dazed state by Timmy and Paula, who ambushed their father as he made his way back toward the Parrs' patio. The children were munching protein bars with which they smeared his clothes. Overriding his requests for a delay, they pulled at him to get him moving on a tour of the block's central park. He gave up and went along. He reassured himself that his children were well and then tentatively questioned them about Mommy. About all he could find out was that she had said she would come back to get them soon.

The tour got as far as the nude pool before its directors deserted to join the Parr boys, who were already in the water. Art sank down on a grassy bank nearby and tried to think, now and then waving mechanically at his offspring when they clamored for his attention.

There were other distractions too. No other men were at the pool—probably most of those who lived in the block were busy this morning, at jobs or tending to their investments—but several women had come to swim. Ann was obviously not the only bluenose radical in this small community; probably people with similar attitudes tended to get into the same blockhouse corporation. Anyway these women came to the nude pool wearing long, loose, only dimly translucent jackets, and they swam as bare as babies, without so much as a sequin pasted on to emphasize their sex. It was hard to say which was the more antierotic, being almost completely covered or completely bare. Some of them cast suspicious glances at the male stranger, who in turn waved at his children to show that he had a good reason for hanging around, and then frowned thoughtfully into space. But only his face was truly thoughtful. His brain was getting nowhere.

In half an hour or so the kids were ready to do something else, and Art walked home with the four of them, reminding them to gather up their clothes. When he got back to the house he found George there, and promptly took him aside.

"George, have you seen her this morning or heard from her?"

"No, Art, I swear."

"I've got to find her. She's my wife and I have a right to talk to her."

George stood there for a while, looking glum and uncertain about it all. Then he said: "I have to agree with that."

Emboldened, Art pushed harder. "I don't want to get you, or anybody, into trouble. But if I can't find her I'll have to go to the police and report her missing. It's that important to me."

George came to a decision. "All right. After lunch you and I will go out and see about making contact."

"How about right now?"

"Just come along and we'll do it my way. After lunch."

So a couple of hours later, after Art had spent some more time with his children, and Ann had fed them all some more sandwiches, the two men went out and got on the slidewalk together, George explaining that he didn't have a car right now, what with one expense and another.

After a couple of kilometers' ride, Art saw a vast domed stadium looming up ahead of them. At about the same time, George came up from deep thought to say: "Understand, it may take a little time to find out exactly where she is. There are several people I want to talk to about it."

"Just so I get a chance to see her, before she commits any irrevocable foolishness. Where are we going now?"

"I expect one of the people will be at the ball game today. You just stand by and let me talk to him."

"All right."

Another kilometer and the slidewalk, by now fairly thick with passengers, deposited them before one of the entrances to the stadium. George said: "Let's not forget to pick up tickets. A dollar is a dollar."

They accepted time-stamped tickets from the jaws of a machine as they passed in through a turnstile. George led Art through cavernous passageways to an outfield grandstand, where they emerged squinting into the sun. A sizeable crowd was filling a good proportion of the seats. The stadium's domed roof had been opened like a set of gigantic jaws and the people were in a good humor under the warm sun.

George chose seats high in the rear, and kept looking around him at the crowd. "I think I see our man," he said after a minute. "You just watch the game, and I'll go talk to him." George moved away.

Art watched the game, which was just beginning, and the crowd as well. The Cubs, the home team, took a one-run lead in the first inning, and gambling in the grandstand promptly became fierce and steady, conducted by arm-waves and cryptic shouts. Ushers and police ignored the betting; Art wasn't sure whether it was legal here or not. There seemed to be no bookies, no formal organization, and no wagers more than ten dollars, but small money passed through hundreds of hands with every pitch. One of the busier gamblers was the man George had engaged in low-voiced talk, who seemed able to keep his gaming and his conversation going at the same time. They were sitting too far away for Art to be able to tell if George was learning anything. Their talk just went on steadily.

So things went until the top of the fourth inning, when the Cubs blundered themselves four runs behind. The emotional climate in the stands changed radically with the score. The majority of the spectators, grown men and late adolescents who wore the gaudy codpieces and indefinable look of the jobless, lost most of their enthusiasm for betting and brooded in sullen silence. Here and there a few gamblers persisted more energetically than ever, jumping and shouting like fanatics when they won, but joyless even then.

George finished his conversation abruptly and stood up, motioning to Art that it was time to leave. They met on the moving ramp going down to street level. A number of other men were heading restlessly in the same direction, taking to the exits early. In the lines forming at the exits there was some jostling for position, and some police were standing by alertly. A huge, disheveled man standing in the next queue glared across a railing at Art and George and murmured something unpleasant about jobholders. In present company Art felt secure enough to glare right back, until the man decided he was getting nowhere and turned away.

"Three innings, dollar and a quarter," droned the Bureau of Sports agent in the booth where Art presented his ticket. Art picked up the coins that came clattering toward him from under the bullet-proof glass. Probably watching a whole game would be worth three

seventy-five. He wondered if they paid over-
time for extra innings.

As soon as they were clear of the stadium
crowd, riding a westbound slidewalk into a
part of the city Art had not visited before, he
asked eagerly: "Did you find out where she
is?"

"We're on the trail. I told you, I'll have to
talk to a couple of people." George, shaking his
head, turned back to look at the slowly reced-
ing stadium, its roof-jaws gaping at the sky. "I
was afraid we might have a little riot. It gets
bad in there sometimes when the home team
loses."

Controlling his impatience, Art looked back
too. "They can get paid now just to sit and
watch a game and keep out of trouble. Or there
are a thousand things people can do to win
prizes. They don't have to be intelligent or
educated, they can win by bowling or pitching
horseshoes. Everyone can win a prize at something. I don't know what they want."

George faced forward again. "Did I tell you,
I may be going on television? Probably not,
though, I think I blew the audition."

"No." Art was surprised.

"That's where I was this morning, audition-
ing. Just a local station. Oh, it's a real triplet of
a mess. They have this monstrous clumsy machine, made up like a woman, for a man to
fight. Let's change to the high-speed walk
here, the next place I want to stop is way out in
a slumburb."

At the interchange, the walk they had been

riding flowed briefly beside an acceleration strip. This strip was of viscous plastic that remained cohesive and hard-surfaced though it flowed like water, the circular stream of it running thick and deep and slow beside the slow slidewalk, and thin and fast to match speeds with the express. With no more balancing than it took to mount a stair, the passengers made the changeover. Once whizzing westward aboard the fast, long-distance belt, Art and George sat down on the continuous bench that moved with their new conveyance.

"So what about this television program?" Art asked, his curiosity aroused.

"It'll be garbage. They want somebody to jump through the air like an idiot and scream, and beat up this giant woman . . . There *could* be a good karate program, showing how the human mind and body can work together. I'd like to do a good one someday but I don't suppose they'd ever let me. I guess I'll do this one if they want to hire me. I can use the money."

Art had a sudden realization of the obvious: a midwife was illegal and therefore must be expensive. Rita hadn't had much money with her. Might she have fallen into the hands of some cut-rate quack?

"George, are you paying for—Rita?"

"I'm contributing something."

"Then why must we run all over the city to find out where she is? Don't you know?"

George calmly shook his head.

For a while they rode through the warm afternoon without talking. The whispering rush

of the express walk, shaded beneath its plastic
awning, bore them at highway speed through
kilometer after kilometer of the great city.
They passed industrial blockhouses, and older
manufacturing parks surrounded by grim
fences, where machines labored night and day
for Man, the master, repairing and sometimes
redesigning themselves, only occasionally requiring any human supervision. They passed
street after street of the two- and three-apart-
ment dwellings in which the bulk of the city's
people seemed to live. Here dwelt the great
respectable mass. Here the head of the house-
hold might work two or three days a week,
here the family owned stocks and bonds
enough to bring some usable income, here they
had success from time to time in winning
prizes. Not really full-time jobholders, most of
them, but that was how they saw themselves.

Vending centers flowed past, public com-
puting terminals, streets and parking lots. A
school. A park, with a young couple naked on
the grass, bodies locked and working toward
orgasm. A Church of Eros, whose twin towers
stood like the raised knees of a supine woman,
flanking the main entrance. A superhighway
interchange for private surface vehicles, fallen
into disrepair, with half its lanes closed by
barricades, grass growing through the cracked
concrete. Nearby, a terminal of the underground long-distance tube complex. More two-
and three-family dwellings, row on row on
row. And scattered everywhere throughout the
clean and sunlit city, the fortified stone walls

of blockhouses springing up.

Now Art noticed with part of his mind that the buildings rushing past were becoming noticeably shabbier; they must be approaching the western border of the city. Thinking aloud, he said: "Suppose she actually does have a child, produces a living child out of this. What will we do then? I tell myself that if it comes to that we'll just ignore what people say, or the looks we get from them. I'll do all I can to keep the third one from feeling unwanted. But I suppose he will."

"I just don't know how that would work," said George.

"And Rita. I don't know if going to jail would bother her as much as being sterilized."

After another little silence George said: "I know the thought of having that done has scared her in the past. Maybe now, though, it won't seem so terrible. She'd never have another baby to worry about, once this one is taken care of."

"If it ever is a baby." Art felt a surge of pity and grief for the unwanted third-to-be, unneeded and detested by a world already jammed. Fetus, why do you thrust with such a mad, blind drive to reach the light? Shrink back to nothing. Go away. There's nothing here in the world for you, that you should fight to reach it. But of course the seed could only grow where it had been planted.

"George, the Family Planning man implied that when some women go through this new method of extracting the fetus and freezing it, then they're content to have the resulting child brought up in an orphanage. I wonder if that's what Rita has in mind. To me it would be worse than having a third child with us, to purity with what the neighbors say. Do you know what she intends? She must have discussed some plan with you."

George shook his head gloomily, staring off into the distance.

"We'd adopt the kid, or something. We'd hang onto him. But it would be pretty grim, and I don't want that kid to ever come into this world. You can see how I feel, can't you?"

"I can see how you feel, and how Rita feels, too. Maybe that's my trouble, I see everybody's point of view. Even the kid who isn't born yet." His eyes flicked at Art and off again. "If abortion's not killing, what is it then?"

Being well rested and in good control of himself, Art could now have brought out the arguments with which to demolish this simplistic point of view. But he had no wish to argue with George, and anyway arguments were no good for changing someone's mind until that mind was ready for change.

The city proper was suddenly left behind. No official boundary or sharp line of demarcation was visible, but within the space of a few blocks the view changed, as what was unmistakably a slumburb came rising about the slidewalk like a dirty wave. Art was a stranger to this part of the Chicago area, but it did not look much different from some sections of Los

Angeles. Here were the endless curved rows of small houses cheaply built, falling apart at the age of twenty or thirty, but still occupied. Not only occupied, but cut and partitioned. There would be no steady jobholders living here, and not many who owned shares of stock or won more than an occasional prize. This was Basic Income territory.

A small vending district clustered around the terminus of the high speed slidewalk. Here all the other pedestrian walks were stat, as rigid and unmoving as the streets. Among the automated vendors a couple of human-attended establishments survived. One of these, a small and dingy tavern at the dead end of a block, proved to be George's destination.

The tavern did not look old, but was already rundown in appearance, sharing the neighborhood's general air of defeat. Daylight was shut out from the interior, and the artificial lighting inside was dim but violently colored. As Art's eyes adjusted he could see obscene words scrawled here and there on the shabby walls, and concealing garments, opaque hip boots and overcoats, crudely drawn. All in all, Art supposed, a typical BI barroom; not that he had seen many such, except in television stories. Four or five apathetic male customers perched on bar stools. Above and behind the bar, the legally required police TV eye roosted like a robotic vulture, now and then turning its glass eye on its scrawny metal neck.

The bartender raised his head, sizing up his two new customers, and fixed eyes blank as the vulture's lens on George, as if deciding he was the one who had to be dealt with.

"Couple of short ones," George ordered, resting an elbow on the bar. When two small glasses of beer had been poured, he asked: "Is Alfie around?"

"Maybe shootin' pool," the bartender grated. There was a back room. POOLHALL $1.00 ADM.

George strolled that way. "I'll just see if he's there."

"That'll be one dollar, see the sign?"

George just glanced back as he strolled. "I won't touch a cue." He went on into the POOLHALL.

The bartender hesitated briefly, then picked up the coins George had left on the bar and slouched sway to tend another customer.

Art sipped his beer, which for some reason tasted quite good. He wished he knew how to talk to these people and act with them. George's and Rita's background was as middle-class as his own, but George had picked up the knack somewhere. Maybe in karate, though he had mentioned once that most of the students and practitioners were not the tough-guy type. Couple of short ones. Get tough with me and I can break your ribs—this last was only implied, of course, never verbalized or even bluntly stated in so many body-language words. He was just this somewhat undersized fellow who was not at all intimidated. What others read into that was what intimidated *them*.

There was a stir in a rear booth and a pair of

B-girls materialized out of the dimness there and come flowing forward to the bar. Art felt a mild twinge of alarm. The girls' license buttons were prominently displayed on their kimonos, but the garments were probably longer and thicker and more shapeless than the letter of the law allowed. The women approached the bar and stood there, closer to Art than to anyone else. Not that they looked at him. Their pale-painted faces were averted slightly, their mouths pinched in professional haughtiness and cool reserve. Art uncomfortably shifted his stance.

George stuck his head out of the back room. "Not today, girls," he called. "Art, get a beer for Alfie, and get us a booth. We'll be out in a minute."

The girls' faces relaxed into more natural scowls and they moved away, resuming some private conversation in bored voices. One pulled off her kimono to scratch beneath her bikni straps. Art bought three more short ones, and carried the filled glasses to an empty booth.

From the booth he had a good view of the tavern's huge television stage. For some reason the ball game was not being shown; maybe the game was already over, or there could be rioting at the stadium. The barrel-sized image of an announcer's head was reading a news story:

"This afternoon in the General Assembly, chief Chinese delegate Lu Ti-p'ing accused a neighboring government, Southern Pan-Asia, of using biological weapons against its own—

the Southern Pan-Asian—people.

"Lu quoted statistics from UNIMED which indicate that deaths from uncertain causes have reduced the SPA population by nearly ten per cent during the last three months. According to the UNIMED report, most of those dying have been the elderly and the chronically ill. According to the Chinese accusation, disproportionately few of the deaths have occured among members of the Patriots' Party, now the ruling group of Southern Pan-Asia.

"Finally the Chinese delegate expressed regret that, in his words, the SPA government has chosen such an inhumane method of trying to strengthen itself economically. Is this, Lu asked, to be the first step on a road of dangerous economic aggression?"

As if on cue the announcer's head was abruptly replaced by that of another, equally big, who with a tryannosaur's smile read hastily through a perhaps ill-timed commercial for a Chicago vending chain. The presentation was so inept that Art assumed this was some small local station, maybe the very one George had auditioned for. Probably there were a hundred of them, though.

Art sipped his beer. The newsmonger was soon back on stage, saying: "Then it was the turn of Cao Din That, chief SPA delegate, to reply."

The enlarged head of Cao Din That now appeared on the stage of the tavern in the Chicago slumburb, where nobody but Art seemed to be paying the least attention, and his translated words were heard, categorically denying all the charges leveled against the leaders of his suffering country. Possibly some foreign government was really to blame for the surplus deaths. If so, let the aggressors beware, they would be found out shortly. In any case, UNIMED was overstepping its authority by interfering in SPA internal affairs.

The tone of the speech became milder. Possibly the deaths were the unforeseen side-effect of a new insecticide, employed in the desperate struggle to increase food production. Also to be considered were the airborne viruses that had been accidentally freed during the recent UN police action against the Nile Republic; no one knew where those viruses might have landed, nor would anyone even admit to knowing exactly what they were. The UN was to be applauded for its prompt action along the Nile, which had liquidated some planners of biological war, but still some of the consequences had been unfortunate.

"Ah, th' world's gone t' repression," said a colorless little old man who must be Alfie, for he arrived at that moment with George. Art slid over to make room.

Alfie seized a beer, drank most of it, and went on talking. "The whole world's crazy. You know what happened the other night? Somebody bombed Vic Rizzo's townhouse. It musta been just vandals. They couldn'ta known it was his."

"That so?" George asked, indifferently. Art wondered who Vic Rizzo might be. After a few

more social noises had been made, and Alfie
further supplied with beer, George got to the
point.

"Alf, you know the city pretty well."

"I guess I do."

"Then tell me something." George dropped
his low voice even lower. "Who might a nice
girl go to see, if she got kind of carried away
and emotional, and wanted to finish an extra
baby? She's got two kids now."

Alfie gave facial demonstrations of thought.
"Married?" he asked, as if being married or
single made any difference in the number of
children a woman was allowed to bear.

"Yes," said George.

Alfie glanced at Art, wordlessly identified
him as the worried husband, and winked at
him. Then obviously pleased to be consulted,
Alfie assumed an air of wisdom and began to
talk. He seldom quite finished a sentence,
however, and his speech was thick with al-
lusions to people and places that Art had never
heard of. Also Alf used a number of slang
words strange to Art, or maybe Art was only
mis-hearing them, because Alf's whisper was
almost too low to be made out. All in all, the
dissertation was perfectly unintelligible.
George, though, kept on listening with apparent satisfaction, now and again encouraging Alfie with grunts and nods, and ordering
more beer.

"Some characters you know," Art reflected
aloud, as he and George rode the express

slidewalk into the east again. Twenty kilometers or so ahead, near the shore of invisible Lake Michigan and farther east than Art had been as yet, the unbelievable towers of the central city rose.

George grinned. "Alfie has his uses."

"I hope you found out something from him. I didn't. Do you think Rita is with one of those people he mentioned?"

George turned to look back into slumburb country, a desolate sea of rooftops beneath the mid-afternoon sun. "I think Alfie may be on the phone to Family Planning right now, trying to sell them the information that you and I were asking about midwifers. The man I talked to at the ball park may be doing the same thing. Family Planning knows what Rita's trying to do, but I want'em to think she doesn't have a midwifer yet. They can't arrest us for asking general questions. All I've been trying to do so far today is put'em off the trail a little."

Floundering well off the trail himself, Art could find nothing to say.

VI

ART MAINTAINED a somewhat surly silence through several slidewalk interchanges. He and George were deep in the city again, moving on a fairly crowded walk that angled to the southeast, before he spoke again to ask: "Where are we going now?"

"The dojo. Fred's supposed to be there at three-thirty so I can watch him work out. And then I have a private lesson to give. Come along and watch."

"Look, George, are you going to help me find Rita or aren't you? If you can't or won't, just say so. Don't keep stalling me along."

George was unperturbed. "Just come along to the dojo. I said I'd help you and I will."

Art puffed out his breath. But he went along; somehow George's words carried conviction.

Under a sign that read PARR'S KARATE DOJO Fred Lohmann was waiting for them, holding up the front of a modest building in a small middle-class vending district. Under one arm Fred was carrying a whitish roll of what appeared to be clothing.

"Art, you and Fred remember each other,

hey?" George unlocked the ground-floor door and stepped inside, waving on the lights with a passage of his hand over the switchplate on the wall.

Art's hand was squeezed. "Sure we do," said Fred, clearing his throat nervously. He towered over the two older men. "Art, how's your wife and kids?"

"Oh, fine. I guess you met Rita yesterday? Over at George's place?"

"Yeah, sure, that's right."

It seemed obvious that Fred wasn't in on the midwifery conspiracy, but still some clue to Rita's whereabouts might possibly be gotten out of him. Later. Right now Fred was all nervous anticipation of whatever test he had been brought here for, and George was present, raising his window blinds, checking his printout for messages, and in general opening up his shop.

The interior of the dojo was mostly one big room, about twenty meters square, and two stories high, so you could have fitted a very small house inside it. The floor was of polished wood. In the front, beside the street entrance, an area separated by a low partition from the big room contained a desk, with phoneplate and computer terminal, and a few chairs, some of them arranged as for spectators. An open doorway in the rear led to some lockers and, Art supposed, a shower. Large flags of the United States, the United Nations, and Japan were formally and correctly displayed together on one wall. The general impression was of functional orderliness.

George and Fred each bowed, not deeply or very ceremoniously, toward the flags. Then they slipped off their sandals and padded back toward the locker room, bare feet seeming to grip the floor familiarly. "Make yourself at home, Art," George called back.

Art put his own sandals into the convenient rack by the front door, then wandered about looking the place over. The smooth floor was not slippery to bare feet.

Something here reminded him of chess. He wondered if it was the square arena of polished wood, or some faint scent of conflict lingering in the conditioned air. Glancing up, he saw four android fighting machines hanging like felons near the high ceiling, above the center of the open floor. He looked about and spotted their control console standing near the desk. Feeling a technician's curiosity, Art walked over and looked at the controls.

George and Fred soon emerged from the locker room, clad in loose whitish trousers and jackets, only moderately translucent, and wearing athletes' codpieces of hard protective plastic. "I guess I just *lost* my own belt someplace," Fred was saying, meanwhile accepting a brown belt, an overlong strip of tough-looking cloth, from George's hand.

George looped a black belt twice around his own waist and knotted it in front, and the two of them began to limber up, swinging their legs like ballet dancers, crouching and twisting and stretching their bodies to unlikely extremes, shaking wrists and ankles as if their hands and feet had fallen asleep. Art stood watching with some interest.

"Ready?" George asked, after a few minutes of this. "Let's go five-time sparring, then." With nearly the full length of the floor clear behind him, he drew himself up facing Fred and they exchanged bows. Then they stood, each with arms slightly bent, hanging down in front of his body, fists loosely closed. "You first," George directed.

Fred snapped into a tenser, much lower stance, poised to attack, his right fist cocked near his hip, left arm curved before him in a blocking position. *"Jo-dan!"* The word came out in an explosive breath.

George grunted: *"Uhss!"*

Fred sprang forward and advanced in long deliberate strides, and with each stride one of his fists drove like a piston at George's chin. George flowed backward easily, staying just ahead of the punches, pressing each of them aside at the last moment with an economical open-handed block perfectly timed against Fred's extended arm. His short legs gracefully matched the speed and rhythm of the long ones driving at him. What he was doing looked quite easy. After he had gauged the first punch, George's eyes moved downward between punches, appraising the movements of Fred's feet and hips.

With his fifth punch Fred halted and stood motionless, arm still extended. Instantly George came blurring back at him with a counterpunch that was evidently an expected part of the ritualized combat; he snapped it to a halt a centimeter from Fred's unmoving chin.

Now it was Fred's turn to draw himself up straight, while George crouched for the attack.

"*Jo-dan!*"

"*Uhss!*"

George charged. Somehow he made his shortness look like an advantage. The sleeves of his white jacket snapped audibly with each punch. Fred retreated stiffly and hurriedly, parrying with heavy blocks that looked comparatively awkward. When it came time for his counterattack he essayed an arm-grab and kick to the stomach which George did not attempt to avoid. The snapping kick just touched George's jacket, as it was evidently supposed to do, but George still seemed to find it unsatisfactory. "Try again," he ordered.

Fred went through the grab-and-kick again. George said nothing. Art got the impression that Fred was failing his test.

George exchanged bows with his opponent, and turned to Art. "Art, switch the andys on, will you? The console by the desk."

Art found the power switch. There came a whispering of cables up above, and the four androids started to descend, hanged men coming down for vengeance. Their wire cables lowered them slowly, as their still-blind faces turned this way and that and their plastic limbs began to quiver and stir. By the time the androids' feet had touched down on polished wood, their legs had life and balance enough to let them stand.

The cables detached themselves and were quickly reeled up out of the way by the overhead machinery. Four men of about average height were left standing in the middle of the floor. Their heads and hands and feet were tan, the rest of their bodies white, as though clothed in beltless karate outfits. At the crotch of each appeared a small, formalized codpiece-bulge. Their tan faces were featureless except for small recessed eye lenses and flattish dummy noses. Like superior creatures lost in their own proud thoughts, they stood with loosely hanging arms, ignoring the three real men who watched them.

George, coming over to the console, called back to Fred: "Want to run through *heian* number four?"

Fred shrugged. "Okay." He frowned at the man-like figures, as if hoping to intimidate them.

The four androids were warmed up and fully active now, and as George set up their controls they obediently arranged themselves in the center of the floor, facing one another like four cardplayers looking across a large square table. Each was crouched in the same attacking position that the men had used for the ritual sparring.

"You don't fight all four at once, do you?" Art asked. "I've seen karate on television a few times, but I confess I never paid too much attention."

George dismissed television karate with a mere lipcurl of contempt. "What speed do you want, Freddy? How about Three or Four?"

Fred flushed slightly. He stood with his hands on his hips, swinging his legs again. "I can handle One-point-five, or Two."

After a moment George said: "Try Two-point-five, then," and set a dial. "Better get a helmet."

"Okay." Fred trotted to the locker room.

Art was interested. "Then he is going to fight all four at once."

"Just in a kind of formalized way, a pre-arranged exercise. They come at you one at a time, and anybody who has some training and who has memorized the moves of the particular *heian* can do it. If he keeps his nerve. And if the speed's set low enough. He wants to do it pretty fast." For a moment George's face said openly: It's his funeral.

Something about the fighting machines fascinated Art. The way they stood there on the polished wood like outsize chessmen, waiting for an act of human control to impel them to ritual battle. He asked: "Is it all right if I take a closer look?"

George glanced at the controls. "Go ahead."

Art padded over to the androids. They did not seem to notice him, as they waited with impassive poise. If you order us to punch and kick you, Lord Man, so will we do. Art peered into dull lens-eyes and wondered what image they made of him. With a cautious finger he touched the plastic knuckles of one cocked tan fist. Not as hard as the proverbial rock, but not what one would call safely padded, either. The fingers of the hand were not really separate, but only indicated by grooves in the one plastic piece.

"Feels as if it could kill you."

"Not likely, they don't really hit like black belts." George smiled briefly. "Does sting a little, though."

"You've been hit, then."

"Oh, sure. Not seriously. Yes, these things can be dangerous. We sometimes put big padded hands and feet on'em for novices. But if there's no real element of danger when you train, you can't really train properly." He glanced toward the locker room. There came the sound of a toilet flushing. "Fred's no novice. But he's nowhere near as good as he's been telling me he is. I just can't hire him now."

"Then why—?" Art gestured at the androids.

"Oh, I owe him a full fair tryout, I guess. And he's got good potential if he'd settle down and practice every day."

Fred game back, fitting on something like a fencer's mask. "I found a face protector. I like it bettern a whole helmet."

"All right," said George, standing by the console.

Fred moved in among the androids, and oriented himself carefully at the center of the space between them, where he was the focus of all their lenses. He drew a deep breath and then stood up relaxed. "Ready."

George touched a red control, and instantly bright red warnings glowed into life in the eyes of each mechanical figure. Somewhere a small repeater chime began to sound, one, two, three, four, five notes and the android at Fred's left lunged at him with a punch too fast for Art to follow. Fred was ready though and his left arm snapped up to block the attack while his right hand came whipping around edgewise to hit home like a hatchet on the tan plastic neck. The aggressor machine was sent staggering back. Meanwhile another was already charging.

Each android charged in turn, was beaten off, reset itself quickly, and in its next turn came back to the attack again, aiming another blow or kick at Fred, or grabbing at his jacket with clamplike fingerless hands. About half a minute passed, while Fred piled up points.

Fred spun from side to side, defending himself with vicious blocks, counterattacking with fists and feet and elbows. His face was rigid with concentration—or was it fear and hate he showed? He reached out and pulled down an android's head, smashing the blank uncaring face against his driving knee. Again he spun around—

Not quite in time. A savage punch glanced off his skull, and down he went.

Art moved with an electronic technician's instinct for the power switch, but George's hand was there already. For an instant the androids hesitated, looking for fair game. Then their eyes died and their bodies fell clattering to the wooden floor.

Fred was rolling over on the floor, gasping and moaning, clutching at his head. Art and George went to him. He rolled just as Art bent down, and Art's hand was besmeared with a drop of Fred's blood.

"They changed speed!" Fred sat up, dripping blood onto his white jacket. "I almost had'em, and then something went wrong . . . ah, triplets, that hurts! I swear they changed on me . . ." Fred was practically sobbing with exertion, pain, defeat.

Having played chess against computers, Art thought that perhaps he understood Fred's feelings. But since he had risked no blood against the chess computers, Art said only: "Lie still, I'll get a towel." Fred's scalp was torn but still the damage didn't look too serious.

George stayed with the victim, gently getting his face-protector off, while Art went to the locker room and found a towel and also picked up a first aid kit that hung there on the wall. He had just gotten back to the disaster area when the street door of the dojo opened and a tall man came in. This man was well dressed in translucent shorts and business jacket, and had dark skin and Oriental eyes. As he was starting to bow to the flags he noticed what was happening, and immediately slipped off his shoes and came across the floor.

"Have an accident?"

"Oh, hello, Doc. Yes," said George, getting

to his feet. Fred also started to get up, then sat back on the floor as the man who had just come in bent to look at his torn scalp.

Accepting the towel from Art, Doc dabbed around the wound. "This looks like it'll need some glue. Ivor, fetch my bag in from the car, will you?"

Another man, youngish and of undistinguished appearance, who had followed the doctor in and then had remained uncertainly near the door, gave a little salute with his fingers like a chauffeur or a servant and then ducked out.

"Doc," said George, "this is Art Rodney, my sister's husband. Art, this is Dr. Hammad."

With a look as of recognition, the doctor nodded, and reached to shake Art's hand.

George said: "Art, when you have a chance, you can consult the doctor about your problem. He's your man."

"I happened to see your wife this morning," the doctor was telling Art a few minutes later. "She's in good health and good spirits." The doctor was hanging his street clothes in a locker, getting ready for his private karate lesson. George was out in the main room of the dojo, discussing some refinement of mayhem with the bodyguard Ivor. From where Art stood in the locker room he could see Fred sitting out there too, the picture of defeat, head resting in his hands, blood drying brownish on his jacket. His brown belt had come unknotted.

"Where is she?" Art asked.

"Understand, I have no direct connection with the place she's staying at. It's been my experience, though, that they do a good job of taking care of guests."

"You have no connection? Aren't you the one who's intending to—?"

"Oh, no, no, I'm not handling your wife's case myself. No, the connection between me and George is too obvious, you see. In such cases a referral to another physician is more prudent."

"Who is he, then? When am I going to see her? When is the operation to be?"

"It'll be soon, I suppose. She's young and healthy, and I would anticipate an uneventful parturition and freezing."

The casual words brought on an icy congealing in Art's own bone marrow. He had no clear idea of what a three-months' fetus actually looked like, but in his mind he saw a mindless finger of tissue, extracted like an appendix and then frozen into an icicle.

He asked: "If a fetus is treated this way, then grown in one of those artificial wombs— what are its chances of becoming a normal child?"

"Oh, very good. Excellent. Is that what's worrying you? Don't let it. Freezing an organism that small and then revivifying it is nothing, these days. And an artificial womb actually offers several advantages over a full-term pregnancy and birth. Development of the fetus can be watched day by day and the flow of nutrients perfectly controlled. It's much more physically convenient for the mother, too, of course. I expect the FDA will release the wombs for unrestricted use with legitimate children soon; they're probably only delaying because more women would want kids if pregnancy wasn't such a bother." Dr. Hammad pulled on his loose white karate trousers; he smiled reassuringly, as if he had just solved all Art's problems for him.

"That's all very well, doctor. That helps to ease my mind of one kind of worry. But now what about my wife?"

"Oh, this is safer for her than a normal birth would be. I understand she's had two of those."

"I mean legally. Suppose she's caught and convicted and sent to jail and sterilized against her will? What's all that going to do to her?"

"See here," said Hammad sharply, "I thought you wanted this child. There are always certain risks involved, for everyone."

"I don't want this frozen so-called child, Rita does. I want to talk to her, to reason with her, before it's too late."

The doctor had turned his face away and was adjusting his jacket, slowly and meticulously. "You'll have to see someone else about it, then, Mr. Rodney. I told you I'm not operating."

"I insist that I be allowed to see my wife, face to face!" Art was keeping his voice low, but he felt it becoming shaky with his anger.

"Now you know where she can be found. And I'm quite ready to stir up trouble, if you refuse to help me talk to her!"

Knotting a green belt at his waist, the doctor glared at Art as if he had found the wrong specimen laid out on a dissecting table. Art glared right back.

"All right," the doctor said at last. "I'll find out if some arrangement can be made for her to phone you. Though it's not wise, phones can be tapped. Where are you staying?"

"No. I want to be able to talk with her in person. Alone."

Hammad was ready now, but he did not go out. "All right, all right. It's against my judgment but since you insist on taking the risk I'll see if there's any way a meeting can be arranged."

"Soon. Very soon."

"All right. Where can you be reached by phone?"

Fred Lohmann stood inside the Megiddo Bar & Coffee House, on the edge of a mean little urban BI district near State Street, not far from the Y where he was rooming. He was alone in a crowd. On a low dais some people with medieval musical instruments were twanging out a ballad about pure-hearted love, and a chill silence had crept into the huge dim room. The place was befogged with the exhaled smoke of several kinds of leaves and synthetic mixtures, tobacco being only one. At every table there were glassy staring eyes, and few of them seemed to be aimed at anybody else.

Fred slouched his tall frame over the coffeebar, nursing what they called a small Turkish, which had coffee and other things mixed in it, along with a vague dull hope that someone might ask him about the little bandage on the side of his head. After all, mighty few men could have handled those andys at the speed they were set for today. Not one in a hundred, probably, even given the chance to train, could do it. Black belt George, of course. Third degree black belt, no less. He probably set them on speed One and knocked them down like bowling pins. Toward George, Fred felt envy, but there was no malice in it.

Karate was a good business to be in. You could get to meet some influential people, people with class, like the Dr. Hammad who had come in and patched Fred's scalp today. Afterward Fred had watched the doctor go through his private lesson, and George had used Fred to demonstrate a point or two, and had Fred spar freestyle with the doctor a little bit, taking it easy.

Now Fred made a karate blade of his hand and chopped delicately, silently, at the edge of the bar. Then he stopped. Who cared? What was the use? George probably could tell without even checking that he had been lying about having a brown belt. Sorry, George had said, no job now. Practice every day and we'll see. George hadn't said every day for how long, but Fred knew it wouldn't be for just a week or two. Months or maybe even a year before he got his stance and his control and everything else up to the standards George wanted in a

brown or black belt, in a paid instructor.
There was not much fun in grunting and
sweating and working like a machine for that
length of time. And there was no guarantee
that he would ever make it, so what was the
sense in putting out that kind of effort?

Up to the bar beside Fred there stepped a
young man who looked like one who knew his
way around. He was of average height, but so
broad-shouldered that he appeared squat.
Around his shoulders he wore the pelt, doubtless artificial, of what Fred supposed was a
wolf; anyway it was a shaggy animal, with
pointy little stick-up ears, beady glittering
glass eyes, and sharp-looking sizable white
teeth in a pink open plastic mouth.

Fred hadn't yet made contact with anyone who knew where he might buy some gladrags.

"Hey," he called quietly.

The wolf-man turned, properly casual, and
looked Fred over. "Hey," he answered coolly.
"You buyin'?"

Fred waited long enough to show that he
wasn't being pushed into anything. "Got my
check today, why not?"

Fred and Wolf ("Call me Wolf, man.") sat
at a table, where they were soon joined by a
friend of Wolf's called Lewandowski, who was
drinking herb tea spiked with vodka. Fred
bought another round for the three of them
and decided it was the last he was going to
buy. He sounded out Wolf and Lewandowski about gladrags, and they assured him

that a man who sold such things would be
around later.

Wolf said he came from New York City. He
let it be known that he had led a gang there
and the New York police were looking for him
so he had come west for his health. Fred could
believe this about halfway. Lewandowski, a
fat, strong-looking youth with empty eyes, was
a native Chicagoan. Once he started talking it
was hard to get him to shut up. He said he was
looking for a job with one of the policy wheels,
legal or illegal made no difference to him; his
old man was a compulsive gambler and he
knew there was no money to be made on the
sucker's side of the operation.

Neither of them asked Fred about his bandage, but he faked a little more headache than
he actually felt and managed to reveal casually that he was a karate expert, working hard
for his black belt. He saw the others hardening
their faces slightly to keep from showing that
they were impressed. Probably they believed
him about halfway as he did them. Well, he
was telling them about half the truth. If only
there was someone he could talk to.

Finally Fred gave up waiting and bought yet
another round, for neither of the other two
seemed to have any money. They both said
they had been on BI for about a year, since
abandoning school. And Wolf said he couldn't
even collect his checks these days or the New
York police would find out where he was and
have him extradited.

Fred began to feel a little drunk and sick,

and his wounded head ached in earnest. The gladrag man finally arrived and was pointed out to him, and as soon as he had the little carton in his pocket Fred went back to the Y. Marjorie wasn't in, or else she wouldn't answer his tapping at the door. Without her unlatching her side of the bed, he couldn't even let his down, and so was restricted to slouching on his spine in a chair with his feet up on his tiny table. He sat there in dizzy silence for a while, staring into the hot eyes of the Y's founder, whose portrait decorated one wall. On another wall was the predictable print of *Love Conquers All*, the naked urchin wearing wings and pretending to be Eros, climbing out of bed and knocking down books and mathematical instruments and trampling a violin. That Caravaggio had certainly known how to paint. That picture would be something to try to carve in wood.

He wanted Marjorie to come back, and to hurry up about it. But maybe she had checked out, and tonight he would have to sleep with some real old-fashioned sex kitten, some real dog who studied an erotic manual every day. He didn't know if he could take that now.

One thing he sure wasn't going to be able to take for very long tonight was sitting here alone. It was only about eight o'clock, not yet dark outside, and he was neither sober nor yet really high on the spiked coffee. He got up and went out, and had nowhere to go. In a little while he was heading back to the Megiddo.

VII

THE PHONE call got Art up from the Parrs' dinner table. When Art had let the caller see him, a man's voice spoke briefly through a blanked screen, giving him directions. "The corner of Belmont and Halsted. Be there in an hour. Don't forget to come alone."

"How will I know—?" but the connection had already been broken.

George, who had been listening in the background, now looked worried, which did not help Art's nerves at all. Ann, smiling though she was worried too, came up to Art. "You're going, then? Give Rita our love if you do get to see her. And listen to what she says. And don't do anything foolish. You won't get lost now, will you?"

"No. No, I won't. Well then, I'm off." He left the house before they could change their minds completely and begin to argue with him not to go. He had prepared himself somewhat by purchasing a map of the city's slidewalk system from an autovendor, and to pick out a good route to Belmont and Halsted was no trouble at all. He even detoured through a busy shopping center with the idea of shaking off anybody who might be trying to follow him.

Chicago was a place where people walked, or at least rode standing on their moving walkways. In this it was unlike most of mid-California, where a man trying to move any distance on foot soon found himself a helpless alien in a world that had been planned and built and paved and spaced for surface vehicles. By night out there a walking man was a blind alien once the particular slidewalk or statwalk he was on had taken him out of the particular region where he lived. The tall islands of glittering buildings seen in the distance all looked pretty much alike, and the daytime mountains were gone. A walking man could think that the passing tides and torrents of headlights and taillights went on forever.

Here in Chicago things were closer together and more reachable, more on a human scale, save for the towers that clustered in the center of the city, the place a few Chicagoans still called the Loop. Here signs named the streets at every corner, address numbers were consistent where they could be seen, and the city was covered by the vast slidewalk grid. But now at sunset most of the walks were only thinly occupied. The crowded shopping center had evidently been fed most of its customers by surface vehicle, for its large parking lots looked nearly full. The people Art saw on the walks kept looking at one another in mutual wariness as they passed.

Art kept to the main thoroughfares, which

Ann had said were fairly well patroled by the
police. Plenty of artificial light fell on the
faintly whispering slidewalks, and on the new,
high, blind walls that now made up so much of
the city's face. Next to the vehicle lanes of the
street there usually came a strip of grass, then
the whispering walk, a wider strip of grass and
trees (no shrubbery, though, wherein a man
might lurk), and then the walls, high and un-
scaleable. Walls of workerless, humming factories, or walls of defended blockhouses like
George's. Art, searching out his path tonight
between the walls, was reminded of a maze he
had once seen in the laboratory of a psychologist who had been experimenting with rats.
With the going of the sun, the trees growing in
the tended spots and strips of grass took on an
unreal, misplaced look. Their June leaves
were as green as signals in the streetlights'
brightness. And the streets' steady vehicular
traffic, dipping or rising as the streets passed
under or over the moving walks, was also quite
unreal to a slidewalking man; the people in the
cars were like fish in an aquarium, dim sliding
shapes bound into their own world.

"See that one there?" the psychologist who
ran the rats had said. "Looks fine and healthy,
doesn't he? Fat and sleek and bright-eyed
compared with most of the others."

"How do you keep some of 'em that way,
with so many crowded in?"

"They're supposed to be crowded in. I'm
studying the effects of overpopulation. And
he's really no healthier than the others are.

He's like a sleepwalker, passive, nonsex-
ual . . ."

"What about the others?"

"Various reactions. See the shabby one with
all the energy? He's what we call a 'prober'.
Hyper- and homo-sexual. Hyperactive altogether, often turns cannibal. Only good point
is he's not a status-seeker as most of the males
are."

Thunder rumbled somewhere. Or was it
thunder? Close above the streetlights the night
pressed down, opaque and prematurely black.
Above the brilliant lights there might be stars
or clouds or watching eyes, nothing could be
seen.

Art ran his maze. After leaving the shopping
center he changed slidewalk directions twice,
navigating with his map. He was sliding east
along Belmont Avenue, calculating the distance to Halsted Street, when a passing police
car slowed, keeping pace with him for ten or
fifteen seconds. Art threw one half-scowling
glance toward the car and just kept on walking, until it pulled away.

A minute later he wished it back. Glancing
down a comparatively dim side street as he
crossed an intersection, he saw a group of four
or five male figures walking together two long
blocks away. They were shouting in rough
voices and waving their arms. Fortunately
they were a little too far off to be concerned
with Art. He would bet that they meant
trouble for someone, though.

Thunder rolled again. Hyperactive, and
they often turned cannibal. But the psychologist with his crowding studies had been too
wise to offer any cure-all for human nastiness.
Certainly not the simple absence of crowding.
There was still plenty of violence on farms.

Art's nerves relaxed a little when the band
of toughs passed out of sight, then tightened
again as he arrived at the intersection to which
he had been told to come. It was a busy place,
the center of a small vending district. He
alighted on a statwalk bathed in the rippling
noon of a barred display window. People
moved around him, shopping or aimlessly
walking. No one moved at once to approach
Art, and as far as he could tell no one was
watching him.

Another police car, or perhaps the same one,
came easing around a corner, and Art turned
away from it, pretending to study the contents
of the vendor's window. He heard the car halt
just a little distance off, and wait there, turbines idling with a muffled whine. Maybe they
were just keeping a protective watch over the
pedestrians in sight. If they were trying to follow him to Rita, surely they would be more
subtle about it than this. But now it seemed to
Art that the police and Family Planning probably knew already where she was. He pictured
Hall conferring with cool and crafty agents, all
of them agreeing to wait until the crime had
been irrevocably committed before they
sprang their trap. We're not out to get her,
Hall had said.

Art inventoried the window until he heard the police car pull away. A few seconds later another car drove up to the curb beside him, one of its windows lowered. A man's voice called softly: "Are you Rodney?"

"Yes." Art skipped across the slidewalk to the curb.

A rear door opened for him. "Get in."

He got in and pulled the door shut and the car moved out. There were two men with him in the car, one driving and the other beside Art in the rear. As soon as the auto had turned out of the busy intersection, the man in back took Art by the neck and pushed him impersonally down to the floor.

"We don't wancha see where we're going. Get under this." A musty-smelling, opaque blanket of some kind was thrown over his head.

Opaque blankets like this one were not commonly found in the possession of proper people. Suddenly all the possibilities of evil began to open. Art could fear that he was not being taken to Rita at all, he was being gotten rid of as a troublemaker. Meanwhile the car purred on, no one in it having anything to say. It stopped and started and turned in traffic. Art no longer had the faintest idea of the direction in which he was moving. There was a faint odor of perfume, or perhaps some kind of drug, in the car or clinging to the blanket. He told himself firmly that his new fears were ridiculous. Anyway, it was too late now to start having them.

He crouched awkwardly beneath the
blanket, breathing uncomfortably and pulling
at his beard. Just let him have one chance to
talk with Rita, face to face. She would not be
able to stick to her mad plan. She had always
gone along with him on the few occasions when
he had really insisted on having something his
own way. If she were able to face him with this
decision, she would not simply have left him a
note and fled. He had to believe that he would
be able to make her change her mind.

How could he have lived with her for more
than three years and not know her any better
than he did? But Rita didn't know him, either,
if she thought he would simply let her wreck
her life this way. That was the important
thing. The number of children and the legal
problems were secondary. To save her was
what he was really fighting for.

The car turned, slowed, turned once more,
crept ahead, and shortly stopped.

"We get out here. Don't look around, just go
straight into the building."

The blanket was pulled away and Art saw
that they were parked in an alley. Anonymous
rough brick walls were close on either hand. As
he got out of the car one of his escorts turned
him toward an open doorway, some kind of
unmarked service entrance, in the rear of a
sizable, dimly lighted building.

One of his guides, a graying, tough-looking
man, came along, walking a pace or two ahead
of Art to show him the way. Art followed down
a long shabby passage between walls of

painted concrete block and up a narrow flight
of stairs whose carpet had begun to wear. The
place was a run-down apartment building, or
perhaps a hotel. This impression was strength-
ened as they traversed another passage, that
twisted past closed and numbered doors. The
building was certainly old, but reasonably
clean and well-maintained.

At last Art's guide stopped and pointed to a
door. "She's in here. I'll come back in fifteen,
twenty minutes, and we'll take ya back where
we picked ya up." The man turned his back
indifferently and walked away.

Art tapped on the door, then turned the old
knob and pushed it open. Rita was sitting with
her back to him, in a worn plastic armchair,
wearing a silvery bikni that sparkled in the
light of the small room's single lamp, and staring out through the one small window at the
night. She looked around, startled, at Art's entrance, and he saw that above the bikni bottom her belly still bulged slightly with three
months' illegitimate pregnancy—he was not
too late. As she recognized him, love and fear
and defiance came into her face, and she
jumped up from the chair. A second later she
opened her arms.

"Come home with me now," Art murmured,
almost sleepily, about ten minutes later. His
voice was half muffled by the single pillow on
the small bed. Rita's hair, spread artlessly on
the same pillow, was silver and gold in the
light of the cheap lamp, as it would be in the

best light anywhere. A gleam of almost the same color came from the plastic armchair, where her discarded bikni lay.

"No, I can't." Her voice was small but did not hesitate. "They'll kill my baby if I do." Unable to lie still after saying those unsettling words, she got up from the cot and went to close the window, against which rain was just starting to splash.

Art also sat up and put his feet on the floor. He had suddenly realized that a good many minutes had passed, that his escort would soon be back for him, and that so far Rita and he had talked very little, and that mainly about how they loved and missed each other and whether Timmy and Paula might be much up-set by what was going on.

He stood up and reached for his codpiece, which had been thrown onto the armchair too. "You're coming home with me, so don't argue about it. You haven't committed any real crime as yet, and there isn't any reason why you can't just walk out of here. A man from Family Planning came to see me, and from what he said I'm sure they won't place any charges, *if* we just turn in this fetus as we're required to do."

"I can't, I can't. I wish you would try to understand. I wish you could stand by me." Her tender body turned in the lamplight, naked and unprotected. His heart turned over.

"Why can't you do it, for sex's sake?" he demanded, more savagely than he had meant.

"B-because it's living. It's my baby, and it's

part of you I have inside me. It would be like killing you. Oh, Art." Even slight pregnancy always made women look ridiculous and she would look more so when she put the bikni on again. Why couldn't anybody make clothes in which a pregnant girl looked less grotesque? Maybe such clothes were made somewhere. But then, Art realized abruptly, Rita's pregnancy was probably going to be ended in one or two more days. One way or another.

Now she got her bikni from the chair and did start to put it on. She looked fragile and vulnerable and ridiculous and he loved her tremendously. Her breasts were fuller than usual; that would be the pregnancy, too, of course.

"I can't go through this again," she told him grimly, meanwhile working on a strap. "I'm g-going to have myself sterilized when this is over, even if the government doesn't make me. But I can't give up this baby who's already here." When Rita got very tired or upset she sometimes stuttered.

"You have two real children, who need their mother with them right now, not away somewhere in one of those places that Family Planning runs, or hiding out here."

"You say they play all day in that b-blockhouse park. I didn't have time to look around there much. Is it safe? Ann's very nice but sometimes she doesn't watch her children closely enough." By now she had gotten back into the bikni, and stood looking into the little mirror on the dresser, trying to pull and tug the bottom to a better fit.

"Very safe." By now Art too was dressed. "Come on, Rita, you're not killing any part of me by getting rid of a fetus. I'll still be here."

"But not inside me. That part of you won't grow anymore, or go on living."

"Bah. How do you know it's even mine?"

She did not answer, or look away from the mirror, but something in her face closed off.

He said: "If I had a diseased appendix you'd want it cut out and done away with."

"What's growing in me is not diseased—"

"How do you know, have you had any defect tests made?"

"—and even if it were, I'd love it."

If this kept on he was going to grab her and shake her. "If you loved it—I mean, if you loved the potential child it might become— you know what I mean—you'd want to save it from a lifetime of being unwanted by the world."

"I want him. His mother wants him." Now Rita was getting angry too. "We should kill him now because he's going to have a very tough time someday? Then I suppose we'd better not take any chances, we'd better knock Timmy's and Paula's heads in because some- day they're likely to have a tough time too."

Sublimation! He knew that he was right, but where was the argument to use? Not what the neighbors might someday say; that wouldn't work with Rita. It came down really to their duty to the overcrowded world, of course, sacrificing a personal wish for mankind in the abstract. For the good of mankind, everyone's reproductive urges, weak or strong, just had to bow aside. But those were not phrases with which to belabor one's suffering wife. How to make the truth sound less self-righteous, speechy and highflown?

There came a knocking at the door. On his way to answer, Art said over his shoulder: "You're coming back to Ann's with me now to get the children, and then you're coming home."

"No, I'm not." Stubborn as a mule, just like her sister-in-law. You might have thought the blood relationship was there.

This time the knock was loud. Art reached the door and flung it open. The man who stood there, the same graying escort, looked at Art's face and hesitated. Then, in a more respectful tone than he had used before, he asked: "You about ready to leave? Don't worry, she'll be outta here in a couple days."

"My wife is leaving with me. Now."

"I'm not going, Art. Don't ask me—oh, I wish you hadn't come."

A pair of young women were coming along the hallway, talking and giggling about something. They eyed Art strangely, and as they passed the doorway they glanced through it into Rita's room, curiosity showing through the pale makeup that masked their faces. They were made up worse than the B-girls in the tavern had been, and dressed worse too, for those two wore loose shrouding robes, totally obscene draperies of brown and gray that no woman would wear except . . . except . . .

"What kind of a place—?" barked Art, glaring wildly at the man who faced him in the hall. The man took a step backward, startled.

Art turned quickly and confronted Rita. Lightning flared, twice, very bright through the window just behind her. In the repeated violence of light Art could see the main front of the building he was in, Rita's room being evidently in a projecting wing. DIANA ARMS APARTMENTS, said a cheap new sign above the main entrance at ground level. Above, molded into the old concrete that arched above the entrance, were other words, not conspicuous but picked out now by perfect light and some trick of the speed-reading brain.

CHICAGO MATERNITY HOSPITAL
NURSES' QUARTERS

"What kind of place is this?" He grabbed at her, while thunder detonated. "Answer me, what kind of place?" He saw his hands shaking her, shaking Rita, with a violence that no one should dare to offer her.

Rita slapped him in the face. Never before. Art backed away from her slowly, as she began to cry. He backed up three steps and bumped into the man who had come to take him away and who now took a grip on Art's arm. When Art tried to pull free, the man said something and only tightened his hold. Art turned in instant rage and struck out with his fist. The blow was clumsy but by chance he got most of his weight behind it and it took his enemy by surprise. Art felt human tissue yield with a

crunch beneath his knuckles and then he was
no longer being held.

Now once more he had Rita in his grip. She
was struggling with him, trying to break free.
She screamed: "Do you think I like it, being
here in a whorehouse? Do you know what I
feel about anything? Let go!"

Even in his rising madness he had no intention of hurting Rita. His only thought was to
save her, get her out of here. After he had gotten her, screaming, out of the little room, there
were frightened faces in his way, and doors,
and scrambling bodies. All these were obstacles that must be pushed or knocked aside.
Strong hands came from somewhere and
fastened—on him, but he struck out blindly
and kept trying to pull Rita free. Her being
here was not to be endured.

An expert foot tripped him, and down he
went on a dirty floor. His arm was clamped
and bent until he must let go of Rita's wrist.
Massive weights sat on him, crushing out what
little of his wind was left.

"Stop it!" a rough male voice demanded.
"Stop. You gonna stop?" It had been barking
the same words at him for some time, and
finally he had to listen.

"Uh."

A hand turned Art's face up from the floor.
"In th' name o' pure chastity, you gonna behave?"

"Yuh."

"All right, let 'im up. Sublimation, we get
'em all in here, every kind of nut there is."

The powerful hands that held Art down reversed themselves and hoisted, and without even trying he was on his feet. He was dizzy, the world was gray with his faintness. Unused to such exertions. Sweat and dirt were in his eyes, all mixed with helpless tears. His chest heaved in wind-broken spasms. There was a pain inside his shoulder, where something seemed to have been torn.

Rita's voice was somewhere nearby, demanding: "Where is he? Let me see. Oh, the fool. If you've hurt him, I'm going to—to—"

"Oh, lady, please, he's all right, see? Just his wind knocked out. He was out to tear the place apart. Look at my chaste eye, excuse th' language, where he slugged me."

Good.

Rita was visible as a blur before him now, and they were speaking to her with respect. Of course she was a boarder here, only a fugitive, not a—no, no, of course she was not that. He felt her cool hands, moving on his hands and his face.

"Don't start him up again, now, lady, please. Let us get him the purity outta here. We'll see he gets home safe."

"Art? Oh, Art, forgive me. Are you all right?"

"Come home with me."

"No."

He nodded. Then he was being led away. He no longer tried to resist.

A man's voice muttered: "Where's the Holy Joe, why don't he look after these celibatin' people of his? I'm sick of the whole celibatin' mess." Then the voice lowered itself to ask a whispered question.

"No! Take 'im back where ya picked 'im up, and just leave him there, nice and safe. Is somebody usin' the car now?" There was a fresh uproar in the middle distance, men's voices raised in some angry quarrel. "What's that?"

"Sounds like the homos again. I tell ya, we get every kind of nut there is. Lemme put this guy in here for a minute."

The grip that had remained on Art's arm guided him into another room. He was released and the door was closed behind him. He groped along the wall in darkness and found a switchplate, which in response to human fingers on its surface turned on a lamp.

The light was dim and his eyes were still befogged with tears and sweat, but he made out that the small room possessed a cot. He stumbled over and sank down on it, still wheezing for breath. He had to regain his wind, and more importantly his self-control. His strong point was supposed to be intelligence, and so he had to think.

Forget that Rita was staying in this whorehouse. Forget that the arrogant nameless obstetrician (Holy Joe, the bouncer had said—a cultist, then? One of Ann's priestly friends?) was using this former nurses' quarters of a doubtless abandoned hospital as his maternity ward.

Remember this, seen in the fortuitous light-

ning flash: DIANA ARMS APARTMENTS. Let them
use all the blindfolds they liked, now he could
locate this place again. To what end? Should
he tell all to Family Planning? Should he tell
George in what sort of place his sister was
holed up? George coming here to drag her out
would likely kill somebody in the process, or
they would kill him. Anyway, it was likely that
her brother would let her stay here since she
wanted it that way.

The door of the room opened quietly, and a
nude girl stepped in, carrying under one arm a
bundle of cloth rolled up as Fred's karate out-
fit had been. Art blinked his eyes and found
that he could focus clearly now. She was young
and blond, flat-bellied and full-breasted, and
her face was made up into a pale, cold mask.

The girl closed the door behind her and then
froze, motionless, staring at him haughtily. In
a cold voice she asked: "Is this the right room?
I don't think it can be mine. What are you
doing here? I don't want men in my room."

Art shifted his weight on the cot, started to
get up, and then when his body made its great
reluctance known he let himself stay sitting
there. He knew, he understood perfectly well,
that he should speak up without delay and tell
the prostitute that for once she was indeed
mistaken. This one time she had actually, really, walked into the wrong room. He understood it perfectly well yet he said nothing. Was
it that he had not yet regained wind enough to
speak? Was something wrong now with his
throat?

The girl now was moving away from the door, edging along the wall opposite where Art sat on the cot. Already she was gradually unrolling the thick, opaque robe that she had brought in under her arm, and now she was beginning to cover her body with it. As she passed the switchplate on the wall she turned the room's light to a cooler, softer glow. In her movement she gave the impression of trying to keep as far as possible from Art. She turned her painted face away from him, fixed in a mask of bitterness and contempt, while her motions, graceful as a dancer's, expressed distaste and even fear.

By now the robe was half unrolled, and now it covered half her flesh. This girl was good, she knew her trade. "Don't make a move toward me," she said in a low voice, tense with raw repression. "I don't want to be pawed by a man. I don't want you even to stare at me."

In his adolescence Art had gone twice to brothels. Both times guilt feelings had hampered his performance, and the results had been unsatisfactory. He was still very nearly a virgin as far as sublimation was concerned. Since his marriage he had come to think of himself as grown above all that kind of thing, and he had never, since marriage, been seriously tempted toward it. If Rita had ever wanted to do anything like this, he hadn't been aware of it. Did he know what she felt about anything?—those were her words. He would have done it with her, if she had ever asked. What went on between husband and wife was nobody else's business.

The girl had nearly reached the window now. "Maybe you don't *want* to touch me, though," she said, turning her eyes on Art as if with dawning hope. Oh, yes, this girl was good. "Maybe you're a pure, chaste man. Maybe you're a person who knows what a human being really likes."

She had reached the window, and now she turned her pale mask of a face to look up and out through the upper panes, left unshaded for this very purpose while the lower were fitted with plastic shields in imitation of stained glass. By now her body from the neck down was completely hidden in the long robe, and now her simulated fear and tension were fading out, were being put aside by something else.

By an exaltation that, once he let it grip him, might be impossible to deny.

"The stars," she said, her voice now more distant and far softer than before. "The stars are very beautiful tonight."

Of course tonight's sky was all clouds and rain, and the stars were only a part of her routine. But that hardly mattered. In his mind the perfect blue-white points of light were there. Her voice and her face and the attitude of her body beneath the long concealing robe made it all true.

Again he realized dully that he must move and speak, he must explain his presence here and make her stop. But for the moment he could not. His breathing, already slowed to normal, became still slower while his eyes rested on the girl. Her hair reminded him of Rita's, and in other ways they looked something alike. This girl was physically quite attractive, as were all the most successful whores. The more lust there was to sublimate, the more the act could mean. Of course nothing to do with sex was ever reducible to such a simple formula as that; but it seemed to Art that with this girl the meaning of the act of sublimation was likely to be very great indeed. To throw down the weight of sex and stand beside her, for the moment straighter, taller, freer, than that encumbrance would ever let you stand. To stand on top of sex, and use it for a footstool, and look with this girl at her imaginary stars and take their light into his being. Tonight he yearned very powerfully to do just that.

He knew it was a wrong and perverse yearning that he struggled with, and once he had thought that such urges were over for him, all safely outgrown. But now in his weakness and defeat they came to trouble him once more. Well, since an act of sublimation promised all the comfort of which he stood in need, why not? Why not, just this once?

No! He was not going to be so spineless, so weak-willed. Art resisted. He called up images of Eros, lust-knotted bodies sweating, writhing, roaring, raging to attain a pinnacle of lust yet higher than the one they slipped and labored on. He fastened his mind upon the remembered image of the girl's bare body as he had seen it when she first entered the room. He pictured Rita's body, spread out invitingly before him. But all the fleshly stirrings that he now managed to arouse in himself would only go as fuel for sublimation if he faltered. And he was faltering. The consciousness of sex-as-God that never should entirely leave an adult's mind was flickering now and fading dangerously in his.

"The stars are beautiful," the girl said again, and now her voice sounded like winter bells. "So beautiful, so far away."

The rain drummed on the window steadily, but had no power to make her words ridiculous. Art feebly tried to cling to images of female nakedness, but all were still and flat and lifeless now, remote and meaningless as old photographs.

Just as he might have gotten up and gone to join the girl at the window, the thought presented itself that the men would soon be coming back for him, and they would have quite a laugh if they came in and found him stargazing. The banal fear was enough to tip the balance on the other side.

"I'm sorry," he said, and stood up with a grunt. His hands and knees were quivering still and his wrenched shoulder hurt. He fumbled in his pockets for some money with which to tip the girl; probably she would make a fuss if he tried to walk out without tipping her. At least she seemed to recall that things had been that way in the brothels of his youth. "I'm not a customer."

She had turned from the window and was regarding him with great surprise. He handed her money and explained: "There's really been a mistake." Mechanically a gentleman, he squeezed the girl's breast through her robe.

"Mistake? I'll say!" The wintry voice had broken suddenly to nasty shrillness. "This is only five dollars you gimme!"

"It's all you'll get," said Art, now dangerously calm in his exhaustion. "I told you I'm not a customer."

With the money in hand the girl rushed out of the room. Art followed, wearily, as far as the corridor, where he stood waiting. In a moment his guide, with a swollen cheekbone but the same indifferent expression as before, and another man, came into sight. "I'm ready," Art told them. "Take me back."

He rode under the blanket again in the silent car, and smiled grimly to himself. *Diana Arms Apartments.* He was let out of the car at the busy intersection where he had been picked up. After all he had just been through, a late trip home by slidewalk seemed nothing at all to be concerned about, and he did not even look around when once there came to him the sound of distant screams.

When he got back to the Parrs, who seemed to have been waiting anxiously, Art did not have a great deal to say. Yes, he had seen her and yes, she still wanted to go through with it. She seemed to be all right, and she said they were treating her well enough.

"What kind of place is she staying in?" Ann

wanted to know. "And what's wrong with your arm?"

"I, ah, twisted my shoulder somehow, opening the car door."

Ann, evidently assuming from Art's defeated attitude that he was now going to let his wife do as she chastely well pleased, became very comforting and motherly. Art let her rub his shoulder with some kind of medicine that George used for his occupational aches and pains. He also let her go on thinking what she liked.

George appeared noticeably relieved by Art's safe return. "I should have gone," he muttered several times.

No, you shouldn't, thought Art. At last Ann released him and he dragged himself upstairs and fell into the guest room bed.

In the morning, he decided painfully, he would go to Family Planning, and have a talk with Mr. Hall. There was really nothing else that he could do.

Sleep was a long time coming.

VIII

"MR. BARNABY of the Homosexual League is here asking to see you, sir."

Oscar Grill, director of the Chicago office of the Bureau of Family Planning, slumped back in his chair and gazed unhappily at the image of his secretary in the intercom plate. "What's he here for?" The same as usual, I suppose."

"I tried to find out, sir, but he was vague. I suppose the same as usual."

Grill made a grimace of annoyance. He had barely had time this morning to sit down and assure himself of what a busy day he had ahead, and now here came Barnaby again. About a year ago the president of the Illinois Homosexual League had begun a series of drop-in visits, coming around about once every two months. Barnaby came, and talked mostly in generalities, and sometimes they had lunch together, and Grill had never been able to understand just what his visitor was hoping to accomplish by visiting. It wasn't that Barnaby was personally attracted to him; that surely would have been made plain by now, and didn't seem too likely anyway, given Grill's paunchy, jowly appearance and the fact that he was sliding fast past middle age.

What made the situation difficult for Grill was that the president of the state Homo League was too important to be casually brushed off. No politician wanted to risk alienating a bloc of votes of the League's size, and Oscar Grill was, among other things, very much a politician. And general elections were coming up within a year.

Grill sighed, mentally trying to rearrange his morning schedule. He wondered which appointments he might be able to put off. "I suppose you'd better send him in right away. Maybe I can cut it short."

"Yes sir."

Seizing the moment of peace before Barnaby walked through the door, Grill closed his eyes and tried to achieve an instant of total relaxation. But his job was difficult, and his thoughts were hard to quiet quickly. He wanted to be sure to get to today's luncheon meeting, with the local heads of other bureaus, Art, Poverty, and Vandalism. Important political decisions were in the offing. And sometime today he wanted to try to talk again with his semi-official contacts at the UN's Chicago consulate, to try to find out what might be delaying the latest population forecast. There was a fog of rumors surrounding that report; probably when he did learn what it contained, he would wish that he hadn't.

The door was opening, and Grill opened his eyes and stood up and came around his desk, setting himself to be courteous but still to ease his visitor out as quickly as he could. At least he had an obviously and honestly crowded desk for Barnaby to notice.

The president of the Homo League entered, moving with his usual slightly feminine walk. His basic physique was that of an average male, but his face was strikingly handsome—or perhaps pretty—and his long hair was a natural-looking bright red. In the League as elsewhere, appearance evidently counted for a lot in getting to be president. Barnaby wore a conservatively tiny bikni not too much different from the standard female model, the bottom lacking the exaggerated fullness of the usual male codpiece. Mr. Barnaby's bra was functional; medical science had given him that much in the way of matching his biology to his lusts.

"How do you do, sir?" Grill asked formally, extending a hand in greeting.

"Not well today, Oscar, not very well." Barnaby's voice was husky rather than deep. He shook Grill's fingers delicately. "I am becoming afraid to travel through the streets. There is an organized harassment that I must endure. Good citizens pay taxes, then find that their government offers them no protection."

Grill said: "Won't you sit down? You mean you're being picketed again by that bluenose group?"

"Again? One might say that it has become almost continuous." Adjusting his shoulder bag with a large hand, Barnaby settled himself in a visitor's chair. "Not only is our headquarters under seige, as it were, but some of these Young Virgins have taken to following my car through the streets. I should warn you that some of them have followed me here to-day."

Grill had seated himself and was toying with the corner of a stack of printout that lay awaiting his attention in his desk, though he had little hope that the hint would be taken. "Well, I can certainly sympathize. I really wish there was something I could do but, twins, we're sometimes picketed here ourselves."

"Yes, I'm sure you are, and by many of the same people." Barnaby crossed his hairless, slightly plump legs. "Oscar, it seems to me of the utmost importance that those of us who lead in conserving traditional values should support one another, for the cause of Eros and the good of society. Men and women of good will should stand together whenever possible, that's all I mean. I realize that you have no power to punish those wretches who are out there picketing."

"I certainly don't." Grill sneaked a look at his clock.

"I did go to the police about the picketing, as I believe you suggested once before." Barnaby seemed unable to keep from exciting himself over the pickets. "I tried to point out to the police the difference between our country's traditional freedoms and the anarchy those bluenoses want. They paint their dirty words right on their signs, and wave them about in public places, and the police and courts will do nothing to put a stop to it!"

Grill shrugged. "I suppose if the police are providing you with physical protection, that's really about all you can expect."

"Oscar," said Barnaby reproachfully. He leaned across the desk and lowered his voice. "Which is the more to be feared, injury to the body or poisoning of the mind? And I am more concerned for youth of the community than for myself. What will happen to them, growing up in a world where nothing is considered obscene any longer?"

Art woke up slowly. There was something very nasty that he would have to face on waking, and so it was pleasant to delay the process. Then he moved, and felt a twinge in his shoulder, and all his memories of yesterday came back. With a groan he sat up in the guest room bed. His watch read half past eight.

His situation looked no better in the morning light than it had in midnight gloom. There was nothing for it but to be a good citizen and go to Family Planning. Mr. Hall had said they were not out to *get* anyone, at least not anyone like Rita. People like her were only the innocent victims of the midwifers and their gangs. And of their well-meaning relatives. Too bad if the relatives got in trouble. Art's first responsibility was to his wife, not to the relatives who should never have gotten her into this mess in the first place. Even if they were only trying to help.

He didn't want to think about the Parrs right

now, but it was hard to avoid while he was in their house. He got out of bed and began to get ready to go downstairs.

While he showered and shaved and dressed he pictured raiding police breaking down the doors of that former nurses' quarters, carting off hysterical whores, handcuffing thugs. Then along came their quietly efficient lieutenant, leading Rita safely out. When she saw Art (who had ridden along in the lead car with the lieutenant) she burst into tears, and threw repentant arms around his neck . . .

More likely she would slap his face again. The scenario was fundamentally unconvincing, so Art had to give up on it and think of something else while he held fast to his determination.

Aromas of coffee and warm food now reached him in the upstairs hall. He promised himself that he would say nothing to the Family Planning authorities about George and Ann. Well, sooner or later he would doubtless have to say *something* about them, for he was going to be asked a lot of questions. But he might make their immunity a condition of his giving information. Something like that. Anyway, he kept telling himself, if they wound up in trouble it would serve them right, for helping Rita get herself into such a mess. His shoulder definitely felt better this morning. He would get Ann to rub it with liniment again tonight, if he was still staying here. If she was still staying here.

After taking a quick peek into the children's

room and finding it already deserted, Art went downstairs. In the kitchen he found George and Ann facing each other across the breakfast table, where Art's place was also set. Dirty dishes and a minor litter of garbage testified that the children had already eaten before going out to play.

Even as Art's in-laws said good morning to him, they seemed to him to be exchanging guilty looks. They had provided Art and his children with food and lodging, but what did they count for, compared with the harm they were doing Rita? Their intentions had been good, of course, but what of that?

George raised troubled eyes. "Art, what are your plans now?"

"I don't know." As soon as Art was seated, Ann began to ply him silently with toast and protein bars and coffee. His fingers fumbled on the jelly jar. He asked unnecessarily: "Are the children out in the playground?"

He was assured they were, and with that an awkward silence fell. He wished he had gone straight out of the house, but that would have been insulting, and besides, being under a strain increased his tendency to get sick if he didn't eat any breakfast.

Still, he couldn't stand to sit there. He gobbled his food and quickly pushed back his chair. "I'm going out." No one said anything to him as he fled the house.

It was a bright warm morning; only puddles here and there gave evidence of last night's rain. Once outside the blockhouse walls Art

breathed a little easier, at least at first. As
soon as he came to a public computer terminal
he went in and obtained the address of the
Chicago office of Family Planning. With a
slight feeling of relief he saw that he would
have to travel a considerable distance to reach
the place; he needed some time to think over
just what he was going to say. They weren't
out to get Rita, though, they were really on her
side. Once on the proper slidewalk, he drew a
deep breath, and again remarked to himself
that the weather was fine today. Who cared?

Reaching the Family Planning office
seemed to take almost no time at all, and
somehow he could get no constructive thinking
done en route. The office occupied a new, fairly large building, one of the foothills surrounding the central Loop's high range. From a
block or two away Art could see that there was
an unusually dense crowd gathered on the
statwalk in front of the place. As he drew a
little nearer he realized this was no ordinary
pedestrian jam. There was a stack of placards
on the pavement, ready for distribution; some
kind of demonstration must be shaping up.
Should he go in? If he didn't make himself go
in and face the authorities now, he never
would. Ignoring the murmuring, jostling
crowd as best he could, he pushed his way into
the lobby.

In the vast ground-floor lobby of glass and
marble he approached a receptionist, a vo-
luptuous girl who smiled at him enticingly
from behind her desk. As befitted her place of

employment she was very conservatively dressed, wearing only a few electrostatically clinging sequins and pads.

Art halted in front of her desk, not as by the application of brakes, but as with a complete loss of momentum. This was it. He was finished. His mind had gone as blank and bare as the smooth expanse of receptionist's skin confronting him. Somehow he had convinced himself that once he got this far all the right words would flow, but that had been a lie. Now here he was, and all the words were gone in fear. To ask for Mr. Hall would be like leaping over a cliff.

"I'm from California," he began with a great effort, helped along by the girl's encouraging eyes. "Still, I have important business with you here. I'd like to see—the director or someone." Art was suddenly and completely sure that he never wanted to talk to Mr. Hall again. He would never be able to convince Hall that George and Ann were innocent, or at least that they deserved a break, not after the tough time Ann had given him. And she and George hadn't even asked Art where he was going this morning.

The girl's eyes turned grave. "The director is a very busy man," she said. "If you'll tell me the nature of your business, perhaps I can help you."

"My business is, uh, important." Of course the director was not going to see everyone who just walked in. One could hope that everyone here would be too busy for that.

The girl's eyes narrowed slightly, searching

Art's face. He had the idea that she could see his guilty knowledge, and was already pressing an alarm button hidden beneath her desk. "I can arrange for you to talk to a social worker. Are you in a hurry?"

"I—" When their computer learned his name it would give him to Mr. Hall, and Mr. Hall would seize upon him, not to be denied a single scrap of information. Art would stumble helplessly into a betrayal of the Parrs, and Rita would hate him for that, even if she were not thrown in jail and forcibly sterilized herself. "No, there's no hurry," he told the girl.

"May I have you name, please?" the receptionist pulled a computer-input slate toward her on its decorative coiled cable, and took up an electronic stylus.

"I—" Ann was at this moment caring for Art's children. George was risking bloody beatings from machines, to pay for safe blockhouse playspace and midwifers and cinnamon-flavored protein bars that tended to turn lumpy in the stomach. Art's thought, now scrambling like a cornered animal for some way out, seized suddenly upon the possibility that Rita's illegal operation was being performed this very morning. If so she would certainly be jailed instead of rescued if Art led Family Planning to her.

In his present state he took this as excuse enough to flee. Without even delaying to pinch the receptionist goodbye, Art took a step back from her desk. He blurted out wild words about returning later. He turned and fled.

* * *

"Radicals and bluenoses, repressors of all
that makes Man at one with a billion years of
his animal heritage!" Barnaby's voice had
grown shrill. "Are we to abandon the youth of
the world to them?"

Looking down, with Barnaby, from an
open window of his office, Director Grill had a
good view of the wide statwalk in front of the
Family Planning building. Two competing
picket lines had just been organized down
there, and both of them were on the march,
weaving and writhing like antagonistic ser-
pents. The lines had formed with a healthy
distance between them but were gradually
being forced closer to each other by the pressure of a mass of onlookers, whose expectation
of a riot was probably going to fulfill itself. It
seemed likely to Grill, who had seen this sort
of thing happen elsewhere, that a critical mass
of active humanity would soon be reached. To
carry the analogy with atomic fission further,
a block away a column of helmeted city police
was marching in, a damping rod about to be
thrust into an overheating pile.

Sporadic shouting drifted up to Grill's office
window, but as yet he had seen no actual violence. He was not too high above the picket
lines to tell that one of them was composed
mostly of radical-looking young people, the
girls wearing their hair long, the men short-
haired and clean-shaven, both sexes dressed in
opaque garments that covered half their bodies or more. These of course were the Young

Virgins, the objects of Barnaby's wrath. In the
opposing picket line, men and women of ordinary appearance were in the majority,
though there was a noticeable admixture of
men in biknis, and women in codpieced, translucent business suits.

"I see your League has some counter-picketers out today," Grill commented.

"Naturally we do!" Barnaby ran nervous
fingers through his bright red hair. "We don't
intend to succumb without a struggle."

Grill decided that the time had come for
bluntness, whatever the result might be.
"Frankly, I wish you hadn't decided on coun-
terpicketing. Not in front of *my* building."

"What? But we must take action. Look, look
down there! A sign that says 'sublimate', in big
bold letters, being waved around in a public
place!"

Grill looked down and saw. He also saw another sign, in bigger, bolder letters yet: STOP
MORAL FREE FALL. He wondered honestly which
side that one was intended to be on.

"Let them go to their monasteries and
lamaseries and nunneries to have that kind of
freedom," Barnaby was saying. "Let them go
behind walls, away from the innocent, and do
what they like."

Grill drew a deep breath. "You know, if I
was coldly logical about my job . . ."

"Yes?"

"Well, I might look with official favor upon
the bluenoses. After all, the less sex activity
there is, generally speaking, the fewer preg-

nancies and the less population pressure."

"Only in the most primitive societies!" snapped Barnaby. But then he fell silent and put on a mask of careful control, which Grill thought was concealing more fear than anger.

Emboldened by this, Grill went on: "I don't know if any society has ever been run on the basis of cold logic. Probably not. I'm sure ours isn't. People's emotional attitudes are the ultimate power, of course. And most of the people are with you, at least in your attitude toward bluenoses. If I were to come out strongly in favor of chastity today I'd doubtless be fired tomorrow."

Barnaby relaxed slightly. "You are joking. Of course there's no excuse for chastity. For a long time our League has shown the way toward the fullest enjoyment of sex without the slightest risk of pregnancy."

"Most people just don't enjoy your kind of sex, though," said Grill deliberately. "At least not as a steady diet. And the monasteries and other religious places you talk about are from my point of view very much like Homo League enclaves—they have a vanishingly low birth rate. So, I may not agree with the bluenoses emotionally, but I'm not going to try to put them out of business. I still don't dare to praise them publicly, but I can tell you off the record that I'm rather glad there are more and more lamaseries and nunneries these days."

There was silence, except for Barnaby clearing his throat. He seemed to be giving some point a deep reconsideration. "Really," he said at last. "I didn't come here with the main objective of getting your help against the blue-noses. I know I let them upset me too much. I can see, they do help you in your difficult job. But we've helped you even more, haven't we? For many years? I like to think that we in the League are your favorite citizens, so to speak. That there's a large backlog of goodwill built up between us."

"Of course." Grill sighed, left the window, and walked back to his desk. He did not want to watch another riot.

Privately, he had no more emotional sympathy for homosexuality than he did for chastity. Professionally, he was glad to accept all the help, from every quarter, that Family Planning and the world could get. The human world was in danger of collapsing by the weight of its own numbers, though you might not be able to tell that by what went on in Illinois.

On the walls of Grill's office the computer-drawn curves of the world demographic charts showed the danger in the form of the ever-worsening pressure of population. More people inevitably ate more food, and while around the world the food suppliers struggled to get ahead, sometimes they could not even manage to keep up. There were now laws restricting births in every country on the planet. It was mathematically, physically, inevitable that at some future time, by some combination of peaceful or violent forces, the world's population growth would finally be stopped—obviously it could not continue until human beings stood jammed shoulder to shoulder on every square meter of solid land. The approximately eight billion people who inhabited the world today could all, in theory, probably be stored within Chicago's borders, standing indoors and out, leaving the rest of the earth on which to grow their food.

Frighteningly many of the eight billion were hungry and sick today, and more would be tomorrow. Science had boosted the world's supply of available energy beyond all foreseeable needs by achieving controlled atomic fusion; by harnessing, as the popularizers of science put it, the power of the H-bomb and of the sun itself. The problems of producing and distributing adequate food, and providing medical care, were not so amenable to research and engineering. The leaders of the have-not nations spent their time in power in states of chronic desperation, weighing and selecting gamblers' moves to keep themselves in power and—sometimes this came first—to help their countrymen.

One aid toward staying in power was to point out a scapegoat or two on which the people could vent their hate and dissatisfaction. If there were any justification for the choice of scapegoat, so much the better. Another gamblers' move was the utterance of overt or implied threats. Often the threats were serious, even when spoken by the leader of a poor but desperate nation against a wealthy and much more powerful one. Today at least eighty nations were theoretically capable of producing atomic weapons, and fifteen or twenty of these had technologies sufficiently sophisticated to perhaps enable them to hide such outlawed weapons from the UN inspection teams. Delivery of a nuclear bomb could be accomplished by stealth if not by missile or aircraft. Biological weapons were easier to make, conceal, and deliver, and could be just as deadly if not as quick as nuclear blasts. Thus the voices of the have-nots must be heard in all the greatest capitals of the world. Thus if a new-born baby in Chicago consumed, statistically, three times the food of one new-born in India, it was considered only just and decent to limit the number of new-born Chicagoans, and the same with Londoners, Muscovites, babies of Peking and Tokyo. The starving child in the Indian village might never see a bite of the food thus theoretically saved for him, but who could say it was not just to offer him at least a chance? Thus, even among the haves, compulsory sterilization and abortion for women who could not limit their fertility in any other way. Thus, the illegitimacy of the third child. We may not feed the world, we may lack the knowledge or the will or the material wealth for that, but we will not let it watch us overeat.

Again, as he looked now at the charts, there darted across Grill's mind the question of why the latest population forecast had been delayed. He felt a foreboding chill.

"It seems to me," Barnaby was saying to

him, "that in fact you owe us a real debt. Very few of the League's members have brought any children at all into the world—as yet."

Something in Barnaby's tone brought Grill's thoughts back firmly to his office. "As yet? Why do you put it that way?"

Barnaby did not answer at once. An alien hardness had come into his face. He continued to stand beside the window, watching Grill.

As Grill stood waiting beside his desk his mind started to relate that odd phrase "as yet" to the chain of Barnaby's odd visits, and to certain other terrible hints that Grill had lately received from other sources. The hints concerned recent advances in surgery, and in hormonal chemistry; until now, Grill had managed to avoid confronting their implications face to face.

Barnaby, as if reading the director's mind, was nodding slowly and solemnly now. "Maybe you've heard something about it? True male to female sex reversal is going to be possible. There've been doctors working on it in Sweden, and lately in Japan, and both groups seem to have been successful."

"Well. That's fine. I suppose many members of the League will want to avail themselves of the operation, to become practically complete women."

"Not just practically, Oscar. Truly complete. I want that. Does that surprise you?" Paradoxically, as he spoke of becoming a woman, Barnaby looked more normal than before, a male trapped in a masquerade costume he could not shed, a man grown weary and desperate beyond all words. "Does it make you laugh, to hear that I will want to bear a child? Two children, if I can."

Grill was far from laughter. "This is—beyond belief."

"Not to me." Barnaby's husky voice quavered. He spoke now as if confessing some terrible crime. "All my life, since I was a child myself, the thought has been in my mind that somehow—if I could have a son—what do you know about me, anyway?"

Like the first thunder of an unexpected storm, the sounds of rioting burst up abruptly from the street outside; Director Grill hardly noticed them. He moved behind his desk and sank slowly into his chair, without taking his eyes off Barnaby. "So," Grill said in a faint voice. "Today you have come here on business."

Art, while inside the building and knotted in his own problems, had forgotten completely about the demonstrations being organized outside. When he emerged from the lobby, practically at a run, he was at once caught up between chanting swirls of picketers and counter-picketers. When he pushed his way free he had been turned around, and stood still for a moment, disoriented, in the middle of the statwalk.

A short fat man carrying an armload of cheaply made, stick-mounted signs appeared at once beside Art, haranguing him. "Get yer

sign, get yer placard here! Do yer *part,* sir,
only a dollar." STOP MORAL FREE FALL, said the
signs, or some of them at least. Others, in-
terleaved, bore the proud legend LOVE CON-
QUERS ALL.

"I'm not involved in this," Art muttered,
trying to get free of the peddler, not knowing
which side the man thought he was on, or even
what the two contending forces were. As soon
as Art spotted a small gap between the picket
lines he made for it. The pickets were chanting
louder and louder, faster and faster, mouthing
unintelligible rioters' warcries. The peddler
would not give up but stayed at Art's side like
a stubborn conscience, trying to sell him a
sign. Moving together they were too big to get
through the gap, and they, or Art at least, col-
lided with one of the lines as it writhed
snakelike toward him. A shout of anger went
up from those he had bumped, followed by a
cheer from the opposing ranks.

"Filthy censor! Bluenose!"

"Smear the queers! Smear the queers!
Smear—"

A tall male figure loomed up in front of Art.
Above the words STUDENTS FOR A CHASTE SOCIE-
TY, handpainted on a dirty, opaque sweatshirt,
the young man's face was clean-shaven, angry,
florid, shouting. Someone bawling a song
about love pushed Art from behind, where-
upon the young man in front struck Art on the
head with his flimsy sign.

Something was wrong, the blow should not
have hurt so much. It was a great deadening

bash that dented a vacuum into his skull, into which a tremendous pain was now about to rush . . .

There was a policeman in view. And other people, he could not tell who . . . Art was down, but somebody had him under the arms and was dragging him along . . . the blow from the flimsy sign should not have been so hard . . . now he was dying, or else . . .

IX

AFTER ART hurried out of the house, George and Ann remained seated at the breakfast table, alone now in the silent house, facing each other with glum expressions.

"I wonder what's happened to Fred," said Ann distantly, turning her head to look out through her window at the patio vines. "And I wonder if Rita has her baby yet." Then she gave up making conversation and brought her hands up to cover her face. "Oh, if Art turns us in today it's going to be all my fault."

"He won't," said George, putting into his voice a lot more certainty than he felt. "He doesn't want to get Rita in trouble. Anyway, there's no use blaming yourself if he does."

"He might." Ann spoke through her muffling hands, around her silver wedding ring. "You and Rita will be the ones who go to jail for conspiracy, but it'll be all my fault. Why did I have to tell her you had a student who could arrange things? Some criminal doctor."

George was irritated. "Hammad's no criminal, or I wouldn't have him as a student. I don't consider arranging births to be a crime, and you don't either. I don't know of anything else he does that's outside the law."

"He arranges births and breaks the law just for money. I don't like that. Why couldn't we have waited until I heard from the Order of St. Joseph people?"

"You might have waited a long time, with their monastery burned down. Anyway, it might even be one of them who's doing the operation. I think it was smart for Hammad to farm it out."

"Someone else is doing it, while he gets paid. Hammad, I don't trust Hammad."

"Now's a fine time to tell me that," George grumbled. "Anyway, Rita's no Christian, she won't care who does it or why." As long as it's done competently. If it isn't—but there was nothing he could do.

Ann was silent behind her hands.

"Art won't turn us in," George repeated, trying to be comforting. To himself he thought that he could hardly blame Art for anything he did today. Art was the one they hadn't allowed for in their plans.

Still silent.

He reached across the table, pried one of Ann's hands down from its job of eye-hiding, and held it softly in his own. "Hey, things aren't that bad," he said. "Hey, lady, do you need some help?"

The first time he had made that offer to Ann they had both been aboard a bus cruising at eighteen miles an hour along the sixty-lane freeway that ran from Bear Canyon to Pasadena, near the middle of Los Angeles.

Five apish young men had also boarded at Bear Canyon, though George had not paid much attention to them then. Perhaps they had gotten on to follow Ann. She had five or six small children with her that day.

The five young men had taken seats just a little forward in the bus from Ann and her brood, and once the bus was isolated from the world in the flow of traffic they had begun talking loudly among themselves, boasting in obscene language of their skills at stealing, fighting, and sublimating. Ann was pretty good at ignoring them, but then one of the apes began to toss little wads of something or other in her direction. "Hey, lady, those all yours? Quintup-lets! Looks like you waited too long, decidin' which two to keep."

By now most of the other passengers had congealed in their seats, seeing and hearing nothing, feeling safer behind pretended walls.

"Hey, girly?" called the youth who had been tossing the spitballs. "Anyone ever tell you you'd look nice wrapped in a blanket down to your toenails?" He turned to a friend. "Red, you got some gladrags with you?"

"Sure."

"Break 'em out. Girly's gonna gaze at the stars with us."

An old women sitting beside George muttered something to the effect that girls who dressed that way were just asking for trouble —and true enough, Ann had on an opaque blouse, and an opaque skirt that came down nearly to her knees. Maybe her dress was one reason why George had noticed her as early as he did. But that was irrelevant now.

"Do you need some help, lady?" he called to Ann politely, as he got up to stand in the narrow aisle, swaying there slightly with the motion of the bus. George was then twenty-one, half trained in karate, proud owner of a purple belt. He stood up with a feeling of necessity, without either much fear or sense of heroism. Vaguely he wished that he could have a chance to limber up.

"Yes, I believe I do." Ann's voice was as calm as if she had dropped a package in an awkward place and a presentable young man had offered to pick it up.

So George cleared his throat like a nervous orator and faced forward. He met the eyes of the five troublemakers, one after another, and wondered if there were any words that he might stop them with. A wise old instructor had once told George that if you were really ready for street trouble the readiness showed somehow and trouble never came, not unless you went out of your way to make it, which wise people in or out of karate never did. What words would have stopped me, George wondered, when I was just a kid and up to something wild? But he had never been as wild and apey as these five were acting now, and magic words eluded him. At the same time he was reassuring himself on a comforting point he had already noticed: the narrowness of the aisle. There might be five of them, but they could only come in reach of him one at a time.

If they were going to come at all. He could see in their faces that he had frightened them just by getting up to face them, and he hoped that his continued calm and that of the girl might be enough to keep them paralyzed. He raised his eyes toward the front of the bus, and met the driver's eyes in a mirror behind the driver's personal shield of armored glass. All around the bus the sixty-lane river of vehicles crept on, cutting it off from the rest of humanity and bearing it along. The driver was already trying to maneuver the bus into an outer lane and reach an emergency stopping bay, but to accomplish the maneuver might easily take ten minutes or so.

Meanwhile, maintaining a calm silence was not going to be enough, perhaps because the five had nowhere to retreat. Now their faces were hardening again; they were more afraid of something else, something that drove them on, than they were of him. They looked at one another and got to their feet and started after George. The old woman screamed.

The eyes of the first youth to come at George changed again when he realized he was in a narrow aisle, and could expect no immediate help. He was a boy of average size and strength, a little taller than George, sixteen or seventeen years old. His face was just a bit too broad to be called handsome, and his red hair was cut so short the top of his head looked bald. His cohort, mumbling obscenities,

shoved forward behind him, pushing him to
the attack, until there was nothing he could do
but lunge at George, swinging his fists in
clumsy desperation.

The bus driver was thinking, as well as
watching in the mirror. At that moment he
tapped his brakes firmly, risking a bang from
the vehicle following, but stalling the momentum of the single-file attack.

George saw the first blow of the fight coming
at him, and ducked just enough to catch it on
the top of the head, where an enemy knuckle
was likely to be cracked. Then he leaned forward counterpunching, just as the sudden
slowing of the bus rocked the enemy back on
their heels. George could already crack two
centimeters of pine with either hand. The foe
went down like helpless dummies, tangled
with one another as they fell. George pressed
forward, hammering at the face and body of
the unfortunate youth who had led the attack,
getting him down and keeping him down so
that the rest were jammed and pinned behind
him and beneath him.

When the police came aboard, only a couple
of minutes after the bus had reached an emergency bay, they found George still leaning on
the pile of inept apes, punching anything that
dared to move. The police heard Ann's matter-
of-fact story, and the driver's, and the stories
of the passengers who had noticed anything
happening. George was identified and allowed
to go his way; the five were removed to a police

copter. The red-bald youth had to be carried, and his face was now far from handsome. George had a moment of sick regret, but no more than a moment, on seeing the damage he had done.

As soon as the police had departed with their catch the bus got rolling again and Ann's reaction started to set in. Her hands were trembling and she had to fight back tears. She understood, probably from experience, that they would have done more than just wrap her in a plastic sheet. And the children riding with her were still in a slight state of shock, sitting quietly and staring at her and George.

George sat down at her side and acknowledged her choking thanks. He now felt ten feet tall, and at the same time shaky with relief. "Relax, it's all over now," he said to Ann. He patted her arm, and slid a hand beneath her long skirt, gently squeezing her thigh.

"Please don't," she murmured, shifting away from him, pressing her knees firmly together.

His quieting pulse speeded up again at her withdrawal. But he couldn't believe she had meant that just the way it sounded. Probably it wasn't really the open invitation it sounded like, but just a nervous reaction from the danger she had been in. A lot of people just didn't feel like sex when they were frightened or upset, and under the circumstances her lack of even a polite pretense was quite forgiveable.

So he restricted himself to holding Ann's

hand, and lightly stroking her arm, which attentions she accepted and seemed to find comforting. "I think I know you," he said with sudden mild surprise. "At least I know who you are. Your name's Ann something, and you're in my sister's high school class. You were there at school one day with a bunch of girls when I went to pick her up. She's Rita Parr. Oh, excuse me, my name is George."

"Yes, I heard you giving it to the police. I'm Ann Lohmann. Oh, why must I start blubbering now, when the trouble's all over?" She was certainly not blubbering, just a little tense and swollen-looking about the eyes. "Thanks to you." Getting herself completely under control, Ann looked around to her children, giving them a smile and a few cheerful words, snapping at a boy to get his feet down off the seat.

"Where are you taking them?" George asked.

"We're just coming back from Bear Canyon Park. I took them out there because so many never see anything but pavement and little strips of grass." The kids all had a BI look. "They're from my Sunday School class."

"Oh, one of those religious schools?"

"Yes." There was a pause. "I remember seeing you, too, now that I think about it. Rita looks a lot like you."

He laughed. "Don't say that about the poor girl. She's all excited about graduation these days. So are you, I suppose."

"Yes, we all are, I guess." But Ann was evidently not nearly as excited as Rita was.

"And about going to college. Where are you going your freshman year, if you don't mind my asking?"

"How could I mind *your* asking anything?" Ann smiled beautifully. She was really quite a good-looking girl. "I might go to Mid-Cal my first year. Or maybe Ha-Levy Junior. I'm not sure."

George also liked this girl's voice, now that he had a chance to listen to it attentively. Girls' voices were important, in his estimation. So were their tempers and spirits. If there was a suggestion of repression in Ann's clothes and manner, well, that was an attractive spice for him. He hadn't yet seen her standing up, but he guessed that she would be no taller than he was. That, too, was nice.

"You're older than Rita, aren't you?" Ann was asking. "Well, naturally you are. Where did you go to college, or are you still going?"

"I didn't go." Not wanting her to think him lazy or stupid, he quickly added: "Oh, I may go yet. But the year I finished high school there was one problem after another in our family, people were getting sick and losing jobs and all. We were almost back on BI. I didn't have much time or money, and I was a little too dumb to qualify for any good scholarships. Then I got into this karate business. Once you get your black belt, it's really a profession."

Ann looked at him warmly. "I can't imagine that you're lacking in intelligence. Anyway, you've proved that you have courage, that's more important." She shook her head as if marveling. "When you stood up there in the aisle, I didn't know what you were going to do. But I knew that you knew."

Unable to find the words to answer that, George changed the subject. "I suppose you're all excited about the Prom? Rita is. She's got her escort all picked out and everything. I don't know if the poor clod knows about it yet."

Once more Ann seemed to withdraw for a moment, as she had when he caressed her leg. "I'm not going to the Prom," she said, then busied herself suppressing a quarrel that had been developing among the children.

George supposed that she had been having a quarrel with her best boy friend, and was uncertain about who her escort was going to be. He never doubted that a girl like this would have a choice of invitations to accept. "I'll bet you change your mind about that," he said, thinking back to the closing of his own high school days. "The Prom's half the fun of graduating, or more than half."

She didn't answer. But *surely* a girl like this had been invited, so he could push and tease and probe a little more without seriously hurting any feelings. "Why," he said, "I'd be tempted to ask you myself, if I was in your class."

"I've been asked." Ann's face was slightly averted so he could not make out her expression, but her voice was unhappily chilly. "I'm just not going."

Ouch. He had managed to hit a real sore spot after all. "Anyway," he said, "your Prom isn't next week. You have lots of time to think about it. Meanwhile, when am I going to see you again?"

It turned out that he saw her next day, at the police station where they had both been summoned for questioning about the fight on the bus. George came near being charged with aggravated battery, but when the testimony of all the available witnesses had been heard, he was not charged.

Later George bought Ann a snack at a nearby restaurant, and then suggested they find some place a little less noisy and copulate.

"No, please, I'd rather not." Again her reply was blunt and seemed to amount to an open invitation to repression. But at the same time her answer seemed so natural and direct, so unembarrassed, that he simply could not take it at face value. He told himself that she had probably been upset all over again by having to testify. She was so matter-of-fact about what she said that she probably didn't realize how it sounded.

He asked her several times to go out with him on a regular date, but she consistently refused. Still, he contrived to see more of her. His sister Rita told him where Ann could usually be found on Monday nights, playing volleyball, and he went to the gym and managed to get in on some of the games.

"Annie, this is fun, but how about you and

me going out someplace by ourselves? You like other sports? Bowling, swimming? Or maybe a show."

"George, I . . . you're nice, and I really like you, but I think it wouldn't be wise."

"Why not?" But now people were yelling at them to get back to the net if they wanted to play. They never had the time or the place for a serious discussion. Ann seemed to be making sure of that.

During this same period of a month or so George made it a point to enjoy sex with five or six different girls. With each, at the most abandoned moments, he found himself closing his eyes and imagining that it was Ann Lohmann's flesh that moved against his own. The popularizers of psychology on television and in the newsprints were always warning that such behavior could be a danger signal. To focus lust on one individual might be a step toward its repression whenever that individual was not available. Brilliant, thought George. It was just staggering how smart those college educated psychologists could be. Anyway, he wasn't worried. A lot of the younger, more radical psychologists held that sexual repression, or all-out sublimation even, did no permanent harm when practiced occasionally. That seemed sensible to George, though he hadn't much personal experience to judge by. He was young and full of health and usually wanted to do nothing with his sex but satisfy it every day or so and enjoy thinking about it in between times.

But now this thing with Ann—this thing with Ann was something else.

Early on the evening of the Prom—living in the same house as Rita, he could not possibly have gotten the date wrong—he obeyed an irrational-seeming impulse and phoned Ann's home. Ann's mother, tight-lipped and looking somehow hurried and harried, answered. When he asked for Ann, she reminded him in a nervous voice that this was Prom night. Still he noticed that she did not say in so many words that Ann had already left for the Prom, or that she was too busy getting ready for it to come to the phone.

After he had blanked off, George sat thinking. Then he went to Rita's room, where his sister was still being fitted into her Prom gown, meters and meters of fuzzy pink transparency. While their mother was out of the room looking for implements or materials of some kind, he took the opportunity to question his sister.

"I really don't know whether she's going tonight or not, George. How does this look in the back?"

"Fine."

"She's an honest girl and a good friend of mine and I love her dearly. If she said someone has asked her, then someone has. Also, if she said she's not going, then that's the way it will be. I love her dearly, as I said, but I wouldn't be at all surprised if she doesn't go. Oh, George, what do you mean it looks fine? I can tell in the mirror that it's terrible."

He wasn't looking into the mirror, or at the dress.

Ineluctably motherly even on her Prom night, Rita came over to him, frowning with concern. "Oh, George, is it really getting serious between you two?"

"It is for me, although I've never even screwed her once. Is she always—like that? You know?"

Rita was worried now, completely distracted from her dress. "I might as well tell you bluntly, Ann has a bad rep with the boys in the class. I mean *I'm* not the most prudish and old-fashioned girl, but *she* is really way out." Rita glanced at the bedroom door to determine whether their mother was still out of earshot. "You know she's been excused from Erotic Orientation classes all along, on religious grounds. Don't get me wrong, she's been my loyal friend ever since sophomore year."

"No, I didn't know that about no EO. But it's not really surprising."

"You say you've never screwed her. If you ask me, no one has." Rita nodded significantly. "I mean it. She's my friend, but you're my brother. I've seen a lot of the boys displaying a certain *interest* in her, if you know what I mean. And more than one man teacher, too. Well, if she hardly ever lets them see anything between her shoulders and her knees, I suppose the men are bound to get the message and come sniffing around. I guess you know what you're doing."

Rita was still looking at him worriedly when their mother returned and George withdrew. A deep excitement was now taking control of him. It had begun on that first day on the bus and had been developing ever since. He went back to his own room and spent half an hour alternately lying on the bed, pacing, and practicing his side snap kick before the mirror. Meanwhile he fought an inner struggle, understanding that the whole course of his future might be altered here and now. Again and again he told himself to put dark ideas out of his mind and phone some other girl with whom he could joyfully and simply spend the night in bed. Then he gave up and started to punch out Ann's phone number again. Then he gave that up too and headed for her house.

The house was all in darkness and he almost stumbled over a small figure sitting on a step in front of the door before he realized that anyone was there. Taking a second look, George saw that it was a boy about ten years old, who held in his hands a carved wooden figure about half as tall as he was.

"You live here?" George asked, his hand hesitating over the callplate on the door.

"Yeah," said the boy. "Nobody's home but my sister," he added gloomily.

George's heart gave a little premonitory throb. "It's her I want to see." He touched the plate and immediately a light came on above his head, giving the TV eye in the door a chance for a good look.

In the new light George could see that the carved wooden figure in the boy's hands was— or had been—a female nude, executed with some skill. The kid was slowly mutilating it now, moodily gouging and hacking it with a small knife. The step was littered with little chips and shavings.

"Hey, what're you doing that for?"

"I carved it, I can do what I want."

"Well. What's your name?"

"Fred."

"I'm George. You can carve pretty good, Fred, if you did that. Why don't you save it?" Though it seemed too late for that. Now one of the house's windows came alight; someone was on their way to answer the door.

"Oh, you're karate-George from the bus." The boy looked up with interest for a moment, but then lowered his brown head again and dug in with the knife. "Why should I save it? Nobody wants to look at it."

Ann opened the door, rubbing her dark hair with a towel. She was wearing a translucent pinkish sarong, not radically concealing, with apparently nothing under it. "Hello, George. Freddy! I thought you were at the Scout meeting. What are you doing, *destroying* that?"

"Nobody cares about it."

"*I* care. I told you I like to see anything you do—"

"You don't know nothin' about it. And nobody else cares." Freddy flung down the chunk of wood and was gone running into the night, across the little front yard and then swallowed up by the shadows along a narrow statwalk beside a slow river of taillights.

Ann called after her brother in annoyance, but evidently without any real expectation that he would turn around and come back. She made a gesture of resignation and then turned. "Come in, George." It was almost as if she had been expecting him.

"Thanks. Is your brother going to be all right?"

"Oh, I suppose so. I think he'll stay in the neighborhood. Anyway I don't know what I can do."

George daringly omitted giving her any slightest pinch or caress of greeting, even on the hand or arm, as he stepped into the house. True to form, Ann did not blush or giggle at the omission, as most of the girls he knew would probably have done, nor did she take offense at it, as the really nice conservative ones might. A bad girl then, as Rita had warned him, and all the signs so plainly showed. But still . . . somehow he couldn't believe she was.

"Let's go out beside the pool," she said. "It's nice outside tonight."

"All right." He followed her through the house. "I called earlier, and your mother sort of implied you were going out, but I just had a hunch and came over anyway."

"I'm glad you did." As they were leaving the indoors for a palm-fringed patio Ann stopped and turned to him. Her gladness, if such it was, was quiet and almost melancholy. "My parents have gone to the Prom, they agreed to be chaperones. They were very upset when they found they couldn't talk me into going, even going at the last minute with them instead of a boy taking me. My mother is Church of Eros, you know, quite devout, and she's been going there for guidance day after day and trying to get me to go. But her church and mine just don't agree. My father went to his playclub and talked to the philosopher. Finally my parents both decided they ought to do what's expected of them even if I won't. So they're chaperoning. I guess that's partly why Freddy is upset. He thought Dad might go with him tonight to some Scout meeting." It was about the longest speech that George had ever heard from her. She seemed farther from melancholy when she had gotten it out.

"I'm glad your parents decided that way," said George. "Now I have you all to myself."

"I'm glad you do. I had to talk a little bit to someone." Ann stopped rubbing her hair and let the towel hang down in front of her. She seemed innocently unconscious of concealing effect. Now for the first time she smiled. "Would you like a swim, George? I just climbed out."

"Sounds like fun." He followed her around the bend of the L-shaped patio to the pool, which was irregular in shape and fairly small, and bordered along most of its perimeter by plastic grass and probably artificial flowers. His mind pictured Ann climbing from the pool, slipping on her sarong, going to answer the door. Suddenly he was sure she had been

swimming in the nude, and his inward excitement—if excitement was really the right word
for this chilling thing—went up another reading on the dial. Of course there was no sensible
reason why a girl alone should not slip off her
bikni and swim nude if she wanted to. Only
the most satyrish reactionaries would insist
that a solitary person wear clothes to emphasize his or her sex. But still the mental picture of Ann floating alone, smooth as a snake,
divorced from sex, all chaste and bare as a
lily-pad, was overwhelming.

"Still, the air is getting a little cool now,"
said George, stalling. Standing beside her on
the edge of the pool, he felt very unsure of
himself. Would she laugh at him for an old-
fashioned clod if he mentioned his lack of a
swimming codpiece? On the other hand, if he
just stripped bare and dove in, would she, after all, be shocked? In spite of the evidence of
her own words and actions he couldn't really believe that she was the bad kind of girl. But
hadn't he come here tonight hoping she was,
trying to prove it, wanting to get from her what
only bad girls gave? Confused as a sixteen-
year old, he chickened out.

"You're right," she said calmly. "I wasn't in
the pool for very long."

They sat down side by side on the pool's
curved grassy edge, and George pulled off his
sandals and dipped his feet into the water. In
his knitted translucent shorts and jacket he
was really quite warm enough, but he saw Ann
shiver just slightly in her sarong with the

damp towel around her bare shoulders. In a minute he would suggest that they go back inside where it was warmer. Meanwhile he wanted to watch her as she stirred the water gently with one toe, scattering a thousand California stars.

Only once, as an adolescent in the grip of a way-out mood, had George visited a brothel. There a pretty girl had draped herself while he watched, and had talked about stars and purity and poetry and other high, mysterious things until she had him sexless as a mushroom. Then he and the girl had lain chastely side by side on her narrow bed and talked. Between other topics of conversation he tried to explain the mental processes of karate to her, how the mind could concentrate the body's force sufficiently to drive the hand uninjured through a wooden slab. At the time he had not really started any serious study of karate, and so he had been facile with explanations.

Probably his dissertation hadn't made too much sense, but the girl was a skilled listener. He supposed most whores were that, and sexually desirable, too. He had heard Japanese speculating about what the old-time geisha must have been like, and he wondered if they were something similar. In the brothel George had never forgotten how desirable the girl with him was, while at the same time his mind had daringly pushed lust farther and father away. A door had opened for him to a bittersweet world of controlled power. Change the

metaphor: free-style sparring, and Eros's feet
of fleshy clay were swept out from under him,
and down he came with a great ignominious
gonad-jarring crash, to be made to bend
his neck before a single rebellious human
slave.

Still, when it was all over, when his half
hour was up and he was being expertly shown
the door, he found himself somewhat disap-
pointed. Was this all that sublimation ever
amounted to? It hardly seemed worth the fuss
that people made about it.

Now, sitting with Ann on the grassy rim of
the pool, he watched a movement of her hips
show through the sarong as she shifted her
weight slightly, and felt a sudden physical
surge of desire for her. He remembered suddenly that he had seen and responded to just
such a movement of the prostitute's body as
she began to wrap herself before him.

"So. I guess you're still working with that
Sunday school religious class, hey?"

"Oh, yes. When I have time."

"Have you belonged to that Christian group
long? I mean, guess the rest of your family
aren't members."

"It's a Christian school, but . . ." Ann spoke
slowly and carefully now. "I'm not actually
baptized into the Church yet myself. I just
help out there. I've been hanging around the
school and church there since I was about thir-
teen. You're right, my parents are much
against it and of course they try to argue me
out of ever being baptized. I guess my

adolescence has been difficult for them, with
me always hanging around Sunday school instead of going to young peoples' orgies in their
church. The philosopher at Daddy's playclub
says I'm looking for a crutch to help me get
through life. And really it is such a tremendous step, being baptized, I mean. In a sense
I'm still free now to do anything I want, but
after baptism I won't be."

"Hm."

"For example I'll be practically restricted
to marrying someone who's also a Christian. If
I get married at all."

"Really?"

"Well, I just mean it takes an awful lot of
work to make a marriage a success even when
the two partners agree on the important things
such as religion. And my marriage will have to
succeed because Christians don't have
divorce, or at least not very often."

"Aren't they divided into a bunch of
splinter sects? I was reading about it the other
day." George had rarely given the subject of
religion much thought, but just recently he
had been reading up a bit on Christianity. He
didn't think it was for him. He couldn't figure
out whether violence was ever allowed or not.
Maybe it was something like the traditional
rules of karate, where you weren't allowed to
use it for real unless to protect yourself or another loved one.

"Christians used to be divided. Now they're
pretty much reunited again, what's left of
them."

"Well, I never even go to Church of Eros any more. I think religion's not for me. They say that some of those churches, once you join them they never let you alone again afterwards."

After a little silence Ann said: "There are a number of thing that never let you alone."

"Yes," agreed George, wondering just what things she had in mind.

"George?" Her voice was different.

"What?"

"Would you like to have sex with me? Here and now?"

"Why, yes," he answered, speaking mechanically in his surprise. "That would be nice."

For long seconds she did not reply. She sat there so motionless that her toes no longer troubled the starry water. George tried to read her face in the near-darkness. Then abruptly she turned her face away. "The way you say that!" Ann said, and made a frightened, twisted sound that was a little like a laugh.

"It's just that you took me by surprise." George slid closer to her along the side of the pool. "Oh, Ann. Annie? You've never wanted me to give you an erotic touch before."

"Oh," she said. "I've wanted." She leaned away from him, supple and graceful in her sarong. Her toes left the water with a tinkle of tiny drops, and she stretched out on her back along the edge of the pool. Now she covered her eyes with one slender wrist.

George could no longer control himself. He

crept very close and bent over Ann, daring not to touch her at all. "Don't be afraid," he said.

"I'm not afraid, I'm not ashamed." Her voice was surprisingly firm and proud, and she was watching him from under her arm. "You don't know me very well, George. But maybe you've heard some stories."

"Yes I have. But I don't care if the stories are true."

"What do they say about me, the stories that you don't care about?"

"They say—" His voice went shaky on him and he had to pause. "What they amount to is that you're still a virgin."

She moved her arm away and now he could see her face in the starlight, her face becoming calmer now with an inner change, the blooming of some beauty that George could not have named. "Yes." She said it without a trace of shame. "That's why I'm not at the Prom tonight. Nothing but one long orgy. George, just now I offered you my virginity. Can you understand what that means to me?"

Watching her, listening to her, he thought he could. As if following some biological imperative his lust now began to recede, while at the same time there rose up in him—something else. His throat ached with his joy. He straightened up so that he was no longer bending over Ann but sitting at her side.

Looking at him steadily, she asked again: "Now, do you want to have sex with me?"

"Yes. Sometime. Right now I want—something more."

Ann nodded agreement and lowered her eyes. Her breathing, that had quickened momentarily, now grew slow. In a gentle voice she asked: "Shall I take this sarong thing off? Or put on something thicker?"

George could not find his voice to answer right away. What had happened in the brothel had afforded him an enjoyable, way-out kick, a fancy kind of reverse mental tickle. That tremendous gulfs of experience lay beyond had been suggested, but no more. In itself the visit to the whore had been not quite worth the effort to repeat it. This thing impending now, beginning now, was going far beyond. A winged thing had been born inside his chest and it was lifting at the roots of his being, lifting and pulling and expanding until it seemed that sex itself might be dissolved out of the flesh and carried outward to the stars.

"Oh, I don't care what you wear." George groaned in a failing voice. "Oh, I love you, love you, love you. Oh, sublimation's such a dirty word, there has to be a better."

"I know," Ann whispered. "Don't talk now." She had done this before. He was the virgin here.

Their hands came together and held, now just human hands more than they were male-female. She raised her eyes to his, and then on past his eyes, and he knew that she was looking at the stars. No turning back now. Never. They rose on the great lifting wings.

X

WAKING UP, rejoining the inhospitable world, was a slow and intermittent and instinctive struggle. Art understood from the beginning of the struggle that he was sick, or hurt, and paradoxically this left him less worried than he had been before. Before whatever had happened to leave him in this state. He was less worried because now less would be expected of him. They would have to take care of him now.

... they? Someone was trying. However he had come to be here, he lay in a bedroom in somebody's home. In one of the two beds crowded into the small cheaply furnished chamber. He had the vague impression of somebody having been in the other bed, and the covers there were rumpled, but now when he looked carefully there was no one. Perhaps, too, somebody had once shared this bed with him. He should have been polite and pawed at their genitals at least but right now he felt tired of genitalia and thank Eros he was sick or hurt and nothing much could reasonably be expected of him along that line.

... should have grabbed and pawed as those little plastic figures were doing to each other, those cheap Church of Eros icons that someone had shoved to the rear of the top of that high plastic wardrobe over there and then forgotten.

It was a BI bedroom from the look of it, or could it be a room in a cheap hotel? Or some rented room where tenant after tenant rushed through, forgetting and leaving things, and none of the haphazard objects in the room fit with anything else. There on the wall was the founder of Christianity nailed up, as in Ann's children's room, but here two pieces of plastic were doing the job instead of wooden beams. And there on the other wall, a reproduction of a painting that looked like a Caravaggio, but a Caravaggio that Art had never seen before. Nothing like Eros trampling the violin, or Bacchus lounging amid bowls of fruit. In this picture there were men around a table doing something, counting money, and on the right two men entering, one of them important, a mysterious figure of light and shadow and power, extending a hand that said: here, *you*, enough of playing with those trifles on the table, more important things are waiting. The summons had come, and everyone in the picture knew about it except the man for whom it was intended.

. . . so he himself was sick, no, he was hurt, for now he remembered something about being frightened out there in the street, and now there was this sexawful pain in his head that only intermittently would go away. And now truly there was a long-haired girl resting, indecently covered, in the room's other bed, and now, whup, a trick of the illusionist's art and she was gone again. Meanwhile it might have been that Art had slept.

Standing before him was a man, tall and narrow-shouldered, with a sandy beard and impressive green or gray or blue eyes, it was hard to tell because the color seemed to change, who looked at Art intently. And this man was a somewhat familiar figure, because he had been standing in the same place an hour ago (a day ago?) and asking Art some questions.

"What's your name?" the man asked now, looking at Art intently. He had a mild, slow voice that contradicted a look in his eyes of being fierce and concentrated and somehow ready to pounce.

"Arthur Rodney?"

The man smiled and nodded, as if this were very good news indeed. He had shut the door of the room behind him; outside somewhere in the background printout was clacking noisily from a computer terminal in need of mechanical adjustment. "Art, what year is this?" Art's second correct answer was just as satisfying as his first. "How do you feel, Art?"

"Not good. I've got a triplet of a headache." All of a sudden the lobby of Family Planning came back, and then the frantically waving picket signs outside, the jam of bodies on the statwalk. What should come after that? He didn't know. He had reached a real blank.

The man stepped closer to his bed. "Let's have a look at that." With what were unmistakably a doctor's hands, professionally sure and gentle, he probed through or around some kind of dressing on Art's scalp.

"Ouch."

"Sorry. Well, that's not looking too bad. And I'm glad you've waked up fully now." The man stepped back, pulling at his curl of sandy beard. "But I still want to make an X-ray or two. Haven't been able to as yet."

"How long have I been here? And where am I, anyway?"

"You've been here several hours. Let's say you're with some people who gave you shelter when it appeared to them that otherwise you'd go to jail. May I ask—what is the last thing you remember clearly?"

Art closed his eyes. His head throbbed. "Coming out into the street, in front of the Family Planning building. There was some kind of demonstration, or riot ... but why should I have gone to jail?"

The doctor shrugged and gave a tiny smile. "I don't know that you would have. Some of the Young Virgins on the scene evidently mistook you for one of their own casualties and brought you here. Some of them think that if a person gets clobbered in the street he must be a good guy, and anyone who's a good guy is automatically in danger of being thrown in jail."

He approached Art again, and with the aid of a tiny light looked closely into his eyes.

"How am I doing, doctor?"

"Not bad, not bad. Rest. It's important that you take it easy for a while. Don't worry about a thing. I'll be back in a bit."

When the door had closed behind the doctor Art lived in silence for a while with the pain in his head, alternately opening and closing his eyes. Somewhere in the distance the faulty computer terminal clacked away again. The room had one small window with bright daylight coming in around the edges of a closed shade. This was some Young Virgins' refuge, then. But he was not back in the Diana Arms; at least, Rita's room had looked very little like this one.

The door opened and a girl in a long, opaque sweater came in, bringing him a cup of something warm and chocolately to drink, and Art was abruptly conscious of being entirely naked beneath the bedsheet.

"Medicine?" he asked, while routinely starting to put a hand up under the bottom of her sweater.

"No." She gave him a cool smile and turned away, so that his hand slid free. "Just a drink. Thought you might like some."

She went out again right away. The stuff in the cup tasted good. Soon he might try getting up. He wondered if his clothes, and his watch and his money, were in the plastic wardrobe, and he wondered what time of day it was. About the time he had finished the drink, sipping slowly, the doctor was back.

He looked in Art's eyes again with his little light and then pulled up a chair and sat. "Art,

I took the liberty of going through your wallet while you were unconscious. Just to see if there was a record of anything, diabetes or allergies or so forth, that might bear on your medical condition."

"No doubt I owe you thanks for taking care of me. And you found out my name. I didn't catch yours."

No answer.

"I suppose now I had better get up and put on my clothes and leave."

"I don't want to scare you, Art, but before you go walking out on the street I must insist we take some X-rays. I hope to be able to make them downstairs here in just a few minutes. If X-rays show no skull fracture we can drive you home right away, take you anywhere in the city you want to go. If they do show a fracture we are going to have to *somehow* arrange to move you on a stretcher to a hospital."

"I—see. Or maybe I don't."

"The point is that your presence puts us here in something of an awkward position. If you do have a fracture, we can't simply call an ambulance to come and get you. And for your own good I wouldn't want you riding folded down and blindfolded in the back seat of a car."

"I know how that works," Art muttered, feeling a little sick.

"Beg your pardon?"

"Nothing. Evidently I'm in some kind of a —secret hideout."

The doctor looked relieved. "I'm glad you understand. It's quite important to a number of us here that the location of this house be kept a secret. And we've realized by now that you're no sympathizer of ours. Nevertheless we wish you well. We don't want to—to make you feel you're being held a prisoner. As soon as the X-ray film I need arrives, which I hope will be any minute now, we'll take a couple of pictures and then you'll be on your way."

Art relaxed wearily in the bed. "All right, all right. I guess you know what you're doing."

"I'm *really* glad you're being understanding about this, Art. I feel a personal responsibility in this matter. For your being in the Family Planning office to begin with, I mean."

Art looked at him, trying to puzzle it out.

"You see, I'm Rita's midwifer."

A couple of sturdy male Young Virgins came along shortly, pushing a regular hospital cart. They got Art's clothes out of the wardrobe—he noticed the strap of his watch sticking out of a pocket, and also the faint bulge of a billfold that had evidently been scrupulously replaced—and helped him put on his codpiece and loaded him onto the cart beneath an opaque sheet. Meanwhile, of course, he was demanding again and again to be told where his wife was.

"She's not here, not in this building," the doctor kept answering him calmly. "The parturition will be quite soon. She's well. And she's worried about you—more precisely, as I interpret what she says, she's worried about whether you'll want her back when she has her third child."

It took Art a moment to understand. "You mean she thinks I might divorce her? But that's foolish, how would that help? It wouldn't help her or the children, and it certainly wouldn't help me." He lay on his back with his head on a low pillow as the two husky Virgins propelled the cart out of the room and along a rambling hallway, through what appeared to be an ancient house of mansion size, or else perhaps the rundown dormitory of some private school. Not at all like the Diana Arms. "Sure, I hope she doesn't have a third baby when she comes back. But even if she does, I most certainly want her. So, you're the one who's doing it. How can you interfere in people's lives like this? How much are you being paid?"

The doctor was walking beside the cart, now and then going ahead or falling behind when the way became too narrow. "I'm not getting a dollar from Rita or anyone in her family. If she's paid out money it must be going to the doctor who referred her to me, or to someone else along the line. In a clandestine business like this you're always going to get some people going into it for the money."

"And you?"

"For the good of my immortal soul. That's how I see it. That I have an inescapable moral duty to do what I am doing here."

The cart rolled into a small, old-looking

elevator. The two orderlies remained behind
as the doors closed and the elevator started
down with Art still lying on the cart and the
doctor standing beside it.

"You don't inspire a great deal of con-
fidence, doctor. If you are a doctor, really. If
you're not you'd better keep your hands off
my wife."

"I assure you I am an obstetrician. And
you'll be glad to hear that I haven't lost a
mother in some years of practice." The slow
descent of the elevator stopped and the doors
slid open. "I haven't lost anyone to a head injury, either. But then yours is about the first
I've treated since I was an intern." And with
that the cart was rolling again.

The opaque sheet came over Art's face in
two thicknesses as they left the elevator. The
voice of his captor said: "I'm covering your
eyes up here, so you won't be able later to
identify or locate this house."

Art only grunted. He felt the cart jolt lightly
over a threshold, and then there came a whiff
of outside air, summer-warm and fragrant,
but he stoically refused to look or listen or
sniff for clues. Once before he had been
granted knowledge that secretive guides were
trying to withhold from him, and knowledge
had done him no good at all. This game was
hopeless, for him at any rate, and he was
about ready to give it up. Not to accept that
his opponents were in the right, but to admit
that they had him beaten. The law and the
bulk of society were on his back but he could

not call them in. When you went into the
endgame a rook down and your clock running out, maybe you had better resign and
save some mental energy for the next game.
There would be a lot of tough games to play
against the world when Rita came home
again, whether she had to go to jail first or
not. If she went to jail who was he going to get
as a steady, dependable babysitter in California?

Now the cart was on a descending ramp.
Impossible to judge whether it went down one
meter or three. When it stopped and the doctor
pulled the sheet down from Art's face, the two
of them were alone in a kind of laboratory or
treatment room crowded with a jumble of
shelves and boxes and equipment, lighted by
some old-fashioned overhead fluorescents.
The windowless walls were lined nearly from
floor to ceiling with shelving, loaded with boxes and bottles labeled in what seemed to be the
jargon of medical technology. The nearby door
through which they had evidently just entered was now closed. It was hard to guess the
size of the room because sections of it to both
right and left were cut off by portable white
screens.

"Now where is the damned film?" The doctor was ruffling through stacks of paper, jour-
nals, printouts, and other impedimenta that
covered a large desk-like metal table. "They
told me that they left it here." Somehow the
archaic swearword, the like of which Art had
not heard since the tridi play went dead on the

tube train, sounded natural coming from this man.

After fruitlessly searching a few moments longer, the doctor muttered an excuse and went out impatiently, closing the door of the room behind him. Art heard another door open and close some distance off.

Apart from his continuing headache, he now felt pretty good. Good enough to have a sense of awkwardness and vague shame at lying here on a cart like an invalid. He raised himself on an elbow and looked about. There on the foot of the cart were his clothes. Should he dress and stagger out into the street, calling for the police? That certainly wouldn't win Rita over to his point of view. No, he had tipped his king and resigned the game.

Near at hand he recognized a portable X-ray machine, a familiar sight from visits to other physicians' offices. An unobtrusive background hum of electric power and electronics permeated the room. And now he became aware of another sound, an old-fashioned watch tick-tick-ticking, except this was a little faster and more irregular than a watch would be.

Still alone, Art swung his feet over the side of the cart and sat up. His head ached, but he felt able to stand and walk. Now if that was a bathroom over there, as a tiled interior glimpsed beyond the top of a white screen seemed to promise, then his physical comfort might soon be brought back close to normal. He slid off the cart and walked around the

screen, past glassy tanks and a maze of piping
and a portable computer terminal set up on a
dimly lighted workbench, and found the
hoped-for toilet.

He was on his way back to sit on his cart like
a good patient when, just around the shad-
owed workbench, he came to a full stop. "Ah,"
he said aloud.

The fetus was in the central glassy tank atop
the bench . . .

The surrounding light was quite dim, and
the tank's only window a tiny aperture that allowed a clear view of the thing only from certain angles.

Art stepped closer, staring, then abruptly
relaxed. There was no umbilical cord, only a
blind knot of tissue at the navel. For a moment
he had thought that the complex of equipment
before him (besides the tanks and piping, there
were three oscilloscopes, counters, and other
gear that Art could not immediately identify)
was in fact an artificial womb, and that the
fetus before him had been frozen and revived,
or was at any rate in some sense viable. But
now he realized that it must be only an abortus
being used in some experiment. Tubes, or only
wires perhaps (he could not be sure in the dim
light) were attached to it inside the tank, but
without an umbilical cord, he supposed, it
could not be receiving oxygen and nourish-
ment. And he could see no placenta, or
analogue of one.

There it sat, or rather floated in an upright

sitting posture. The thing that so much fuss was made about. It was small, only about the length of Art's middle finger. Its proportions were much different from those of a normal full-term infant, and of course even further from those of an adult, but the thing was unmistakably *genus homo* all the same. What other species would develop a bulging brow like that, or hold up two such human hands? When Art bent closer, the fingers were fully distinguishable, as were the toes at the end of the insignificant legs and feet. What with the shadows and the angle of his view, the sex was not quite visible.

He jumped back a step with a quick intake of breath, and only then was aware of the doctor standing watching him at the corner of the screen a couple of steps away.

"Feel all right?" the doctor asked. "You shouldn't be on your feet unnecessarily."

Art raised a hand to gently touch the side of his head, at a good safe distance from the wound. He turned his gaze back to the tank. "It moved."

"Oh yes, they move. I've located the X-ray film at last. Get back on the cart if you will and we'll finally be able to make sure about that head of yours. Yes, the little girl in there happens to be about the same developmental age as Rita's fetus is right now. About three months as near as I can tell. At that age they've usually been moving spontaneously for several weeks, though the mother usually can't feel the movements yet."

Art walked away, pausing at the corner of the screen to look back once. "I didn't know it was . . . there was no cord."

The doctor held out a hand to give support if needed. "Oh. But we usually take that off at parturition. Tapping into the circulatory system elsewhere serves the purpose, and has some technical advantages. Yes, she's very much alive and growing. That's her heartbeat you can hear in the background, sounds like a clock or watch? And with those scopes back there we're continually monitoring brain activity; that won't settle into the regular rhythms for a few more weeks."

Art lay back carefully on the cart, settling his head down gently on the pillow. "Is that a living human being?" he asked the fluorescent lights above. The vision of the grotesque, half fish-like head was still before him, and the tiny hands, that seemed about to be raised secretively, protectively, before the face. "Is it?"

"You tell me," the doctor grunted, moving the cart in the direction of the X-ray. Art now noticed the thick shielding hung between the machine and the artificial womb at the end of the laboratory. The doctor continued: "Frankly, I've had my doubts. Sometimes I feel I don't know where to start in thinking about it anymore." His tone was mild and preoccupied; now he had begun a delicate positioning of Art's head beneath the X-ray snout.

Art, still looking at the ceiling, said: "Maybe it doesn't matter if a fetus is a human being or not. Maybe such a question is meaningless."

"Take a deep breath—hold it, don't move." There came the usual audible hum. "All right, you can move. What do you mean, it doesn't matter? You know, if these embryos and fetuses turn out not to be individual human beings after all, then I and some of my friends have gone to a hell of a lot of trouble and broken a hell of a lot of laws for nothing."

Art twisted on his cart. "You just said that you yourself have doubts."

"Doubts, yes!" The man was vexed. He waved a piece of blackened film. "I might have very strong doubts that there's a child under that overturned box I see in the middle of the road, but that doesn't justify my running over it with a truck, not without some life-or-death reason to run it over. Damn, this one didn't come out as clearly as I'd like. Let's try again. Turn on your right side this time, if you will."

"How about the welfare of society as a whole? How about over-population, people starving? Aren't those life-or-death reasons?"

"To cut off the life of that little girl in there? In a word, no. Take a deep breath, hold it. That's fine."

Allowed to move again, Art got up on one elbow. "I suspect neither of us is going to be able to change the other's mind on this by arguing."

Art said: "All right, I know that thing in the tank has the potential for someday being a full human being, with all the rights thereof. But not yet, surely not yet. It may generate a brain wave or two but it can't think, it may twitch but it can't act. It couldn't survive for three minutes without artificial help."

"Neither could you if you had a really massive coronary. And she could have survived quite well in her natural environment, had we been able to leave her there." The gray-green eyes gave the pictures a final stare and then turned to Art with evident relief. "You're all right. This second picture makes it unanimous. No fracture. You ought to take things easy for a while, but you can go."

"Tell me. Why does that have to be a baby? Why must you break the laws, as you admit doing, to make that point?"

The doctor sighed, and let himself down in a chair beside the paper-burdened table, as Art sat up on the cart and reached for his shirt. "Art, I can't make it a baby or not a baby. I can only try to determine which category it already belongs to, and conduct myself accordingly." He wearily rubbed his eyes. "Damn it, it *looks* like a baby now, right? In a few weeks it may begin to suck its thumb. A cute little human touch, hey? Not necessarily convincing."

"Wait a minute. How about gill-slits? Doesn't it still have those, or didn't it at an earlier stage? Are they cute little proofs of humanity too?"

"All right, the gill slits. What do *you* think they prove?"

"I . . . nothing. How am I supposed to know?

You're the scientist, or at least the expert, though most of the scientists and experts don't seem to agree with you on this. What has you so convinced?"

"Art, I know of no solid scientific definition of man. What can I communicate to you? Only facts, and people interpret them in different ways. Both parents of that organism in the tank were human, of course. But its cells are different from either of its parents' cells; it is now a genetically unique individual.

"It . . . no, I have to say *she*. What you see as a thing in a tank I see as a little girl. But if you try to pin me down on when she began to be a little girl, I'll have to admit that I just don't know. Teilhard says that the beginnings of all things tend to be out of sight. Was a unique human soul infused when the sperm first pierced the egg? When the nuclei of the two parent cells were first completely united? With implantation of the blastocyst in the uterine wall? Maybe a few days after that, when the time of possible twinning had passed."

"If you're bringing souls into it, you're leaving me out." Art was off the cart now, getting dressed. In the background the steady tick-tick-tick went on, soft and rapid. "Just let me get out of here."

"Of course." As if caught derelict in his duty, the doctor jumped up and went to push a button near the door. "I can't help bringing souls into it, though I tried. I'm a Christian priest as well as a doctor, you see. I suppose if

one's humanity is questioned one must try to
prove it by appealing either to God or to a
board of review of other human beings, who sit
in judgment. I know which I prefer to do."

"No one is questioning your humanity, doctor."

"Not now. But some future government
might decide that I belong to an inferior race.
Governments in the past have made such pro-
nouncements about people. Or, if I suffered a
stroke tonight and still hadn't come to by next
week, my fellow physicians might by then be
questioning my continued humanity." He rose
from his chair, hands clenching. The naturally
fierce look in his eyes grew more intense.
"Maybe it *would* be the kindest thing in such
a case to let me die. But I would still be a *human being dying,* not a—a specimen reacting!"

"All right," said Art, in slight alarm, speed-
ing up the fastening of his shorts. "Take it
easy."

"Yes, I'm sorry." The tall man let himself
slump back into his chair. "In my opinion
there are a few rare situations where abortion
may be justified, at least if there's not an
artificial womb available. But it's still a *human being dying,* being killed, and there's not
many reasons to justify that. Surely not some
non-specific good intended for the world in
general."

Art, dressed now and putting on his watch,
shook his head. "Do you think a single human
being dying matters that much to the uni-

verse? Appeal to your God if you want, the rest
of us haven't heard anything from him lately.
We have to look out for ourselves as best we
can."

The priest-doctor pulled himself to his feet
once more. "Let me go and find someone to
drive you home. We'll feed you something first
if you care to wait for it."

"No, I'm not quite through talking yet." Art
moved to stand between the other and the
door. "You are about to inflict a third child on
me and my wife, because your God wants you
to. The least you can do is listen to me for a
minute longer."

Abruptly the priest turned fierce again. "I
am sincerely sorry for the danger and expense
and inconvenience that the third child is going
to cause you. But it is still better than inflict-
ing death on your third child. If you find his
presence unendurable, why there are people in
the world who will take him in."

"People in the world! Yes, I'll say there
are." Now they were standing almost toe to
toe, Art with his arms folded like an umpire.
"About eight or nine billion at last count. And
how many of them are starving now?"

"Quite a few are starving, Art, quite a few.
Maybe you've seen more of them than I have.
Maybe you've fed more of them. Maybe you
promote contraception more enthusiastically
than I do."

But Art seemed to have stopped listening.
He stood staring, with an altered expression,
into a corner of the room. The priest looked

there and saw only a red picnic cooler with a white handle.

"Art, here, sit down again. I'm sorry, we shouldn't have been arguing."

"No, I'm all right," said Art. But then he did sit down in the chair the other brought for him. "That cooler over there. I believe I may have carried that across the Mississippi a few days ago. It was very heavy and very cold. Now I'm just realizing what must have been inside it. That was while your monastery out there was burning down."

"You were there?" The priest sat down again too, and leaned anxiously toward him. "Can you tell me anything of what happened? I've seen and read the news stories, but . . ."

Art told what he could, leaving out the name of the girl for whom he had carried the container. "And the man with her said, 'That was Steve' before he took off running into the woods. That's about all I can tell you."

The priest-doctor nodded, hands clamped on his knees, squinting as if in physical pain. "Yes. Those two men were both my friends. Neither of them mentioned in the official accounts. Maybe the police never knew they were there."

"I'm really sorry," Art said impulsively. "At the time there didn't seem to be anything I could do."

"Of course not, Art. It's not your fault. Listen, I'd better get you on your way home before I'm charged with kidnapping. But you must be hungry, let us feed you something first."

"Maybe just a protein bar. I never got around to thanking you for this patch-up job, did I?" Art brushed a hand gingerly over his scalp bandage. It wasn't nearly as big as he had expected, and very little of his hair had been removed.

In a few minutes one of the stalwart Young Virgins brought him a couple of bars on a plate, and a glass of milk. As he munched, the priest-doctor asked him: "Would you object very strongly to a blindfold when you leave? I'd accept your word if you gave it, but some of the other people here might not."

"Blindfold? Oh, I don't care." Art was abstracted again. Foodbar in hand, he got up suddenly and went to push the white screen aside.

Like an idol in a temple, he thought suddenly. Surrounded by its screens and paraphernalia like an idol, or a statue on an altar. Suddenly the minuscule statue frowned at him, averted its blind face, then stretched an arm.

Not an idol, then. Far more than that. Inscrutable as a flower or a nebula, it could only be contemplated, not understood. Tick-tick-tick. And again the firing neurons in its developing brain smeared green traces across the three oscilloscopes.

Shaking hands with the doctor on his way out, Art said: "Thanks again for the treatment. You know if I could find a way I'd still stop Rita from going through with this. Because of the kind of world we have to live in. But I wish it wasn't so, I wish the world would let your way be possible. Anyway, you tell her that I want her back, whatever happens. I want that most."

"I'll tell her, Art. I'll be very glad to pass that word along."

XI

AT ONE o'clock in the afternoon Art, once more shrouded in an opaque cover (this one smelling more medicinal than musty), was led out of the laboratory and out of doors, across an area of long weedy grass and uneven paving stones. Then he was put into the back seat of a car, where without being told he hunkered down so as to be invisible from the outside. The car when started jolted slowly over rough terrain for about a minute, before getting onto any kind of a regular road. Shortly Art began to hear the noises of other traffic around him.

"You can come up," said one of his Young Virgin escorts, in apologetic tones, only about five minutes after the start of the trip and somewhat before Art had expected any such permission. He pulled the blanket gingerly from his sore head and eased himself up to a normal position in the seat. The car was traveling through some middle-class, jobholders' residential neighborhood that Art could not recognize. One of the two youths escorting him sat beside him in the back.

"Sorry, we're not going to be able to take you all the way to the Parrs' house," the driver said, apologetically. "It's possible their place is being watched—you know how it is."

"I don't know whether I do or not. Not any more."

"Pardon?"

"It's all right. I can walk."

"Oh, oh," said his other escort, swiveling his head to peer back through the rear window. As it turned out, Art didn't have far to walk at all. The police car with its blue lights flashing came alongside and nudged their vehicle neatly to the curb with its foamy plastic bumpers.

From the questions the police asked before the van arrived to cart the three of them off to the station, Art gathered that his escorts' car had been somehow identified as one used by participants in the morning's infamous Family Planning riot. All its present occupants were under grave suspicion, the sullen one with the lump on his head being no exception. When they unloaded at the lockup he was taken underground to a large cell with padded walls. He recognized it as what they called a DD, or drunk-drug, tank of the tv crime dramas. In real life he found it crowded not with thrashing drunks or druggards, but with loudly vocal Young Virgin types, several of whom complained steadily to the walls (where perhaps there were microphones to listen) of their real or supposed injuries.

Nobody else was listening. "Shuddup in there," advised a loudspeaker in the ceiling, from time to time. In reply to this the Young

Virgins would usually break out into a verse of all but unintelligible song. Approaching Art through this milieu, smiling as if at an old friend, came a suddenly familiar face: that of the sign-peddler of the morning.

"It's just a mistake I was picked up," Art could hear the sign-peddler saying, as the latest outburst of song was ended. "My signs were useful, weren't they, to let the world know what was going on? A man tries to be an influence for peace and communication in the world, to mediate the intelligent expression of differences in the community, and this is the thanks he gets. Hey, bud, which side *were* you on?"

"Shut up," said Art Rodney.

Now another fifteen or twenty prisoners were being brought in a group, adding to the crowding and confusion. These looked like Young Virgins too. Presumably any Homo League members arrested were being held somewhere else, in the interest of relative peace. The corridors under this station seemed to be lined with these tank-like cells, and through the corridors drifted the steady animal murmuring of innumerable inmates. There was also a noticeable amount of dust in the air, and the muffled roar of heavy machinery at work nearby. Maybe more cell space was being excavated.

At last three policemen came to the door of Art's cell, and set up a table there for processing. "One at a time now, people. Form a single line. Come up here and present your identification and we'll take your fingerprints. Then you can make one phone call. Form a single line."

A Young Virgin girl, a beautiful girl with dark devilish eyes, pushed herself forward to the table and demanded: "How about separate facilities for men and women?"

The policemen who had already spoken eyed her warily, his lined face on guard against any of these young punks attempting to get smart. "Separate what?"

"Latrines!" The girl waved at the open urinals and water closet at the rear wall of the cell. "We want to have separate latrines for each sex, with walls closing them off."

The cop's hardened face showed disgust. "Oh, and no doubt you'd like to open a brothel in here, too. You'll take what the city gives you, and do your carryin' on outside of jail."

As if that were the answer she had hoped for, the girl stepped back smiling. With a gesture and a yell she started up another loud song, all the Young Virgins within earshot quickly joining in. But their rebelliousness now seemed strictly verbal; they were not slow to line up before the table for processing. Jail probably grew quite boring in a couple of hours, and it was now time to call one's parents to get one out. Art used his weight and his elbows in self-defense, refusing to be pushed to the rear.

Someone shouted at him: "Do you know the song?" It was a comradely voice, coming from just behind Art in the newly formed queue.

The speaker was a tall young man, wearing a sweatshirt with STUDENTS FOR A CHASTE SOCIETY handpainted on the front; something about him looked vaguely familiar to Art.

"No, why should I know your song?" Art answered, as soon as the noise of it had trailed off into silence and he could talk without shouting. "I was just caught up in all this by mistake."

"That's the way it was with me," said the voice of the sign-peddler, from up near the head of the line.

"Are you with us, though?" asked the devil-eyed girl ahead of Art. As the line was just about formed she had squeezed her cloth-shrouded body in just ahead of him, her eyes daring him to protest.

"I'm not with you or against you. I just happened to get caught up in this."

The girl's eyes, those of a determined persecuter, attacked Art's beard and the conservative translucency of his clothing. She was silent, perhaps making plans.

The tall young man demanded: "Sir, if you're really not with us, *why* not?" His tone was meant to be not threatening but inspiring. "Now I judge you're a man who has supported the Establishment in the past, who has upheld all its out-worn dogmas and twentieth-century creeds. And now it's thrown you into jail anyway. What good has worshipping the sex gods and goddesses ever done you? Think about it."

"Oh, shut up," said Art, and shuffled forward with the line. If it came to posting bond, he didn't have a great deal of money.

He never knew what Rita was feeling—those had been her words to him. Why couldn't he have started, sooner, to find out? Until he knew what she was feeling it made little sense to argue with her. Of course she should have shown him similar consideration, talked to him more, found out what *he* really felt. Maybe they weren't so utterly, terribly far apart as it had seemed when she ran away. He didn't want her having another baby, of course . . . but if she was going to, anyway, if she really had to do it, then he wanted to be with her while it was going on. Now it was too late even for that. He wouldn't be able to reach her until the thing was done.

"Everybody be careful!" cried the devil-eyed girl brightly. She had been whispering with a couple of girl friends, and now she was ready to have some more fun with Art. "Everybody on their proper behavior while Mr. Whiskers is here. Maybe we should all undress a little."

"Now, Eunice," chided the tall young man. She wasn't helping his recruiting drive at all.

At least Art was soon going to have a chance at a phoneplate. Did he have the nerve to call George and Ann, tell them that he had been caught in a riot in front of the Family Planning building, and ask them for help? Not if he could help it. Better if he never saw them again until this whole thing was over—but of course, his children were there. He had no choice but to call the Parrs.

"I do hope they let us out soon," said Eunice. "I want to pack as much sin into my life as I possibly can!" She stepped defiantly up to face the sour policeman at the cell door. Art followed in his turn.

After being fingerprinted and filling out a short routine identity form, Art got his chance at the phoneplate. Behind him other prisoners were waiting. Reluctantly he punched the Parrs' number, and felt more relief than anything else when he was answered only by George's recorded voice telling him that he might leave a message if he wished. He left no message and after a moment's thought his relief turned sour. Maybe the Parrs had been arrested too, and his children were now in some orphanage.

He was allowed one completed call. Who else in the city did he know, where else might he turn for help? There was the dojo, but he couldn't remember either its name or address. There was Dr. Hammad. Ugh. After thinking a moment longer he dug a piece of folded paper from his wallet and, without much hope, punched numbers on the phoneplate once again.

"Jamison residence," said a male voice, answering through a blanked plate on the other end.

He cleared his throat. "I'd like to speak to Rosamond Jamison, please."

"Who shall I say is calling?" The voice had some thick and awkward tones in it, those of a man who would rather be doing something more manly than taking messages on the phone.

"Tell her it's Art Rodney. Tell her the man she met on the tube train from California. She'll remember."

"The tube train. All right, wait just a moment."

Art waited, gazing around him. The prisoners in line to use the phone looked in their frozen impatience as if they expected him to forget about his call and get out of their way at once. And now the nearby police were all watching Art, silently, with peculiarly blank, controlled faces. He hadn't noticed them doing this when other prisoners were phoning. If it was just a game they were playing to make him nervous they were succeeding.

"Hello?" It was Rosamond's voice. Then on the phoneplate appeared the image of her pretty face, the cat's-eye lenses gleaming. "It *is* you, my handsome protector! I'm so glad! I've been hoping you would call, and Daddy has too, he's wanted to thank you."

With the corner of his eye Art noted, without understanding, that the nearby policemen had suddenly all lost interest, were turning away and getting back to their jobs. "I'm glad I could reach you," he said. "I'm afraid I need help, and I don't know where else to turn. The police have made a mistake, and they have me in jail here—"

"Wha-at?"

"I innocently accepted a ride with some

strangers," which was quite true, "and it turned out the police were looking for their car. So now I'm being detained for questioning, as they put it. I'm held for investigation on a charge of conspiracy to riot, something like that. I'm not sure I have it straight. I was hoping you might be willing to call a lawyer for me. Or something. I'm afraid I don't have much money with me, and—"

"Oh my, oh my. Poor Art. How do you spell your last name? And what station are they holding you at?"

He spelled his name for her. "And the sign here says Tenth District Detention."

"Just wait there, wait!" Rose counseled him excitedly. Then she blanked off.

Art took a step away from the phone and a policeman was there to touch him on the arm and beckon him away. This officer, for a change, had a friendly-seeming smile. He led Art down a corridor to where a bulky, middle-aged man in civilian clothes was sitting behind a desk. On the desk were computer printouts whereon appeared small photographs of Art, both full face and profile. The bandage on his head with the small bald spot around it showed on the photos, and he wondered when and how they had been made.

The bulky man looked up. "You're Mr. Arthur Rodney? I see here that you're from out of state. Did you know when you accepted a ride in that car that the police were looking for it?"

"No, I—no."

"Well, we find that there's no evidence to the contrary. We're very sorry about the inconvenience, but you can understand that we can't take any chances."

"I suppose not."

The man behind the desk nodded in a friendly way, and the interview seemed to be over. Another smiling policeman, this one in uniform and with an unusually large number of stripes on his sleeve, was holding open a door at one side of the desk as if he expected Art to pass through it. Beyond the door was an ascending escalator.

After he had started up, and realized that what appeared to be a public lobby was at the top, Art asked: "This means that I'm free to go?"

"That's right, sir." The smiling sergeant had come with him onto the rising stair. "By the way," he added, his voice lowering, "if you're talking to—anybody, you can let 'em know that the men on the force are a hundred per cent behind the campaign to get tough with the apes and get 'em off the streets."

"Huh?"

They had reached the marbled public lobby on the station's ground floor. With a gesture the smiling sergeant directed Art's attention to where the air-curtained main doorway stood open to the world.

"I'd better wait here for a while," said Art. "I think someone's coming to see about getting me out."

"That so?" The sergeant winked. "Tell 'em

they needn't have bothered. Still, you're welcome to wait for 'em here if you like. Have a seat. Excuse me, I'd better get back to work."

"Certainly." As soon as the man had gone, Art went to a public phone booth in the lobby and tried the Parrs' again. To his surprise, Ann answered the phone almost at once.

"Art, what's up?"

He stood with his head held high; maybe the bandage wouldn't be noticeable at that angle to the plate's pickups, with his hair sort of piled in front of it. "How are the kids?"

"Why, they're fine, fine. How are things with you?"

"I tried to get you a few minutes ago, but no one answered."

"I was just out in the park with the children. George is working. Where are you calling from, Art?"

"I'll—be talking to you again, soon, Ann." With that he blanked off.

He went to sit in the marbled lobby, and watched the public flow in and out at a brisk rate. All these people were involved with legal trouble in some way, even if they were only reporting it, so he supposed it was natural that they should look frightened or dazed, or indignant or stony-faced. What bothered Art was that now when he looked out the window at the throng passing the station on the slidewalk, the faces out there looked much the same.

He had been sitting there less than ten minutes when Rose came in. She spotted him at once, smiled, and came marching clack-

clack across the lobby on new hard-heeled sandals. It struck him now that her walk was somewhat too childlike and bouncy for a normally mature young woman. She was wearing a red bikni, daringly opaque all over and almost padless. Art stood up and greeted her with an embrace.

"My good friend Art! How have they treated you?"

"Fine, ever since they heard me talking to you on the phone. Before that they practically had me sentenced, and now they tell me I'm free to go."

Rose laughed prettily, and linked her arm in his. "Then let's be going. We have lots to talk about on our way."

He walked out of the station with her, asking: "Did you call a lawyer?"

"I thought you couldn't be in any serious trouble," she said obliquely. "Here, get in." She was unlocking the door of a very expensive car parked right in the NO STANDING zone in front of the police station. The Illinois license plate was number four. *Four*. Great sex, had his luck changed at last?

He got in obediently. "Where are we going?"

"I want to take you home with me, Artie. I told you, Daddy's been anxious to meet you."

Once in on the driver's side, Rose scanned the readiness indicators on the dash, as a cautious driver should, and then punched keys quickly. Then she sat back and turned to Art, giving him a long, unfathomable look while the programmed car started its engine and radared its way out into traffic.

"Artie?"

"What is it—Rosie? Do you like being called Rosie, by the way?"

"Yes, I do like it." She tilted her head, making the lenses shimmer beautifully. Probably in days of calm she practiced with them before a mirror. "Artie, my father's a very nice man, a kind man. He's not one to fly into rages or anything like that."

"Well. That's fine." He supposed she wanted him to ask some favor of her father for her. "Just who is your father, by the way?"

"He's the bishop, silly. Church of Eros archbishop of Chicago. Everybody in Chicago knows him. Artie, we really are good friends, aren't we?" Taking Art's hand, Rose swung his arm back and forth over the seat between them. It was a childlike action, and when a basically sexy girl like Rose did it, a man could be tempted toward serious repression. Especially a weary man drained of his energy to fight. The vision of her crouching on the riverbank, veiled by his dirty shirt, rose in his mind's eye but he managed to thrust it down.

"Of course we're good friends, Rose. Any time I can do you a favor I hope you'll let me know."

"Today I just want you to meet Daddy." She giggled.

"I'm looking forward to that. Especially . . . Rose, I won't lie to you. Especially now that I know he's someone with influence." An hour ago Art had been ready to resign the game, but now things might be just a little different. "Because you see I have a problem, one that I really need help with. I hope your father may be able to at least give me some advice on it."

The cat's-eyes seemed to offer sympathy. "It isn't a really big and nasty problem, is it? Oh, I hope not."

He laughed feebly. "Big and nasty enough. Oh, I haven't murdered anyone, so far."

Rose snatched her hand away. "Don't say things like that! Don't even make jokes about them!"

"I'm sorry." He hadn't realized how sensitive she was to even the suggestion of violence. He looked around them. "Do you live nearby?"

"Not far." The neighborhood through which they were now passing looked much like that around the Parrs' home, except here the blockhouses were set even further from the street, occupied larger plots of land, and their walls looked even higher. Just ahead was one whose granite walls were extra high.

"We're almost home, my big handsome protector."

The car measured the traffic and the traffic-spaces around it, chose an opening and shifted precisely to the street's curb lane, then signalled for a turn and drove onto a ramp that swept it down beneath the granite walls. A man in a guard's booth gave Rose a casual wave which she returned while switching the slowing vehicle back to manual control. The steering gear folded out of a panel into her hands and she drove on.

Here as in the Parrs' block the underground garage was divided into visitors' parking areas and private stalls. Rose turned into what appeared to be the largest stall, with two cars parked in it already, and room for several more.

She switched off the turbines and turned to Art again. "Artie, if your problem is—nothing like the horrible thing you joked about—then you can tell me what it is. In fact I think you'd better tell me, before you go in and meet Daddy."

"Rose, it has nothing to do with violence. It's somewhat similar to—your problem. To the problem you were faced with when you and I first met."

She had pretty teeth and moist, full lips. "However did you figure out what that was?"

"Oh, just putting two and two together. I know now what you must have had in that picnic cooler."

Now her lips were pouting. Was she going to cry? It seemed to Art that without eyes her weeping would be tearless and therefore repulsive. "Not that I care what you were doing, Rose, not that I'm in any position to talk. It's just that my wife is now having difficulties along a somewhat similar line. I don't know that your father would be able to help me with that kind of problem, or that he'd want to get involved in it."

Rose dabbed with a tissue at her nose, and yes, at her lidless lenses too. "I'm glad you understand, Art. What happened to my fetus is another thing my father mustn't know the truth about." *(Another* thing?) "Of course he thinks that I simply had it aborted. But I can't even think about such violence, let alone permit it inside my own body. Ugh." A final dab and a deep breath, and she smiled and was back to what passed for normal. "Now you'd better listen to me for a minute, Artie. Because I haven't told *you* everything yet."

Something about those words was ominous. Art leaned back in the car's luxurious seat, closing his eyes for just a moment's rest. He checked his watch. A little past three. Then he turned and looked into Rose's lenses. "What is it you haven't told me?"

Once more she took his arm. She became clinging. "Oh, Artie, I was just desperate. You see, there's a man I . . . like. I like him very much indeed. In fact I've come to—to revere him."

"Revere!"

"Art, I put my fate into your hands. I know you won't betray me. Just recently my father has found out that I'm having an affair, or at least he's become very suspicious. But he doesn't know who the man is, and I didn't dare confess the truth, because . . . anyway, I didn't dare. So today I told him that it was you."

"Oh." Art closed his eyes again. He supposed he could push Rose out of the car, seize the controls, and go roaring up out of the garage, perhaps crashing through the barrier at the door. Transporting illegally frozen fetuses. Rioting. Midwifery. Auto theft, gate-crashing.

Was there a crime called gate-crashing? There would be. No previous convictions, or even arrests, that Rodney must have been a clever one. But sooner or later the most cunning criminals trip themselves up. They say he seduced a bishop's daughter, that's what really wrote finis to his career. They say just the other day he was in the Family Planning office, bold as you please, talking about an appointment with the director himself. They say . . .

"Artie, dear?" Rose's voice dripped honeyed anxiety. Probably she didn't even like to be called Rosie. "Artie? I was just desperate, or I would never have done it. I had no one else to turn to, and I just had to keep Daddy from finding out who my true cavalier really is . . . Art? Oh, I promise it won't be so bad. Daddy really did want to get you out of jail, even after I told him you were the one."

Art nodded slowly, meanwhile keeping his eyelids firmly closed. If he could somehow get out of the bishop's dungeon here and reach the Parrs' castle, maybe Ann could hide him under a bed and no one would ever find him. Drape him in an opaque sheet. But that might constitute another crime. Oh, chastity, what a mess. Maybe he was dreaming.

"I was just in despair, Art, when suddenly you called. Then it seemed so logical for you to be the man that I told Daddy you were. Don't you see? Art, are you all right? *Poor* Art!"

Poor Art opened his eyes. Now then, what did he have to do to attain success and happi-

ness? Meet the bishop and prove himself innocent of Rose's seduction. Then, with or
without ecclesiastical help, find Rita and get
her safely aborted, while keeping George and
Ann, and Rita and himself of course, clear of
the law. That about covered it.

He opened the car door and slid out. The
situation was clearly beyond worrying about,
and from that fact he derived a kind of second
wind. Bring on the bishop.

"Shall we go in, Artie?"

"Oh, why not?"

Rose led him directly from the parking stall
through a double door that might have served
to guard a bank vault, and up a private escalator. The door at the top was opened by a
huge man, rough-looking though well dressed,
who eyed Art with suspicion. Art in turn suffered a momentary fear that this was the
bishop himself.

Rose said: "Jove, this is a friend of mine,
Mr. Rodney. Daddy wanted me to bring him
home so they could get acquainted."

Jove grunted. "Have 'im wait here and
I'll see. Or would you rather go in, Miss
Jamison?"

"No, you go, I'll wait with Art." She took
Art's arm and they stood there in the elegantly
carpeted hall like a couple waiting to be married.

"The bishop's chief bodyguard?" Art asked,
when the giant was gone.

"Yes. Don't mind Jove's rough manners,
he's really quite sweet." She squeezed his arm

meaningfully. "So's Daddy. Now I put all my
trust in you, darling."

Jove was already coming back through the
plush hallway. "The boss says you should
bring him on in. Hey, Miss Jamison, you're
looking real hot. I'm off duty in a little while,
could we maybe get together for some sex?"

"All right, Jove, I'll see you in the chapel.
Art, dear, let me introduce you to Daddy
first."

At the end of the hall Rose tapped on an old-
fashioned wood-paneled door, then pushed it
open without waiting for an answer. The room
revealed was a large study, the walls lined with
bookshelves and tape-racks. A massive,
brown-skinned old man rose from an armchair
and favored Art with a mild smile of greeting.
The bishop wore the exaggerated white
codpiece of his office, under a vaguely transparent robe.

"Daddy, this is Art. I've been telling him
how nice you are, and that he really had nothing to be afraid of, meeting you. Now I want
you to be nice to him."

"Why, I'm generally sociable, dear." The
old man accepted his daughter's kiss on his
worn sagging cheek. "Dear, why don't you
buzz away now for a little bit? Mr. Rodney
and I are going to have a chat."

"Sure, Daddy. I expect I'll be in the chapel
with Jove if you should want me." Turning toward Art with an expression that was doubtless meant to be encouraging, Rose stepped
past him and out of the study. Art, who had

reached out his arm mechanically, caught himself at the last moment and let her go without a good-bye pinch. They were supposed to be having an affair, and possibly, just possibly, he would want to maintain that fiction.

Bishop Jamison was still smiling. "Mr. Rodney, that sofa there is very comfortable. And how about a drink? I have vodka and bourbon and beer and even a little sherry on hand."

"Uh, thank you, sir. Your Potency. Bourbon on the rocks would be fine." Art sank resignedly into the sofa while his host turned away. Poison in the whiskey, maybe? He would drink it anyway.

The room might have been the study of any successful and conservative man, though, not surprisingly, there was a somewhat heavy emphasis on religious art. Rodin's *The Kiss* in nearly lifesize reproduction. *Leda and the Swan*, there on the wall, by one of the newer photographic masters. Painting had been dead for a century now, along with poetry and story-telling, or so most of the critics said. And there of course above the mantel, *Love Conquers All*, Caravaggio's Cupid trampling triumphantly the symbols of the occupations by which man sometimes allowed himself to be lured temporarily away from his true master, Lust.

The old man was back, holding out a glass, and Art half rose to take it from him. "Thank you, sir."

With a wheeze, the bishop settled his bulk

in his own leather chair; his own drink he held
in a tankard around the outer surface of which
some kind of Oriental orgy marched in bas relief. "Mr. Rodney, Rose tells me that you and
she have become quite good friends."

"Uh, yes sir, we have." Art's intended sip of
bourbon somehow transformed itself into a
gulp.

Jamison emerged from his tankard with a
trace of beer foam on his dark lips. "She's a
lovely girl in her way . . . her mother was a
lovely piece, and I oughta know, though I was
an old dog even then . . . how was it you two
happened to meet? On the tube train coming
in from Iowa, wasn't it?"

"That's right, sir." Art drew in a deep
breath. "Bishop, I don't mean you or Rose any
harm. Far from it. So I'm just going to tell you
the truth. I don't know what Rose may have
told you, but the fact of the matter is I hardly
know her. If she has any, ah, involvement with
any man, it's certainly not with me." So far
the news was being received with apparent
calm. "I'm sorry about her problems, Your
Potency, and yours, but I have problems of
my own that are just as bad. I'm sorry."

Jamison leaned forward a little. "Would
you like a refill on that drink?"

"I'll get it myself, sir, thanks. Another beer?
I'm telling you the truth, bishop, I never was
any good at lying."

The bishop indicated with a headshake that
his tankard had no need of refilling as yet. He
swiveled his chair to keep facing Art, who was

now at the bar. "Some people never realize they're not, and it gets 'em into endless trouble. Most of the time honesty simplifies things, if it doesn't always pay. You really did help Rose, out there in Iowa, didn't you? Her own story is a little muddled. She was coming back from visiting some girl friend in Dubuque, I guess, when that riot broke out."

"Oh, yes sir, I had the chance to be of help to her in a small way." Back at the sofa, Art sank down with relief and took a sip, this time truly no more than a tiny sip, of the excellent bourbon. "But believe me, there's been nothing wrong between us. We made it all the way, right there in the park, while we were waiting to get on the train to Chicago."

Jamison was nodding slowly. "Arthur, I find myself believing you. I know my own daughter, and she just gave me your name too suddenly and too willingly. I don't suppose you know the name of the man she is involved with, as you put it?" Then before Art could try to answer, the bishop scowled and waved a white-palmed, wrinkled hand. "No, I withdraw the question. Don't want to put an honest man like yourself on the spot."

"I really haven't the faintest idea, anyway, who it could be." Numbly relaxing, Art sipped at his icy whisky. His head ached, but not as bad as before. It seemed that he had managed to avert any new and disastrous trouble; and what more could a man hope for than that?

The bishop set his tankard down carefully on a small table. "Not that I care an awful lot

what kind of fun she has with men." His
steady black eyes peered at Art from their
time-ravaged face. "Probably that shocks you,
coming from a church-man like me. But if she
wants to sit with some young fella and gaze
at the stars and forget all about sex for
ten minutes, I can't see how society is
harmed."

"Yes sir, I am surprised to hear you talk
like that." It would really have shocked Art,
too, if he hadn't been somewhat numb with al-
cohol, and emotionally exhausted by still more
shocking things. "If what your statement im-
plies is true, that society isn't harmed by repression, that it doesn't matter what people do
with sex, why do we have the Church of Eros
then?"

The bishop heaved himself erect, his
erotically-decorated tankard in hand, and
walked over to the dark fireplace. It looked a lot
like George's, except this one was bigger.
When the bishop switched it on, a realistic imitation of burning logs, probably a hologram,
appeared in the dark cave. The logs crackled
audibly and flared and seemed to send smoke
up the flue.

"This thing is a fake," Jamison mused, pat-
ting the mantle with one hand. "Lots of fire
and noise, but no smell. And no real heat." He
set his tankard on the mantlepiece and turned
to Art. "You know why it is good for man to
worship sex? Why it really is good? Simply because the poor fool has nothing better before
which to prostrate himself. Eros as a god is far

from perfect, he's just the best of a bunch of failures."

Having a little time to think over what the bishop said, and looking at the old man closely, Art was not so very surprised after all. There were such cynical bishops in modern fiction sometimes. And Jamison wasn't just old, he must be decades over a hundred. He must have spent his youth in the period of moral vacuum before his Church became established. Art had sometimes heard other very old people express similar startlingly modern and radical views.

Standing massive besides the fireplace, Jamison told him: "The war-god and the wealth-god and the heaven-and-love god all have failed. Heaven-and-love came the closest. Best example is the man they nailed up on the cross. He spoke to a lot of people, that one did. He was about the best, except for sex. And then Allah and Jehovah and Mithra and all the rest.

"And then there's the man-god. You know what I mean by that? I mean god made by man in man's own image, humanity in apotheosis, we will all be god someday and maybe our great leader is god right now—he's the worst, the most dangerous, and we're not through with him yet. Damnation, are we ever through with anything?" Jamison's voice, which had taken on the tones it might employ on Saturday nights in the pulpit above the orgy, fell back to conversational pitch. One other man in Art's recent memory had used such ancient expletives. "Mr. Rodney, man was made to worship something, and no god he finds is worthy of him. That's what the ancients would have called a tragedy. Sex does the least harm, I would judge; and sex is fun. Oh man, yes man, it sure is fun."

The bishop smiled at Art wryly, and made his way to the bar to get a refill on his beer. Then back to his leather chair to let down his weight, he and the chair wheezing together. "The only thing is, if she does like some young man in what to her is such an extra-special way, then I'd like to know his name and what he's like. Rose has had enough pain in her young life already. She tell you about that ape-assault where she lost her eyes?"

"No sir. I didn't know that was what had happened. It must have been terrible."

"That it was," said Jamison shortly. "My much-publicized crusade against the street-apes and the dope-peddlers, which you will hear a lot about if you stay long in Chicago, stems in large part from that assault on my daughter."

"I believe I heard something about it from the police. They were in favor."

"I myself am not a non-violent man," the bishop said. "Not always. Eros does not counsel turning the other cheek except for a caress."

Art failed to understand the reference.

Jamison sipped at his newly foamy beer. "When I was a boy, a lot of people thought it was having brown skin, what was then called being black, that made young men go out and act like apes. And there was a grain of truth in what they said, a grain of truth, because brown skin could be a real burden then. It could make a man feel desperate and just lash out."

Art grunted something. He was growing sleepy and would have to be careful that he didn't doze off, what with the drink and the hypnotic fire.

"Arthur, if you should ever quote me as saying what I said about stargazing being not so bad after all, I shall of course deny it. Likewise with my speculations on comparative religion. On the other hand, if you should want to mention to me now your own problems that you said were so bad, I can at least guarantee secrecy. Maybe I could even offer help."

Art was abruptly wide awake again. "Well, my problem involves my wife. And the Bureau of Family Planning. It's a rather serious . . ."

Jamison was already shaking his head and putting up a hand to stop him. "No. Not Family Planning trouble, I'm staying clear of that. Sorry, no, it wouldn't do for a man in my position to get involved. Too bad, my boy, but I can only wish you luck."

"That's all right, sir, I understand. And I wish you luck. And Rose. Understand, bishop, I'm not having an affair with her, but she's a very attractive girl and I can understand how a man might wish to do so. I mean that as a compliment."

"Hmf," laughed Jamison, a single laugh,

not loud. He was staring into the glow of his artificial fire, and looking into the long scroll of his memories he found Art's words amusing. Then he was silent for a while, and Art was almost dozing again before Jamison asked suddenly: "You're not angry about what Rose did to you today?"

"Telling you I was the man? I almost fell through the floor. She didn't spring it on me until we were here and I couldn't run out. But I'm not angry now. She didn't do it out of meanness."

"You're right about that." Jamison nodded. "There's no meanness in her. But ever since that assault she's been not quite right in her mind. Too much frightened of any least hint of violence. I think she's scared that I'll have violence done upon the real man, should I discover his identity. Now who could he be, that she should harbor that idea?"

"I really wish I could help," said Art. "But I guess there's nothing I can do."

"She saw psychiatrists right after she was injured, and now she's talking about going to another one, but I don't put any faith in 'em. Doctors, computers, modern science, and we still live in caves with the doors blockaded. Not that I want to damn modern science, not me with my artificial heart and arteries." With a seeming effort Jamison roused himself from his musings, and once more got to his feet. "Go with Eros, my son. Is there anything else I might be able to do for you?"

Art put down his glass and stood up. "I

guess not, sir. Thanks again for getting me out of jail. I really was innocent."

When he emerged from the study, Rose, who had changed her red bikni for a transparent dress, jumped up from a sofa in the hall and hurried to him eagerly. "What happened?" she stage-whispered. "Did Daddy believe you?"

"I think he believed everything I told him."

She was so delighted she jiggled up and down like a child. "And he didn't explode?"

"No, he didn't."

Rose squealed. "My faithful protector! You took such a risk for me." She threw her arms around Art and kissed him with a kind of innocent chastity. "Poor Daddy, sometimes at his age his mind wanders. I hate to deceive him. But I knew you'd manage somehow. Oh, how can I thank you?"

"It's all right."

"It isn't all right. You've done so much for me, that now I *must* do something in return." Her voice turned suddenly cool, and she retreated from him half a step. "If I wasn't pledged to be chaste with only one . . ."

"Please, Rose!"

"You're right, what must you think of me?" She tugged Art down the hallway. Looking toward the door to the escalator, he could see that a different bodyguard was now on duty. Rose snuggled one breast against Art lustily. "I'm not promiscuous, you know," she whispered. "Not like some of those bluenose girls, those terrible ones they throw in jail."

"I can tell you're nothing like that."

As they were going down the escalator she said: "I bet they didn't feed you properly in that awful jail. And, knowing my father, he gave you nothing but drink. Let's go out and get something to eat, and we'll talk."

"All right." He had nowhere else to go at present. It was almost four hours since they had fed him at the midwifer's hideout, and the whisky he had just taken was biting at his empty stomach. "Where shall we go?"

"I know a place. I'm buying."

That seemed no more than fair, and he went along. They were just getting into the car again when Rose squealed, suddenly enough to make Art jump. "Artie, I forgot all about your problem, trying to help your poor wife save her baby! Did you get a chance to mention it to Daddy? What did he say?"

She had the problem backwards, but he saw no point in enlightening her. "I did mention it to Daddy? What did he say?"

She had the problem backwards, but he saw no point in enlightening her. "I did mention it to your father. He can't do anything."

"Tell *me* more about it."

She sympathized and persisted until he had to elaborate on his story a little. Obviously she had the idea that he was trying to help Rita avoid an abortion, and he let her go on thinking so. Why upset the poor girl for nothing? He would share a meal with her, and maybe some sex again, and go his way and never see her more.

"But where is she right now?" Rose questioned anxiously. By now she had driven the car into a drive-in automat of the better class and they had placed their orders.

"Here in Chicago . . . really, Rose, it's painful for me to even talk about it. And there's nothing you can do." He reached to take a tray of food from a robotic servitor at the window. When he looked back at Rose she was shaking her head slowly, and smiling as if in mischief.

"Artie, as soon as you've eaten you're coming with me to get some help. I know people Daddy doesn't know!"

XII

ROSE URGED him to hurry through the meal, and shortly they were on the road again. "But where are we going?" Art kept asking. "Who is it you want me to see?"

When he began to grow angry, Rose at last stopped being coy. "We're going to visit my psychiatrist, in his office."

"Rose, that's not the kind of help I need. I'm not trying to adjust to my situation, I want out of it."

Rose dismissed such quibbles with a shake of her head. This time she was driving manually instead of riding on autopilot, proceeding slowly and cautiously, with fierce concentration on the job. They were headed straight toward the center of the city.

"It's a good thing Daddy hasn't started having me followed yet."

"Why do you say that?"

No answer.

"Rose, I'm sure you mean well, but I don't see how this is going to help me in the least."

"I know you don't. But wait and see."

Art slumped back in his seat. He could demand to be taken somewhere else, but where?

Probably by this time Rita was waiting for him at the Parrs', with a red picnic cooler frosting over at her side, her belly flat and perfect once again. All right, Rita and George and Ann had won. So let them do the wondering and searching for a few hours. Meanwhile, let Rose lead him where she would.

She parked in a public garage on the edge of the no-private-vehicle zone encompassing the city's center, and from there went on with Art by slidewalk into the multilevel knots of moving pedestrian ways that in their plastic shields threaded the deep canyons between the skyscrapers. At about forty stories above ground level they entered an office building, and boarded an elevator which bore them much higher still. From the elevator they walked an elegant, skylighted hallway, to stop at last before a door lettered

RAOUL RIZZO M.D.

D. PSYCH.

Rizzo. Art had somewhere, recently, heard that name. He followed Rose into a doctor's waiting room, small and luxurious but empty. Not even a receptionist. There was an alarmingly remote look on Rose's face, and she put sexless fingers on Art's arm. "Hush. Wait."

After a moment an inner door opened. The well-dressed young man who emerged from it was of no more than middle height, but so emaciated that he looked taller. His eyes did not turn for even a moment to Art, or in any other direction away from Rose. "My lady fair," he said, his tense voice hardly louder than a whisper.

"My true knight," Rose breathed in answer. Her expression was becoming even more remote, moment by moment. "Oh, my champion."

They stepped closer to each other. They raised their right hands, and each caressed the air a few centimeters from the other's face. Not once did they make actual physical contact. Staring woodenly over each other's shoulders, they reminded Art of opposing chess pawns set down slightly off-center on their respective squares.

Art just stood there. If they didn't mind his watching, why should he?

At last Rose turned, breaking off the non-embrace. "Raoul, Raoul my cold one, this is Art, the man who helped me on the tube train. You remember my telling you."

"I thought that today I would have you all to myself, Rose, rose petal, rose essence, dear specter of a rose." The psychiatrist sighed, still staring into the air. At last he roused himself and put out a hand to Art. In Art's grasp the thin fingers felt as weak as they looked. Raoul's gaze was penetrating at first but then it kept sliding self-consciously away.

"Raoul, dearest. Today Art was kind enough to help me *again*. Now he has a problem of his own, and we've just got to do something about it for him."

Raoul thought this over for ten or fifteen seconds, nodding slowly. He dug a pipe out of a pocket in his translucent shorts. He looked from Rose to Art and back again. "Come in then, all of you," he invited in his solemn near-whisper. He held open for them the door by which he had come out into the waiting room.

In his inner chamber Raoul pushed a pair of reclining chairs together side by side, and gestured for Rose and Art to seat themselves. Looking out the window as he sat down, Art saw the June sun working its way lower in the northwest sky, beyond a palisade of towers and a groundcover of distant, much lower rooftops,

Raoul perched himself cross-legged on his desk and lit his pipe. Judging by the aroma of the first fumes, the tobacco certainly contained an admixture of something stronger.

"Mr. Rodney." Raoul paused and puffed. "You witnessed the greeting that passed just now between Rose and myself. Have you ever beheld even a brother and sister going to greater extremes of anti-erotism? My purpose in posing the question is not to shock you."

Art, watching the lowering sun and wondering if Rita could also see it, had not been paying close attention. "Are you brother and sister? But I thought . . ."

"No, no, we are not. Perhaps I failed to make my meaning plain. Would you have described our behavior as obscene?"

No, thought Art, just exhibitionistic. He doubted that the greeting would have been quite so extravagantly repressive had there been no audience. But, wanting to be a good fellow, and uncertain whether Raoul wanted to be thought obscene or not, he answered: "I suppose most people would call it that."

It was Raoul's turn not to listen. "I just wonder," he murmured, as if to himself, "why did I employ that sibling analogy? Brother and sister may repress a mutual sex attraction and the repression is tolerated by society."

"Of course." Art glanced over at Rose, wondering if she still hoped that he would benefit from this visit. Her inscrutable lenses were aimed steadily at Raoul.

Raoul rocked back and forth on his desk and puffed his pipe. "Taking a larger view, are not all men and women in some sense siblings? What then is more natural than our occasional urges to escape from sex? We are all of us subject to the deep powers of the subconscious. Modern science tells us that dreams, produced in the subconscious, are attempts of the ego to flee the restrictions of the body. In every human adult lies the buried wish to return to sexless infancy. In all honesty, isn't letting these urges out into the open the only healthy course to take?"

"I suppose." If Art spoke honestly he would say he thought his healthiest course would be getting up to leave as soon as he could think of someplace to go. Rose meant well, and he didn't want to hurt her feelings, but this was quite ridiculous.

With an unfolding of bony legs Raoul got down, or rather stood up, from his low desk.

"Personally, I have never conducted an analysis in which I did not uncover a strong, buried celibacy-wish in the subject. Our differences from other animals are inescapably part of our natures; and we ignore them at our peril."

"You may be right." Now she was going to have the chaste baby anyway and he was not going to be with her when she needed him the most. That was all his campaign to rescue her had accomplished. What had he done? But what else could he have done?

"Face these things in yourself," Raoul was saying, in a brooding voice. Behind him on his walls were abstract photographs, and a couple of Vandalist splash-paintings, up-to-date and arrogant in expensive frames. Yes, the art had been dead for a century, all right. "Face them squarely, and they will begin to lose their power over you."

Art cleared his throat.

Raoul's eyes fastened on his, this time not to be easily driven away. "Face the truth about what has happened between you and Rosamond! When you first saw her she was alone, she was frightened, she was in danger."

"She wasn't exactly alone."

"Immediately you went to her aid. Your relationship thus began with no erotic values, but society tolerates that in an emergency, and you yourselves did not realize that in your hearts you wanted it that way.

"When the immediate danger was past, perhaps you turned to sex? Yes. *Then,* when your

lust was temporarily in abeyance, there came
the moment of temptation. The forces of the
subconscious were no longer to be denied. The
fragile remnants of your lust were to be sacri-
ficed upon the altar of repression. You wanted
to flee with Rose from the world of flesh, to
climb a crystal stair to an ethereal palace, to
enter the world of sublimation. Yes. Perhaps
you draped her body—"

"Enough of this." Art pushed away his suddenly vigorous memories of that sunset with
Rose on the bank of a wide river. He tried to
get to his feet forcefully but the reclining chair
betrayed him and he staggered and had to
make an effort to keep from falling. "Look
here, I haven't asked you—to analyze me."

Raoul fell silent, gazing at Art with what
seemed a mixture of pity and antagonism.

"Dearest?" Rose spoke up timidly. "Raoul?
The reason I thought you might be able to help
Art is because his wife is looking for a midwifer. Art want to help her save her baby, but
there are obstacles."

Raoul, professionally unshockable, took the
news in stride. "I can help him live with the
situation, provided he wants to be helped."

Rose shook her head. "No, my chill one,
that isn't what I meant."

Raoul blinked. "What, then?"

"Oh, for you to see your father about it, of
course!" Rose was lovingly irritated by her
lover's obtuseness.

At mention of his father, Raoul's face
twitched, and he laughed bitterly. He sat on

his desk again and tried to relight his pipe.

"Please, dearest. You mustn't be jealous. Art and I are *not* having an affair. He and I are strongly erotic together, really we are."

Puff and pause. "Why do you say that?"

"Who is his father?" Art asked, standing now with his arms folded.

Rose flowed easily to her feet; probably she had some experience with these chairs. "I say it because *you* are my knight. Do you think I could ever want to sit coldly beside any other man?"

Raoul closed his eyes and let his pipe go out.

Rose hovered near him, pleading. "My champion! Won't you do this little thing for me? Take Art to see your father?"

"Who is his father?"

Raoul's eyes opened. His whisper had a broken sound. "For you, my lady, my chaste one, I will do it. Sometime tomorrow."

"Tomorrow might be too late for his poor wife. Couldn't you do it now?"

"I thought that you and I would have this evening alone together."

"Please. Take Art to your father now. I set you this task, to prove that you revere me."

"Then I have no choice but to obey." Raoul came to life and slid off the desk. "Will you wait for me here, my lady?"

Rose squirmed as if with repressed desire and took a step back, avoiding any possible physical contact with her knight. "I'll wait here all night for you, if need be. When you come back, maybe . . . we'll play chess."

"My lady, not that childish game, I beg of you. Anything else."

"Who is your father?" Art asked the ceiling. "And what good is seeing him supposed to do me?" Like as not Rizzo Sr. would turn out to be the head of Chicago's branch of the Family Planning office. Soon everyone in the city would know about Rita's warped reproductive cravings and her illegal plans. No one would do anything to save her, but everyone would know, even irredeemable idiots who thought chess was a childish game.

After staring incredulously at Art for a moment, Raoul asked: "You don't know who my father is?" And then he laughed bitterly and long.

Still not knowing, Art went along with Raoul, first in a taxi to a garage, and then in Raoul's car. In spite of all, a nagging hope persisted.

Whatever his occupation might be, Rizzo Sr. had evidently made a success of it. The blockhouse in which he lived was every bit as high-walled and luxurious as the Jamisons'. The Rizzo garage space was even larger than the archbishop's had been, and protected by heavier gates. As Raoul eased his fine car to a stop and turned its turbines off, Art was once more nagged by the sense of having recently heard the Rizzo name in some other connection. Was it something about this very structure, Rizzo's townhouse?

In a short passage connecting the garage with an underground level of the Rizzo home, a pair of non-uniformed guards were stationed. They looked meaner than the Jamisons' Jove, though neither of them was quite as large.

"Who's your pal, Doc?" one of them asked.

"A man I know." Young Rizzo smiled wryly. "A man with a problem, I expect my father will be able to help him, if he wants to help."

"Maybe you shoulda just phoned," said the other guard. "The Magnifico's sorta been lying low for the past few days."

The what? thought Art.

"You know how my father likes to do business face to face."

The pair of gate-blockers looked doubtfully at Art. He could place them now. They were the ones who had sat on him in the brothel. Not the same men, but the type. Rizzo, Rizzo, he almost had it.

"Well, let's see if you're carryin' anything. Doc, the boss is in his study now, if you wanna go up."

"I'll be back in a minute, Rodney," said Raoul, and went on ahead. The two guards began to pat Art's pockets and bulges, searching him. Rizzo. Little old Alfie in the slumburb tavern, saying Vic Rizzo's townhouse was bombed. Oh, great stargazing quadruplets.

Rizzo Jr. was soon back from his filial visit. His face was flushed, but seemingly not with joy. "He says I can bring him up."

"Awright."

Art rode up with Raoul in a large and fanci-

ly paneled elevator, which disgorged them into
a room like the entry hall of a small art
museum. Marble columns supported a high,
vaulted ceiling, and across one end of the room
there burbled a complex of waterfalls and
fountains and pools, complete with fish. For
all its size the hall was almost crowded with
paintings and statuary. On the wall opposite
the elevator, in a place of dominance over the
other objects d'art, was an ancient life-sized
crucifix of wood, done in a realistically gory
Spanish style. Its paint, once red and brown,
had aged into a grayish dullness that with the
cracks and holes gave the figure a look of
frighteningly patient endurance.

Raoul led Art across the museum hall and
opened a massive wooden door. "In here," he
ordered tersely.

The room behind the door was also quite
large, with a beamed ceiling and woodpaneled
walls. Might it all be real, virgin, tree-segment
wood? Anyone whose house had fountains and
waterfalls—

Art caught one breath-tripping glimpse of a
girl, heavily garmented, even her face veiled,
before she moved out of sight behind some
opaque woven draperies. And there, almost as
startling as the girl and the paneled walls, was
a huge genuine fireplace that appeared to be
consuming genuine logs.

At least four chess sets, of stone or wood or
metal, all large and ornately carved, were visible on tables or in display cases. A suit of armor stood at Art's right hand. What appeared

to be medieval torches standing in brackets on
the wall bore warm and writhing electric
flames. Upon one paneled wall there hung a
crossed pair of long, pointed weapons, pikes or
lances of some kind; on the opposite wall a
brace of submachine guns were mounted in
the same way. Walls and furniture bore many
framed photographs evidently reproduced
from twentieth century newspapers or films,
showing men in the obscenely heavy garb of
that time. The men smiled unpleasantly and
many of them were carrying firearms. From
the upper walls there looked down at least a
dozen paintings of a more distant time, mostly
of men in archaic contume wearing swords
and accompanied by crouching dogs. These
paintings looked old and dim enough to be orig-
inals. The Magnifico, the guard had said.

The Magnifico came forward amid his
treasures. His small torso was plump beneath
his shimmering, partially translucent dressing
gown, but his face still showed some of the
leanness of his son's.

His flat voice came out around a cigar. "So,
you're the man with the troubles. I was
curious to see you, I wondered what kinda
man my son would bring here to get his troubles fixed."

Art made himself look straight into the
Magnifico's direct and seldom-blinking eyes.
The reality of power before him was as apparent as the hardness of the suit of armor at
his right. Art could feel the world and all its
probabilities shifting again, crazily and un-

predictably beneath his feet.

Art cleared his throat. "My trouble is a fairly simple one."

"So. I guess my son can only fix the high-priced troubles in his office. The simple ones he still has to bring to me. What's yours?"

"My wife is in a birth-mill, here in Chicago." Facing the reality of power in Rizzo's eyes, Art had a moment of weakness, of indecision. But now his choice was clear-cut, inescapable. "I want to stop her from going through with it."

"So, who says I know anything about birth-mills?"

The fireplace roared and seemed to make the room too hot. Somewhere behind Art, Raoul fidgeted. Art said the next thing that came into his head: "I see you're a chess-player." Every time he glanced around the crowded room he spotted another set somewhere.

Rizzo removed his cigar from his mouth and raised his eyebrows. "You play?"

Art smiled faintly. "I'm a master."

"No! You are?" The cigar went flipping into the fireplace. Rizzo almost bowed. "Come in here—whazza name? Mr. Rodney? You come in here, there's somethin' I want you t' look at."

He held open for Art the drapes behind which the veiled girl had vanished. At the same time he raised his eyes to stare coldly over Art's shoulder. "Hey Raoul, go fix yourself a drink or something. Or get out. Hey, if

you see Penny around maybe she'll wanna
screw. She's been sublimatin' her urges quite a
bit lately.''

The only answer was the sound of the heavy
wooden door softly closing; probably, Art
thought, it could not be slammed. He went on
through the drapes and Rizzo followed, into a
smaller adjunct of the study. The girl was not
in sight.

''You say you're a rated master, Mr.
Rodney?''

''Yes. However not in this state. In California.''

''I'd appreciate it if you'd take a look at this
position I got set up here. Tell me what you
think about it.''

On a board on an antique table were ebony
and ivory men arranged in an intricate early
middle game or late opening position. At first
glance Art took it for one of the new computer-
discovered variations of the neo-Shapiro de-
fense, but one of White's knights was oddly
placed, changing the whole complexion of the
game.

''Interesting,'' said Art. It really was. ''One
of your games?''

''Nah, not a real game. Oh, Mr. Rodney,
meet Penny.''

The veiled girl had returned from somewhere amid velvet hangings, moving on soft silent feet. Under the Magnifico's smiling but
watchful eye, Art kissed Penny hello with a
fervent show of lust, and pushed a fondling
hand inside the innermost of her voluminous
garments.

Rizzo chuckled benevolently. "Now run along, little lady."

Penny paused to blow an openmouthed kiss to Art before she let the drapes fall into place behind her.

Rizzo, staring at the place where she had vanished, released a small sigh. "That son of mine just don't know how to keep a woman." Then he brightened. "That reminds me. You hear the one about this traveling salesgirl, she stops at a lamasery to sell blankets?"

"I'm not sure."

Evidently he was not going to hear it now. Rizzo was still looking after the girl. "That Penny, though. She's been livin' with me here almost a year now, and I've never touched her. Imagine." He sighed again. "I hardly seen a centimeter of her skin in all that time. I did see her ankle once, when she was walkin' upstairs, and I nearly went dizzy. I tell you, when I finally get rid of that girl she'll prob'ly take a lot of loot along, but she's been worth it, everything a man could want. Whaddya think about this opening setup, now?"

"Interesting." With some relief Art turned back to the board.

"Y'see, I'm foolin' around with a little analysis here. I like to take the book theory, you know, and try t' find improvements in it. The fellas who write them chess books sometimes don't know much about the practical side of the game. Chastity, I'd like t' get out and play in some tournaments. But I got too much business to think about." Rizzo glanced

up from the board. "I'm a investment counsel-
or."

"I see. I was hoping to play in a big tournament myself, but then this trouble came up
involving my wife. That makes it very hard to
concentrate on chess."

"Oh, yeah. She's in some birth-mill, you
said. Tell me about that."

Art recited his story. By now he had it down
pat, like some politician's standard speech,
that could be edited a little here and there to
suit the day's audience even as it was being
delivered. "Possibly it's too late and the
operation's already over. But if at all possible
I want to stop her from going through with it.
For her own good."

"And you say you talked to this doctor
who's gonna do it, but you don't know his
name?"

"Right. He's one of these Christian priests, I
know that much. Tall fellow, kind of narrow-
shouldered, with a sandy beard."

Rizzo nodded thoughtfully and started to
pace the room. For the time being chess was
forgotten. He lit a fresh cigar and squinted
through the smoke of it, studying Art's face.

"Whatever people she's paid, or promised to
pay, can have their money," said Art, as free
with George's substance as with his own. "But
my idea is this: the pregnancy can just be terminated legally, and as far as my wife will
know, something just went wrong. The fetus
turned out not to be viable, or whatever the
medical term is. That's simple, and there's no

trouble in it for anyone."

Rizzo smiled faintly. "I kinda taken a liking to you, Mr. Rodney. Course you understand I don't know nothin' about midwifers—but what did you say your wife's name is, what does she look like?"

Art told him, and ran through the standard speech again, going into greater detail. His tongue stumbled reluctantly at times. He felt afraid to start hoping again.

Rizzo heard him out, then nodded decisively. "Yeah, I see. Too bad. Any day now she's gonna have the operation, huh?"

"I got the impression it might be at any hour."

"Uh-huh. Some of these priests don't stick to religion, they're real cultists and mix into things where they don't belong. Excuse me a minute, I got a phone call to make. Look over this position here meanwhile, hey? Tell me how do you like White's chances."

Left alone, Art heaved a tremendous silent sigh. He sat down at the chess table and leaned his head forward into his hands, letting his eyes close. A great exhaustion was coming down upon him. It came with a disturbing sense of permanence, as if he might never be able to rest long enough to recover. But his feelings didn't matter, if Rita could be saved. Someday he would be able to tell her what he had done, and someday she would understand and thank him for it.

Art opened his eyes and found the chessmen

waiting. Rizzo would expect a masterly evaluation of the position, and that was little enough for him to ask.

Four or five minutes of Art's flawed attention sufficed to convince him that the Rizzo Variation was a bust. Rizzo evidently thought that White's advanced knight could not be readily dislodged from its fine post, but Rizzo had overlooked a thing or two, and White was going to have to retreat and waste a tempo, and stand poorly in the middle game. These were the facts, but they had better be conveyed diplomatically.

In a few minutes the Magnifico was back. His mood had brightened into something like joviality. "Like I said, I know nothin' about any birth-mills. Still, I got a hunch that things are gonna work out okay from your point of view. Just a feeling. Well, should we have a little game? How about a drink, somethin' to eat?"

"Certainly." Art got off another sigh, like a man dropping a weight. But there was the weight still clinging to his shoulders.

He began to rearrange the chessmen to begin a game. Someday she would understand.

XIII

LYING CHASTELY beside Marjorie in the dark bed between their darkened hotel rooms, Fred was pouring out his heart.

"Ah, who'm I kidding. I'm not ready for even a brown belt yet. I could be, if I settled down and worked at it. I dunno, though, if it's really worth the effort. All the lumps and bruises, and you never get rich. Karate just gets you flunky jobs, like this part-time body-guard thing I got going now with this Dr. Hammad. Ivor, he's the regular bodyguard, says the pay never amounts to much.

"George does all right, though, running his own dojo. He must, you should see his house. I don't know what he charges for private lessons. If I could only get myself a set up someplace like he's got. And his brother-in-law does all right too. Ann, that's my sister, says Art holds down an electronics job *and* wins prizes. He must have bread comin' out of his ears. He wins his prizes playing chess, real good at it I guess.

"You know something I was good at, though, besides karate, was woodcarving. I won a couple prizes when I was a kid. My folks showed off the trophies, but they never paid any attention to the stuff I carved. Finally I didn't carve any more. Maybe if I'd kept up with that I could set myself up handcarving chess sets. Art would probably give me some clues on what sizes and shapes the players like and where to sell them. You know, I carved a nice religious cross once for Ann, when she got baptized. I did it from pictures in books. That was after she left home and married George. She still has it on the wall in her kids' room. George don't go for that religious stuff himself, but he don't care what Ann does."

Fred raised himself on one elbow in the bed, making his plastic glad-rag cloak crackle faintly all around him. Marjorie's form, similarly draped, lay still and straight beside him. The room was too dark for him to read her face but still he could perceive the tenseness of her body. A tinny, tiny sound, so faint that he could hear it only intermittently, leaked out into the room from the earplugs of her pocket hifi. Fred could not make out any of the words but he thought it was Orlando, one of the season's top recording stars, reciting his own verse. Marj had said she liked to have Orlando on for background music whenever she got started outward to the stars.

"Anyway," Fred went on, "the carving business is not bad in some ways if you can get a reputation as an artist, but there are certain drawbacks. You have to have the right wood. And when you go to sell your work, it's hard to prove it's really handcarved unless they've ac-

tually seen you do it. I mean there are wood-
working machines that can be set to take off
little irregular chips and leave little marks just
like a hand knife, and the machines do the job
a hundred times faster. It's like man in the
modern world has to contend with machines at
every turn, you know what I mean?"

Marjorie was nodding, nodding gently. She
could understand, she could understand it all
and heal him of the pain of it. Above Orlando's
tinny moans Fred now could hear another little moan, but in his girl's warm breathing
voice. Could it be that she was weeping for
him? He reached to chastely touch her hand,
and tried to think of words to tell her how
much it meant to him to have her here tonight.

Marjorie's little moan swelled quickly into
an exasperated snarl. She sat up in her crack-
ling cloak, and with the hand he had touched
she reached up to pull her earplugs out. "You
twin!" she stage-whispered angrily at Fred.
"What's the matter with you? I've run into
some horny stallions in my time, but . . . what
do you think I am, your shrink? If you can't
talk it chill any better than you do, just fall
back in your plastic and let me listen to someone who can." She flopped her head back on
the pillow and turned up the volume on the
hifi slightly.

Into the silence, Orlando's peculiar, almost
metallic voice recited:
 . . . *up on gladrag hilll*
 you left me so chilll . . .
Fred almost hit her. Why didn't he? Only

because he was afraid she wouldn't be hurt by
his blows at all, wouldn't cry out or fold up or
bleed, but would just ignore his efforts the way
his dream-opponents usually did.

Hands shaking with the urge to hit, he got
up slowly on his own side of the bed, and
pulled the stiff opaque plastic poncho off over
his head and threw it down. He turned away
from the bed and pulled his clothes on and
went on out of the room without once looking
back.

Outside the sky was darkening and the
streetlights coming on. In the Megiddo Coffee
House Fred spotted Lewandowski and the
Wolf sitting at a table together, teetering restlessly in their chairs. Making sure that his own
face was hard, he walked to their table amid
the baby-crying music that at least was not
Orlando's, and amid the smoke, and saw their
faces harden, challenging and welcoming him.

"Let's go cruise, men," he said, standing
beside their table. Wolf's pelt turned to look at
him, with the movement of Wolf's own head
and shoulders turning, and the two sets of
teeth showing Fred their grins.

"Quads and quints, I'm with ya," said
Lewandowski, stretching to his feet. "I been
sitting here five hours now, let's go find some
live fun."

They cruised out of the Megiddo and right
away Wolf began talking about how to or-
ganize a street gang and establish a territory of
streets and blocks. Fred heard without listening, without caring. As they passed some park-

ing meters Fred tried to smash one with a kick, but it was too strongly built and he only hurt his foot. He thought he managed to keep the pain in his foot from showing in his face, as he was still managing to keep a lot of other things from showing, but it was all coming to a head.

They cruised the narrower, dimmer slidewalks. "Hey," Lewandowski whispered, stopping the other two, "here comes fun."

It was a young couple walking alone. They slowed timidly as they drew near, but that only made their fate a certainty. Fred and Wolf and Lewandowski crowded them right off the walk onto the well-manicured grass.

"You're a jobholder, ain't you, pal?" asked Fred, slapping the young man. The youth began to wrestle ineffectually, and Fred slammed a fist into his ribs full power. The young man collapsed, croaking. Fred bent down and seized one of his manicured fingers and wrenched it back savagely until he thought it must be broken. "Now try and work," he said.

The young man sat on the ground yelping and stuttering with his broken finger and cracked ribs. Fred had had enough, so instead of shutting him up he walked away. After a quick glance around to make sure that no one was coming to interfere, he looked to see what Wolf and Lewandowski were doing with the girl.

"Don't hurt me!" she was squealing. "Take my money, wrap me, but don't hurt me!"

"Who'd want to wrap you, sister?" Lewandowski laughed. He had her purse tucked under his arm, and he was tearing off her electrostatically-clinging costume, while Wolf kept her from running away. Lewandowski peeled the last bit of silvery film from her plump body, and then shoved her away so she fell, sadly naked and unattractive. She sat there quivering flabbily, staring at them in abject terror, while Wolf and Lewandowski rifled her purse.

Some people at the end of the block were looking their way and pointing. "Come on, let's go," urged Fred, starting away.

Wolf delayed a moment, bending over the girl. She screamed loudly and he jumped up and came hurrying after Fred and Lewandowski. For some reason the three of them started running. They ran for a block, switched slidewalks athletically, and ran again, looking over their shoulders. There was no pursuit, and they slowed to a casual walk. Fat Lewandowski was puffing hard.

Wolf was holding up the head of his pelt, waiting for the other two to notice it. Fred saw that the sharp-pointed plastic teeth were reddened. "I left m' brand on her, where it counts," Wolf snickered, and Fred wondered, without caring, where the place that counted was.

Lewandowski still had a handful of silvery film, and was tearing it into little bits which he scattered like confetti. Good-humoredly he demanded: "How much bread that guy have on him, Lohmann? Hey Fred, you get the bread?"

Lewandowski laughed at his own rhyme, and they all laughed, feeling good. Fred's sense of power and self-assertion, brought to a peak by the terror with which the girl had looked at him, was not spoiled by the realization that he had forgotten to take the young man's money.

"Naw, I didn't get it," he admitted cheerfully. "But what th' purity."

"Didn't get it? Why?" Lewandowski too was more amused than upset.

"Cause I didn't give a quint about it. What the purity!" But now the omission did begin to bother Fred a little, mainly because the young jobholder would be comforted by having retained his money and his papers. All right, next time Fred would make up for the oversight. Fred had never done anything quite like this before. As a kid he had been in fights, but never launched such an unprovoked attack. But already he knew that there would be a next time, and then he wouldn't stop with just breaking a finger and maybe cracking a rib or two. Next time? Quintuplets, yes, there would be one.

The Magnifico, when he finally returned, furrowed his brow over the chessboard and took half an hour to make twelve moves. Then Art managed to let him win a pawn. Rizzo was an intense and serious player, with a drivingly aggressive style that would probably win him most of the amateur games he played. Though he mentioned vaguely having taken part in some tournaments, he seemed to have little

competitive experience since he accepted a
pawn from a master without apparent suspicion. Maybe he had played in prison somewhere. Art, headache-ridden, wished he had
given away a knight or bishop and so provided
himself with an excuse to resign. But no, that
might be putting it on too thick. The best thing
was to arrange a draw. If only Rizzo would not
take so long to move!

A man opened the study door. "Chief?"

Rizzo grunted in exasperation, got up, and
went out. Art shifted in his chair, took a bite
from the tasteless sandwich that had been provided for him, took a sip from the accompany-
ing drink, and looked at his watch. Nine
o'clock, almost. It would be dark outside. His
headache was waxing fat. He could ask for
aspirin but it wouldn't mix well with the
drink.

He meant to spend a lot of time and effort,
from now on, making it up to Rita for what she
was losing, or thought that she was losing.
Right now, for some reason, all of Rita's weak
points—mostly insignificant things, of course,
like her occasional stutter—kept popping up
in Art's thoughts; but all in all she was a good
wife. What was he thinking? She was a purity
of a good wife, the best of wives, and someday
she would understand. When that day came it
would be a great relief to be able to tell her
how he had managed things, and to have her
understand and thank him for it. It wasn't as
if he had had a real child of hers done away
with. It wasn't anything at all like that, even if

they could move. They would smile over all this then. Over all their foolish ideas and fears.

Someday they would. Still only nine o'clock. Yes, his watch was still running. Twins, how this night seemed to last and last.

The Magnifico came back through the draperies, smiling and rubbing his hands together, looking eagerly at the board. "Where'd you move? Like I said, I don't know about these places where they have your wife. But if I was to give you advice like a father I'd say don't worry, these things have a way of working themselves out."

"I moved my queen here. And I want to thank you."

"For advice?" Rizzo's laugh was deep and rich, and still it managed to be nasty. "Advice is cheap."

The door opened again. "Chief?"

"Oh, Gramma's chastity. Look, Mr. Rodney, you don't mind, hey? I guess we can't continue our game tonight."

"Of course." Art stood up, trying to hide his relief. "Some other time maybe. We'll call this one a draw."

"Sure, sure, maybe another day. Look, I'm gonna have one of my friends see you safely on your way."

A taciturn man nearly as big as Jove came out to guide Art on the slidewalks and ride with him; maybe Rizzo's cars were all out on business. The guardian rode silently and protectively at Art's side until they drew near the Parrs'. Art didn't want him coming to the door. "It's all right, you can go back now. This is a safe neighborhood."

He rode on under the black sky and the daylight streetlights that somehow were nothing like the day at all. What would he tell George and Ann when he got back to them? Nothing. Why should he have to tell them anything? Never mind, some words would come.

He looked sharply over both shoulders; his escort was well out of sight already, and there was no one else in view. He glided past a clock in a vendor's window, and checked it automatically against his watch. Only a little after nine; why did he bother to worry about the time? If only this headache would let up.

At an intersection he heard loud voices in the dark, coming from along the walk that came to cross his at right angles. A streetlight must be out, it was so dark in that direction. He saw an arm wave, though, an extended imperious hand, and a voice called: "Hey. Hey you, hold up." At least he thought those were the words.

Art ran. Each jog of his body sent a stab of pain flaring up from the base of his skull to exit on his pate. The voice, or voices, were raised now in a babble of threats and pursuing feet came pounding in his wake.

He tried to yell for help, but only the tortured wheezing sounds of an exhausted runner left his mouth. The wall of gray faintness, that he had last seen following his struggle in the whorehouse, rose up quite soon to mask the world.

Art stumbled, and had the sensation of losing consciousness for just a moment as he fell. Were they kicking him, hitting him already? No, it was only the pain in his head and the indirect jarring as he fell to elbows and knees on the smooth and smoothly moving walk. Where were his attackers, then?

With a grateful shudder he realized that there was no one nearby. They had left him for more sporting game. Or had he really managed to outrun them all?

Rizzo sent them. Rizzo sent them, said the irrational panic inside his buzzing head, but that made no sense at all. Rizzo liked him, and anyway Rizzo's agent would not have been so easily eluded. But still Art could not get rid of Rizzo's name. It kept coming up like something that had to be vomited.

Art glimpsed a street sign and knew that he was still on the correct walk. He tried to get up on his feet again but couldn't, not right away. He rode on all fours, in terror of meeting someone.

The guard at the pedestrian entrance of the Parrs' blockhouse took no chances on being tricked out of his bulletproof booth. First he shut the steel grillwork gate behind Art's crawling figure, then got on the house phone, and only then came out of his booth to try to help.

A few moments later George came running up, his face a taut mask. Once they helped Art to his feet, he was able to stand. The faintness

returned for a moment but then abated swift-
ly, although the headache pain went on and
on.

They asked him where he had been hurt,
and which way his attackers went. These days
if you saw a human being knocked down,
squashed like a bug beneath a run-over box in
the road, you just assumed some other human
being had done it to him.

"I—I got away from them somehow. I'm
just winded. From running."

George said to the guard: "I wouldn't call
the cops yet, hey Casey?"

"All right, no law says I have to in a case
like this. Wouldn't do any good anyway."

"I'm all right," Art muttered, finding he
could do without support as he and George
passed on into the interior of the block. "How
are the kids?"

"Okay. Come on in and rest, Art. You look
like you've been through the mill." At the
Parrs' patio door, Ann came to meet them.
"Put that thing down," said George. "We're
not invaded."

"Ohhh," she murmured, sagging briefly
against a wall. Art saw now that she was carrying a carving knife with a gaily decorated
blade in her right hand, holding it as if ready
to thrust. For a moment he could also see in
her face all the strain of the last few days, and
he could see how she would look when she was
middle-aged and when she was old. Then she
turned away to take the knife back to the
kitchen.

George pulled forward a chair in which Art gratefully sank down. Then George said: "We've just now had word from Rita's doctor. The one who operated. She's all right."

"Operated?" Art started to his feet again. "Then—?"

"Sit down. She's all right. I got the code-word message on when and where to pick up her and the baby."

Suddenly this was all, in essence, very familiar. Old stuff. It had happened to him twice before, with Timmy and with Paula. "How's the baby?"

"Oh, the birth went okay. Codeword for a healthy boy." George bent down, squinting at Art, his face going all blurry in Art's vision. "You all right?"

"I'm all right," said Art. "All right now." He was crying.

XIV

TONIGHT Dr. Matthew Hammad was working late office hours, and he happened to be performing an abortion on a teenaged girl when the phone call came in.

"Says to tell you it's life or death," his receptionist informed him. "Really vehement about it." Behind the receptionist's image on the intercom he could see on the wall of his outer office, just some grapes and Bacchus' elbow showing in part of a painting visible there.

"What name?" Hammad asked, looking across the supine figure of his abortion patient. He was irritated at the interruption and yet professionally unwilling to ignore the possibility that the life-or-death claim was true.

"Said he was calling for a Ms. Chester. But I didn't know that you had any patient by that name."

"Oh." Hammad glanced down. The young girl draped in translucent sheeting on the treatment table had the music earphones on, and the look in her eyes was faraway. "All right, I'll take it in here." He touched the girl on the arm and when she had loosened an earphone and looked up inquiringly, he said: "We'll just let this work for a minute. Are you comfortable?" Resting on the table between her raised knees, the Autobort looked something like a small vacuum cleaner, or some unearthly alien in sexual union with the girl, its slender sterile organ of plastic and flexible glass extended into her body.

She said: "I'm starting to get a cramp inside."

"Well, next time come in sooner, and we can do a simple menstrual regulation. Those are a lot easier, you know. Next time don't wait until you're this far along."

The girl, pouting at the mild lecture, put her earphone on snugly again and Hammad went over to the phoneplate. He punched the button to take the incoming call. "Ms. Chester" was a code word, and one that Hammad knew he had better not ignore.

The caller kept his own phoneplate blanked, as Hammad expected, but the doctor recognized the voice from a few previous calls. What the voice said this time was guarded and indirect, and the message was being relayed from someone else, but still the message came through plainly.

"Yes, yes, I understand." Now Hammad was frowning. "Well, it wasn't my intention to make trouble when I made the referral. Mrs. ah, Chester's whereabouts are not known to me now with any certainty." Now Hammad understood why this call was being made; every time overlords of illegal business had the

chance, they tried to embarrass the operations
of their rivals in midwifery, the religious cultists who ran their birth-mills without paying
tribute for the privilege.

"I can only guess whether I'll be able to
reach her and, ah, provide the therapy." Even
while he was engaged in this difficult call,
Hammad kept a conscientious physician's eye
on the progress the Autobort was making. The
girl was now quite relaxed, soothed by light
sedation and music and the mild sexual stimu-
lation of the machine. Through the tubing into
the receptacle of clear glass on the vacuum
cleaner's back there now flowed the debris
from the dismemberment within the womb.
Now a few ribs, fishbone clear and soft but
recognizable to the trained eye. Now a knee
joint, which Hammad also could readily identify. Now parts of the skull and brain.

"Yes, I understand." His frown deepened as
he stood listening to the phoneplate voice. Certain powerful people, those who made it possible for him to continue in the illegal sideline
of his profession, were displeased that he still
made referrals to the cultists. "Yes, I'm
sorry." Try to help out a friend whose sister
was having problems and look where it got
you. Now which would he rather have angry at
him, George Parr or Vic Rizzo? There was
always South America, he thought to himself.
Meanwhile, George Parr need never know
everything that went on, while Vic Rizzo
evidently already did.

"All right, then, I'll do everything I can. At

once. You can depend on me to take care of it."

His caller blanked off. Looking grimmer than ever, Hammad kept the phoneplate in hand and punched a number rapidly. Waiting, he continued to keep a dutiful watch on his tabled patient. She was coming along nicely. "Hello, let me speak to Ivor. This is Dr. Hammad. Oh. Well, whenever he comes back, or as soon as you can reach him, will you tell him to call me back at once. It's rather urgent. Thank you." He blanked off and at once began to punch again.

When Fred got back to the Y and found the message waiting for him at the desk, he wasted no time in hurrying to Hammad's office; he wanted to hang onto his job, part-time or not.

Hammad ushered him directly into an inner consultation room and shut the door. "Lohmann, there's something very important that's just come up, and I haven't been able to get hold of Ivor. It can't wait. You haven't been working for me very long, but I think I can rely on you—right?"

Fred nodded at once, and felt the butterflies start up in his stomach. His big chance—could this be it?

"Fred, the situation is this. There's a fetal specimen that has to be reclaimed. This woman—she's not one of my patients. I'm doing this for a colleague—has carried off a specimen that according to law should have been destroyed, and she's likely to get several innocent people in trouble by doing so."

Fred nodded.

"There'll be a nice bonus for you if you can carry this off. We'd prefer that the police not be involved in this at all, if you understand me."

"Yeah, I got the idea."

"Good. Now, from past experience with the people who have been encouraging this woman to do the wrong thing, I can tell you just where she's likely to be waiting to be picked up by some of her relatives or friends. It's down on South Shore beach. Do you have a reliable friend or two to take along in case of trouble?"

"Yeah, sure." With any luck at all he would be able to find Lewandowski or Wolf, or both of them, back at the Megiddo. Lewandowski, being a native Chicagoan, would certainly be able to lead him to South Shore beach, and either of them would be a good back-up man if he should need one. "I can handle it for you, chief. If she's there and she's got it with her. Don't worry about a thing."

Art and George had time for only a few hours' sleep before they started out on the slidewalks at about an hour before dawn. When Ann came to wake him, Art sat up with a start, but he felt rested. The pain was still there in the top of his head, but not bad enough to keep him from concentrating on other matters.

George had dug out a couple of old fishing poles and some other fishing gear for them to carry, to provide a plausible reason for being out if they fell under the eye of the police. He said a lot of fishermen went to the lake in the early morning, this time of year. They briefly considered calling a cab for the trip, but with cabdrivers required to file complete reports on all passengers for the police computers, that was about as risky as being stopped and questioned.

On their southwest passage through the city's nearly deserted predawn streets, they twice underwent brief surveillance from police cars but were not stopped. They also had one near-brush with a small group of rough-looking youths, but at the last moment the others avoided open confrontation.

In the grayness before sunrise the slidewalks brought them to the edge of a green strip of parkland that George said ran continuously along the city's lakefront. Streets and buildings behind them now, George led the way into the park, across a wide, grassy athletic field, now otherwise deserted. Art thought he could smell the lake nearby, fresh dampness without the tang of ocean salt, and billows of morning fog drifted into their faces as they trudged toward the east. The fog made vague green mounds out of stands of trees, and limited visibility drastically in all directions.

"Looks like nobody's following us," George muttered, after he had glanced over his shoulder several times. Traffic on the street they had just left was so light as to be practically non-existent, and at the moment nothing was

moving there. The ghosts of fog stalked in
from the lake to cut them off from the city behind, and when he looked to the east Art could
not see nothing but fog. Now in that direction
he could hear a couple of distant radios or
recorders blaring out pop music.

"We should see some people soon," George
told him a low voice. "There are always fishermen. She won't just be sitting out here utterly isolated."

"I was wondering." He kept wondering too
if she would really have the picnic cooler with
her. According to George the code message had
indicated that she would. Rose had carried her
own fetus home—or somewhere—but that had
been under emergency conditions. Maybe illegal parturition was always an emergency situation. Maybe normal birth and life were, too.

Out of the thick fog there loomed abruptly
athwart their path a chest-high wall of
massive stones, looking at first sight like part
of some ancient fortification. Art realized in a
moment that just beyond this rampart was the
lake. They came up to the seawall and
stopped. Four or five more tiers of the gigantic
blocks made a rough stair going down to the
water, where waves materialized out of fog to
lap against their base. It was impossible to see
out over the water for more than a few meters.

"This chaste fog," George muttered. He
checked his watch. "She's supposed to be waiting right around here somewhere. Look, we'd
better separate. You go south and I'll go north,
along the rocks. If you find her, give a whistle.

If you need help, yell out good and loud and keep on yelling. I'll be there as fast as I can."

"How far south do I go?"

George considered. "I'd say half a kilometer or less and you'll come to a harbor where a lot of private boats are tied up. Some fishermen will be around there too." The radio music was coming from that direction. "If you don't find her between here and the harbor, better turn and come back this way. I'll go north about the same distance and come back. If we can't find her we'll meet again about here."

"Right."

Fred and Wolf came out of the park to stand beside the seawall amid the drifting billows of fog. There they paused uncertainly. At the moment there was no thin blond girl carrying a container—or anyone else—in sight.

Fred wished he had been able to find Lewandowski, too, but there was no use wishing. He said: "This must be the place. I guess we better split up. How about if you go that way and I go this?"

"All right." Wolf and his neckpiece showed their double grin. "Watch out, man. They say there's a lot of apes hang out in these parks."

Fred laughed nervously, and with a tentative wave of his hand set off toward the south, walking parallel to the seawall. Wolf watched him go. Almost at once he was swallowed by the fog.

Wolf set out at a deliberate pace in the opposite direction. Despite having been up all night, he felt alert and cheerful. It was fun to have something interesting to do with his time, fun to help out a pal, and there might be some money at the end of it. He didn't know what the whole thing was all about, except it had something to do with illegal midwifing, but he didn't really care.

He knew the moment he saw the girl that she was the one they were looking for. She was a few meters inland from the seawall, waiting amid some carelessly stacked stones left over from its construction. Thin and blond, and doing nothing but waiting, she was sitting on the lowest tier of one of the stacks of stone where she was pretty well sheltered from view. And there was what he had been told to look for—a container of some kind, which turned out to be a white-handled red picnic cooler.

Her head swung around sharply when she heard the tiny scrape of his sandal on the stone he had mounted in order to see down into her sheltered spot, and at the sight of him she gave a little cry and started to get up. She was wearing a translucent skirt and open Cretan bodice.

Wolf grinned his knowledge at her and came hopping down the stair of stone to where she was. Conscious of being menacing, he watched her face, enjoying the little series of masks she was trying on, masks of unconcern, of welcome, of defiance, trying to hide the fear inside and keep him off.

He came right up to the girl and reached out, but not for her. He put his hand instead on the handle of the cooler. Maybe she would be smart and simply let him take it and walk away. But no, when he turned around she jumped at him silently from behind, and he smiled a little because he had been half expecting it.

But the attack on his face and head was too fierce for him to go on smiling. He had to drop the cooler and use both hands to shove her off. She went down on the grass with a little cry of pain. "Wait!" she called down. "Wait, can't we talk about this?"

Wolf could feel the blood trickling down his face from where her nails had raked him. He sighed. This was business, and Fred hadn't passed along any instructions that the woman was to be beaten up. People who hired this kind of business done usually spelled out just what they wanted, no more, no less. Anyway, Wolf had gotten all the urge to hurt people out of his system during the night. He shook his head, mocking and chiding. "Lady, lady. You know this thing don't belong to you anyway." He picked up the cooler again, noticing its unusual weight. And cold. Well, he wasn't being paid to be curious.

She got up, pulling her bodice together, hiding her breasts provocatively. "Please," she called, first quietly, then louder. "Please, it *is* mine. Isn't there something you want more?"

Wolf gave a tiny laugh and turned, shaking his head. She wasn't bad, but this was hardly the time or place. He started off again, the heavy cooler pulling at his arm.

To his utter amazement, she jumped him
from behind again, this time screaming as she
landed. This time the attack almost brought
him down because it was so unexpected. He
dropped the picnic cooler on the grass again,
once more fended off the clawing fingers from
his eyes, and twisted around to get a good grip
on the girl's arms. Without much difficulty he
avoided her clumsy attempt to knee him in the
balls. This time he gave her a violent shake or
two before he let her fly. This time she went
down harder and lay there sobbing. "Lady,
you're pushin' your luck."

Then there was the sound of running feet
approaching. A little guy carrying a fishing
pole and tackle box dashed out of the fog and
into the little arena among the stones, where
he came to a sudden stop. A short guy with
blond hair and goatee who looked enough like
the girl to be her brother. Wolf had fifteen kilos on him easily. He picked up the cooler once
more and took a step in the way he wanted to
go, scowling, but the little guy only threw down
his fishing gear and took a step to stay in front
of him.

"Hey, it's a quin-tup-let," Wolf said easily.
"And this one must be the runt of the litter."
Now here came another pair of running feet,
and he reached into an inner pocket for his
knife, but it was all right after all, it was just
going to be a little extra fun, for it was
Lohmann who came charging up.

Lohmann slid to a stop, though, with a look
on his face so sick that Wolf had very rarely

seen the like before. "George, Rita," said
Lohmann, staring at the other two people
there, and speaking in this low, sick voice. "Oh
purity. Oh chastity no."

"George," said the girl in a low, fainting
voice. "It's my baby. Stop him."

Wolf snarled and held out the knife to make
sure little George stayed where he was, and
here he came anyway with a skip and a dart.
Wolf, good with the knife, aimed at the oncom-
ing flat belly. The body before him twisted
away, though, going down very low, and Wolf
never saw the upthrusting back-kick coming,
only felt his breath driven out of him and his
heart stop momentarily as the kick smashed
into his ribs and broke them inward. And then
he felt his knee with his weight on it break
sideways from some terrible impact, with blind-
ing pain, and then he felt a jolt that went all
through his head and tore part of the world
away and came again and again like a long
echo, until the world was gone.

Art Rodney, puffing and lumbering toward
the sounds, saw Fred backing out of the arena
among the huge stones.

"George, I didn't know," Fred was saying.
"George, I swear." And then Fred turned and
ran, just ran flat out, almost knocking Art
down in his passage. Art could still hear the
long strides pounding when Fred had vanished
into the fog.

Advancing again, Art took in the scene with
a glance. Knife on the grass, man on the grass,

George looming over him, looking down and rubbing his knuckles automatically. White-handled red picnic cooler on its side, Rita sitting near it, sitting awkwardly and in pain.

"Oh, darling, easy," she said into his ear. "Don't squeeze me. Oh Art, you didn't bring the police down on us, did you? The doctor said you wanted me still."

"Oh, yes, yes, yes I want you. Never mind about all the rest of it. Let's get you home."

"My baby." She was pointing at the cooler and he went to set it right side up, as if that could make any difference to what was encapsulated inside. Then he looked over at George, who was prodding the fallen figure with a toe. "What happened?" Art asked. "I got here as fast as I could when I heard a commotion. I thought I just saw Ann's brother Fred run past me just now."

"It was." George shook his head and seemed to rouse himself. "Let's get out of here."

"And who's that?" Art moved a little closer to look at the man on the ground. The man's eyes were open, blankly, above what looked like a fur collar of some sort. His face was scratched and marked with trickles of fresh blood. "Will he be all right if we just leave him?"

"He'll be dead," said George, in a voice that wavered once and came back strong again. "He's dead right now. Let's get going." And he moved and picked up the cooler with one strong hand and helped Rita to her feet with the other. "Art, get our fishpoles and stuff."

"Oh. Oh, chastity." Art looked once more at the dead man and pulled his eyes away. Somehow he picked up all the fishing gear that he and George had carried here and dropped, and then went on after his wife and her brother into the fog. When he caught up, he demanded: "Rita, did that fellow back there hurt you?"

"No, no, only pushed me down. And my bottom is still sore from the parturition, and I have cramps, but the doctor didn't have to make any incisions. I can walk, but I'm so tired I don't know how far." Now she was clinging to Art's arm while George walked a little ahead of them carrying the cooler. They moved through the fog toward the sound of Orlando's voice on several radios.

"Art. George, if anything happens to me, this is the situation. He's on the waiting list for a womb, but it may be months. The doctor says the safest place for him in the meantime is the Loyola School of Medicine, cryogenics lab. They seem to have some safe depository. I don't know where. Loyola's on the north side of the city, Art. Ask for Gwen or Larry. I said we'd get him there. The doctor said he was afraid he had to flee the city right away or be arrested. Maybe there are worse things than that for us to fear. That man back there was no policeman, but he was after my baby, not after me."

Art felt a pang. Rizzo. He patted his wife, hugged her, murmured soothing words.

"I tell you he was. He would have taken this

basket and walked away if George hadn't stopped him."

Art, head throbbing sickly now, stared at George's back, moving three paces ahead of him through the mist. Over his shoulder George said: "We'll deliver him where you said, Sis. Hey, what's his name?" Art stared at the red cooler, seeing instead the dead body they had left behind them on the grass. He and George both.

"I haven't talked that over with his Daddy yet. I think George Arthur. Or maybe Arthur George, though Art used to say he didn't want a junior."

They came abruptly to a little rise, and at its top encountered the seawall again. Almost below them, amid thinning drifts of fog, several long piers extended at right angles to the shore. The piers were edged in places with moored pleasure boats and elsewhere occupied by fisherfolk with their poles and nets and buckets. The sun was up now, turning fiercely white above the watery horizon, visible between great lake-borne mounds of the dissipating fog.

Here a road of recycled plastic gravel ran just inland from the seawall. A few fishermen's cars were parked along its edge. As the three of them reached the road, they simultaneously saw a police car cruising in the middle distance, a face turned out of its window in their direction. In unison they altered course, and there was another car approaching along the road where it bent inland.

"Split up," said George succinctly. He thrust the picnic cooler into Art's hands and with the same movement took back his own old tackle box. "Rita, take the bait jug," he added, and in the next instant was gone, sprinting toward the south. Now both police cars were accelerating, but the trio on which they had been closing in were gone three ways at once.

George went around a clump of bushes, and back onto the seawall, where he dashed past a group of fishermen. Then he slowed to a trot, and then to a quick walk. He looked back frequently, and cursed. Obviously neither of the cars had come after him, though he was staying near the road to lure them on. But now at last there came a uniformed policeman in pursuit of him on foot.

"You there, halt!"

George was purposely deaf to the first yell, figuring they would give at least one more before they started shooting. If they were serious enough to shoot, which they probably weren't as yet because the dead man could hardly have been found and reported to them so soon.

He heeded the second, closer shout, and looked around with polite surprise as an athletic policeman of dark brown skin came running up.

"All right, hands in the air."

"What's the matter, officer?" He set the tackle box down and put his foot on it and raised his hands.

He was patted down for weapons. "What've you got in there?"

"Show me a search warrant and you can search me completely."

"I'm conducting a weapons search, mister, get your foot off that thing before I shoot it off."

George got, moving two steps away and keeping his hands up. The policeman peered into the box and then looked at him expressionlessly. "All right, come along. Bring this box of junk if you want it."

The officer sheathed his pistol and took a good grip on George's right sleeve just above the elbow with his left hand. With this grip he walked George north again. It must be a technique they taught at the police academy, how to be ready to subdue resistance by the suspect. The grip was not bullying, and yet quite firm enough for business. Not bad for an amateur, not bad.

Fishermen stared at them as they passed. Now only one police car was in sight, parked, with a scattering of the curious observing it from a little distance. Rita sat alone and composed in the back seat while a man in civvies sat twisted around to face her from the front.

"Do you know this man?"

Her eyes turned neutrally to George, waiting for a signal.

"Of course she knows me. I'm her brother."

"George, this gentleman says he's Detective Simmons."

"What were you running off with, George? Empty tackle box, maybe? Don't you know it's against the law to interfere with police carrying out their duties?"

It wasn't really empty, but too close to empty to be convincing to a fisherman. George held it under his arm and remained silent. The man sighed and informed him that he was under arrest for conspiracy to violate the Population Control laws, and made the little speech detailing his constitutional rights.

With George and a patrolman in the back, and another uniformed man up front with Detective Simmons, the car began to move, cruising slowly north, going off the plastic road and over grass, following the lakefront. Then they turned and cruised the other way again, and stopped and let out one of the uniformed men, who stood looking over the piers with quick twistings of his head, then walked away, talking on a wrist-radio.

The man in civvies turned once more. "We're bringing along your tackle box and your empty bait-bucket, George and Rita, to show the judge what kind of tricks you try to pull. We're also going to bring that red picnic cooler and the fat man who's carrying it. We're going to pick that up in a minute. Why don't you tell me something about it now, just to show you're willing to cooperate? Where were you taking it?"

"My sister and I want to see an attorney before we answer any more questions at all. This sounds like something serious."

"What do you think something serious is, George? What were you two and your sister's husband doing here today? No reason you can't tell me, if it wasn't anything wrong."

"Let us talk to an attorney," Rita said. "And then we'll answer questions."

A message was coming in on the car radio. DOA found on the rocks near South Shore Beach. Police number-jargon followed. The two policemen still with the car exchanged looks but did no more. George held his hands down so that the callus pads might not be seen. Sooner or later somebody might make the connection. At the moment he felt no guilt or fear; at the moment he was still steady as a rock. Attorney, attorney, where will I find you? He had a couple of them among his students, but none in criminal law.

Another radio message was coming, this one on Simmons' wrist-radio. From the back seat George couldn't quite make the message out, but abruptly the car was rolling again. It accelerated strongly, turned on its siren for a blast or two, then almost at once screeched rocking to a halt. "That's Hall," Simmons in the front seat said, opening his door and getting out.

Out of a small crowd a lean, stooped man was coming toward them, plodding with slow weariness as if he waded through mud; that was not pure figure-of-speech, George saw, for the man was wet as if he had just fallen into the lake. From the business socks inside his sandals a little puddle sloshed out at every step, and water plastered down his thinning hair and dripped from his translucent shorts and jacket. Simmons jumped to meet him, asking excited questions.

"That fat fathering breeder!" was all Hall said at first, in a voice choked with anger, as he stood there trying to press the water out of his clothes. "That quintuplet-siring crowder!" Some of the onlookers gathered at a little distance smiled or giggled at the earnest vileness of the man's speech, while one or two appeared sincerely shocked.

Simmons was holding his wrist-radio ready. "If he shoved you in the water I can put in a call and charge assault and resisting arrest. That'll get us some more manpower out here. Which way did he go?"

"I don't know. Anyway, I don't care to press those charges." It seemed that a little strong language had served to discharge Hall's anger. He put up a hand as if to ward off the detective's glare and exclamations of disgust. "He didn't hurt me. I don't think he even intended to knock me in the water, just to get away." Hall had taken off his jacket and now began to wave it like a distress signal, trying to dry it in the morning breeze. "I called out to him, when I saw that I had him cornered on a moored boat, I said just hand over the specimen and save yourself a lot of trouble. You and your wife and the whole world will be better off, I said. But then he came off the boat with this picnic cooler under his arm like a football. Just put down his head and charged, and he must weigh ninety kilos . . .''

Hall had looked at Rita several times, but had offered her no recognition until now. ''Well, Mrs. Rodney, I suppose you and your husband and brother here are getting yourselves a lawyer. From the way you sit there looking so serenely into space, I suppose too that you've heard about the report.''

Rita, chin high, was studying the horizon. George asked: ''Report?''

''The new population forecast from the UN. The one we've all been afraid of. A real surprise. If the latest trends continue, world population is going to reach a peak of around ten billion in the next forty years and then start down, maybe even a rather sharp decline. Not that that will help the people who are going to go hungry in the next forty years, of course, but it's going to make it a little harder to convict people like yourselves before a jury.'' Mr. Hall was now standing nude and shivering slightly in the dawn, wringing out his shorts, his dripping codpiece slung over one shoulder.

''World population's going down?'' said the detective, sounding rather dumb. He couldn't seem to grasp it right away. George couldn't either.

Hall said: ''Oh, we all knew it had to happen someday, one way or another. The only question was how and when. Still, when it does happen, we feel surprise."

Simmons was busy with his radio. George asked: "But what is it? The Homo Leagues? I know they're growing fast."

"They were allowed for in previous forecasts. No, the thing that tipped the balance, that wasn't foreseen, was all this religious celibacy. Half a dozen religions booming today, young people pulling themselves out of the reproductive pool by the tens of millions. People will think it will ease the population pressure right away, though of course it won't. It was hard enough before to get convictions, with bleeding-heart lawyers and frozen fetuses to cloud the issue. Now this. But we're going to try, sir, we're going to try. I'll see you in court, whether we manage to recover the specimen or not."

George, riding north along the Outer Drive in the back of the police car, going to some police station where they would have to let him see a lawyer before he said a sublimatin' thing, held his sister's hand and looked out over the lake. The waves were coming in stronger now with a freshening breeze, starting to crest into whitecaps near the shore. The fog had gone. Get through, Art, get through. Loyola School of Medicine, cryogenics lab, ask for Gwen or Larry. I've killed a man to save that kid, and you'd better not lose him now. I'd kill any other son of a bitch who tried to kill my nephew.

He smiled a little for the new man born so

strangely into the world, and at the same time he was very worried. The waves came in from the clear horizon, cresting into white. The crest of the wave has been reached. And now, to see which way the world slides down.